HELLGIRL
RISE OF HELLION

MARY RAMSEY

ISBN 978-1-956010-52-7 (paperback)
ISBN 978-1-956010-53-4 (digital)

Rushmore Press LLC
1 800 460 9188
www.rushmorepress.com

Printed in the United States of America

CHAPTER

The city knew me as 'that homeless girl.' I was the skinny little gymnast with hair like fire, who performed tumbling passes along the boardwalk. I'd been doing it for years, making just enough money to buy a candy bar. (While I shoplifted a fifty-cent package of oatmeal and a banana.)

"Goodbye Mrs. Jenkins," I said as I slipped out the door, letting the cheap bell ding behind me.

"A little girl like you should not be on the streets," said the old Indian woman. At least I assumed she was Indian. And we all know 'to assume is to make an ass of you and me.' A great example of this is how every adult I meet seems to assume I'm a minor, just because of my height. (I'm not.)

Long story short, I ran away from home older than I should have been. I was never a brave kid, and (by the account of all bystanders, teachers, local police) my life was absolutely fucking perfect. I was a star gymnast, a natural talent. I never did enjoy competing; all my life I wanted to perform, I wanted to dance. But you hardly ever get what you want, in this messed up world.

For example, I would have loved to have a place to sleep indoors, instead of leaning against a dumpster. Or maybe a mother who would have chosen me over a town full of rumors and victim-shaming. But that's a story for another day.

"Fuck it's cold." I fished through my jacket pockets as I pulled my knees to my chest. Turns out, after a long day of screwing around, I had a solid sixteen dollars to my name.

I wanted something warm and at the late hour of the night, the easiest place would be a nearby gas station. Standing up, I could see the lights of the pricing sign, no more than a few blocks away. Hopefully, they kept their coffee machine on. I made the short walk, making sure to flash a wad of dollars as I entered. "I'm just here to get a coffee."

I'd gotten the cops called on me before, just for the fact that I was a homeless person wandering around so late at night. But it turns out my distraction was unnecessary.

As I filled my paper cup I could hear the sound of a man shouting, in what sounded like Russian. He appeared to be yelling at a female companion. Moving closer I could see she was a thin, frail, girl, nervously counting out change.

She was a good foot shorter than him but with similar ash-blonde hair and pale complexions. He looked like he could be her father. But that idea made me feel sick, anyone with half a brain could tell he was her pimp.

"Yo, Pops!" the young Hispanic cashier said to the older man (with a truly moronic lack of situational awareness.) "How about you float your girl a couple of bucks so we can keep the line moving?" There was no line.

I was mentally preparing for gunshots. But instead, the man grabbed the girl's arm, jerking her backward with an aggressive tug. He whispered something in Russian that sounded like a threat, before turning to leave.

A part of me hoped that he was going to abandon her, forcing the cashier to call the police and have them haul her away. It would've made sense, the perfect way to get rid of a girl you no longer wanted.

Instead, he waited by the front door smoking a cigarette from a brand-new pack.

The girl pushed her items away. "I apologize," she said in a soft European accent as she turned to follow her male friend.

"Wait!" I whispered quickly, close enough for her to hear. "How much do you need?"

The cashier replied. "To be able to buy the food she needs 12.44, to get out of here without me calling the cops, she needs 7.99."

"Because her friend just walked out with the cigarettes," I sighed. The man clearly sent her in, to pay for his smokes by any means necessary. "How much are you short?"

"I only have six dollars."

"Oh, ok," I said as I discreetly laid out all my money. "I got this."

The cashier counted out the money, it was enough for my coffee, her snacks, and her friend's smokes.

"Thank you." She grabbed her items and turned to leave. But paused with a noticeable uncertainty.

"Are you afraid of him?"

She nodded. "I'm Anya."

"You can call me Lena," I said sweetly. Not my real name.

"You think you can help me?" Anya glanced at the cashier who quickly put on headphones. He seemed to know what was going down.

"I can try. If nothing else I can pose as a diversion."

"You would do that for me?"

"I would have wanted someone to do it for me." This wasn't the first time I had the opportunity to play superhero. I carried a knife and was quite skilled. (At least in my head.) "What's his name?"

"He goes by Alexi or Pasha."

"Pasha?" I asked, biting my lower lip. I knew that word as a Russian nick-name but in my head, it seemed like a kinky pet name. "Let's do this."

I walked out with Anya, hand in hand like old friends.

Alexi raised his chin and smirked. "Hello there."

"I thought you and your wife might have some use for a girl like me."

"My wife?" he asked, his voice deep, menacing.

"Your wife, or your friend." I lifted his hand kissing his knuckles. I could feel thick scars, but he tasted clean, like cedar scented soap with a hint of menthol. I licked him down the shaft of his ring finger, aiming for an engraved gold band. It was a trick I had used in the past to steal jewelry from sex-deprived men. Soon I was sucking his finger, while looking into his blue eyes.

"You looking to party?" he asked, shifting his stance.

"I'm looking to sleep on a nice warm bed."

"You have a pimp?"

"Nah," I said, releasing his hand. My next answer was important, it would be the lynch-pin to the character I was trying to portray. 'I'm just a kid.' No, that would be too obvious. "I got into town, right now I'm a free agent."

"I think we can work something out." he placed his hand to my lower back, groping the shape of my hips. I figured he was checking if I was armed.

Lucky for me, where most girls wore their hearts on their sleeves, I wore my knife on my ankle. I invited his rough fingers to explore lower, to my six-pack stomach. My coach always liked my abs, he had a thing for thin, athletic girls.

Anya looked shy and a little horrified. But she bowed her head as she spoke with a slow, heavy accent. "Her name is Lena, I kind of owe her for her assistance. That, and she is very beautiful."

"You did well, Anya," he replied, still looking at me. "My friend and I, we're staying at the Hotel St Regent just up the road."

"I've heard of it." I pulled myself closer, leaning into his warm embrace. My main goal was to prove myself to be a suitable replacement for Anya.

We walked in silence, with Anya staying a few feet behind. The hotel approached, casting a hellish shadow as if it had risen from the night itself. "Wow."

The front doors seemed to blend in with the darkness. I actually didn't even notice the presence of a doorman until a tall dark figure opened the stain-glass Gothic panel door.

Alexi held me close, covering my face with his tan suede jacket as we made our way to the elevator. "Have you been here before?"

"Not beyond the lobby." I'd once spent an afternoon pick-pocketing, slipping through the sea of wealthy guests. But it never looked this sinister. After a few minutes, the doors opened and Alexi led the way to their room.

Room 405 was nothing special; a single king bed with a high-backed office chair, a desk, and a TV. There was also a mini-fridge and a nice bathroom, but it wasn't the suite I was expecting. "Got anything to drink? or should I just make myself comfortable?"

Alexi sat on a chair, pulling me on to his lap. He leaned back, as he punched in the code to a safe (which appeared to be nothing more than a desk drawer.) He pulled out a dark, unlabeled bottle. "You drink?

"Vodka?" I asked innocently, maintaining character. Clearly, it was not vodka.

"Let's say it is." The color was a strange shade of blue and it smelled like a mix of lemonade and cough syrup.

I glanced at Anya who was shaking her head with a nervous tick. That seemed to be my cue to not actually swallow it.

"I'll take a drink," I said, taking the bottle to my lips. Despite how it smelled, the actual liquid tasted like motor oil. I held it in my mouth for only a few seconds before kissing Alexi's lips. "But I also want to get a little more comfortable."

I hoped to God that I could distract him, forcing the majority of the liquid into his mouth. But I could still taste it and it wasn't long before my brain felt like putty. 'Oh, shit...'

The sudden rush of sleepiness took all of my strength, threatening to knock me out. I had to get naked. I knew that once I felt his touch on my skin, my mind would be shocked back to high-alert.

I quickly took off my sweatshirt, revealing my small, perky breasts. It also revealed the fact that I hadn't shaved my armpits in a while. Hopefully, that wasn't a deal-breaker. "I think I want to go to bed."

I was bracing for a slap in the face, or worse. But much to my surprise, he held the kiss, all while coaxing my legs around his waist as he carried me to the bed.

I could feel his erection against my leg, and it made me want to vomit. It was the same as when my coach used to help me 'stretch,' for better flexibility. In a matter of seconds, he would be on top of me.

I couldn't let that happen. Alexi was much too strong, I needed to present an alternative where I had the power. I kissed his neck, tracing my tongue along a black lined tattoo of a church.

This was enough to get him to pause. I reached between his legs, feeling for his raw heat. "It's not going to suck itself," I said in a whisper, taking a long breath, "Pasha." It didn't take much to get Alexi on his back, opening his shirt to reveal a slender, muscular chest covered in mafia tattoos; nautical stars, angels and saints.

I cupped his face with a tender kiss. His breath smelled like cigarettes, and it was really testing my gag reflex. I switched to sucking his lower lip, alternating between soft kisses and love bites. I watched him close his eyes as I worked my way down his chin. I sucked on his rough facial hair, looking every bit like a sex-crazed little slut. The trick worked so well, Alexi didn't even notice Anya securing his arms, and wrists to the bed.

Using his shirt as a thick dense rope, she made a series of knots, pinning his arms above his head. I have to admit I was impressed. Alexi's hands were bound so well he couldn't break free even if he wanted to. Not that men like him ever want to.

I tapped Anya on the shoulder, motioning for her to switch positions. "I got this."

She smiled and snickered, like a true femme fatale. No words were necessary to express what we needed to do. (And likely she had done it before.) Sitting on his chest, she went after his pants opening his belt, then his zipper.

Anya made sure to lock eyes with me as she took him in her mouth.

I licked two fingers, being sure to make loud drooling sounds. (In case Alexi was even paying attention.) With my saliva drenched hand, I lubed up the handle of my knife, spitting a massive wad for good measure. I was actually pretty good at fucking men with my knife, bringing them to the edge, while not cutting my fingers on the slippery blade. Unfortunately, this ultimately resulted in my favorite knife getting caked with feces. (Thank God for hand sanitizer.)

I couldn't see if Anya was fully naked (in a 69 position) or just administering oral sex while choking him with her legs. Either way, she had his full attention.

I could tell when he was close to orgasm. I tapped Anya on the shoulder, as a word of warning before the next stage of my plan.

Anya nodded and sat up. She was still positioned on his chest, with his head between her ankles. She mimed a silent stabbing motion. (So technically this was her idea.)

In one swift motion, I removed the hilt of the blade from his ass, turned it around, and sank the knife into his thigh, making sure to cut nice and deep into his femoral artery.

This caused a sudden geyser of blood to hit Anya in the face and chest. She giggled, and without missing a beat she switched up her technique. Instead of oral sex, she was aggressively jerking him off, as if milking a cow.

I forced my knife hilt deeper and deeper, moving in and out as if I was using my fingers. Alexi was moaning in Russian, but he wasn't begging for his life. He was begging for a release. He had to know he was going to bleed to death in a pool of his own semen. Or perhaps he didn't feel it?

It was actually kind of fun. This was everything I wanted to do to my father, my coach, and everyone else who hurt me. This was for all the men. I stabbed him again, severing off a large chunk of flesh from his thigh. That was when he finally cried out in pain. I wouldn't call it a scream, more like the roar of a lion.

Anya turned and punched him in the mouth with an unexpected amount of force. Over and over she busted up his face, breaking his nose, eye sockets, and jaw.

After what felt like a long time, she gripped her wrist. "Ouch."

"Hey, Anya, you good? Are you hurt?

"No just a little sore. I always knew he had a hard head." Her work done, Anya got off the bed and went to the bathroom to wash her hands.

"So, thumbs up or thumbs down?" I asked, reinserting the handle of my knife into his ass. His muscles were tense, throbbing, that was when I realized he was yet to ejaculate. With all the blood rushing to Alexi's hips, he would bleed out quite easily if his genitals were to be forcibly removed.

Anya sighed, as she emerged from the bathroom. "Alexi was not the man who killed my father, but he was the bastard who purchased me off the dark web."

"I saved your life," Alexi cried through blood-covered lips. "They were going to sell you off in pieces."

"I would rather have died," she replied as she rifled through his jacket. "But then again, that is why I feel death is too good for you." When she had a good collection of cash, credit cards, and his cell phone, she approached Alexi. "Maybe we should ask our new friend to determine your final fate."

I smiled proudly at the sight of Anya's newfound confidence. "I think you should buy a ticket back home, or to wherever you want to call home."

"Maybe he'll bleed out, maybe he won't. But I won't take his life until I know you're safe."

Anya nodded. "Since I already took the time to wash my hands." She handed me her smartphone and pocketed (What I assumed was) Alexi's flip phone.

I wanted to keep my promise and wait until she called, before fully deciding Alexi's fate. Turns out that would not be up to me.

Anya left, and I turned to Alexi who had gone silent. I dragged my blood coated fingers along his jawline. "What do you have to say for yourself?"

The man shook his head. "There is nothing to say. I will not stoop to begging a timid, underage girl, as if you are an equal."

"But you'll fuck one." My words made me sound braver than I really was. I wanted him to beg, to tell me he was a human being. "So, what's your deal? Did your daddy beat you? Maybe he sold your ass on the streets?"

Alexi smiled, revealing a mouth full of bloody teeth. "My childhood was quite lovely."

"Do you have a wife and kids?" I asked as I attempted to remove my knife from his ass.

Alexi was clenching, his body threatening to swallow my blade whole. "Do you truly believe all men are like your father?"

"What?" My mind went blank. I remember taking a single breath. The world around me went in slow motion, before fading into darkness.

Next thing I knew, a woman grabbed me by the neck. "What's your name kid?" she asked with a strong, Latina accent.

"Go to hell," I replied with a gasp. She appeared to be the leader of the team that was securing the room.

"Hell?" she said with a laugh. "That's kind of cute."

"What?" I had been distracted with finding Alexi. The bed was covered in blood but there were no remains to be seen.

"That's what I'm going to call you, Hellion." The woman pointed me towards the fire escape.

"What can I call you?"

"You can call me Maverick."

"Like the Tom Cruise character?"

"Exactly," she said as she cuffed my wrists. "If you'd said anything about that cowboy-shit, I wouldn't have hesitated to punch you in your pretty little face."

The woman's humor seemed odd for a cop. "Am I under arrest?"

"No, I think you're going to make a great addition to my team."

"Ok, sure." And yet the cuff stayed on. I took my last look at the city before being led to the roof and shoved into a waiting helicopter. This was either really good or really bad. But at least Anya was safe. Enemy of my enemy is my friend, that's the way the saying goes, right? "Where's Alexi?"

That caused Maverick to laugh. "He's alive and able to answer our questions about the human trafficking ring." She pulled out a black cloth bag. "Head forward if you please."

Before I could respond, she forced the bag on my head. "Sorry, sweetie, it's just protocol."

I nodded under the hood. "Is Anya safe?"

"Yeah," she said patting my shoulder. "Anya's safe."

I felt the helicopter taking off. After a while, we seemed to have reached cruising altitude. That was when I heard footsteps coming from the pilot's seat.

"I told you she was great." The approaching voice was Russian, female, but not Anya. She sounded older, like someone in their thirties who'd smoked since the age of ten.

"Anya?"

"I'm here," the voice replied. "You did great."

"What did I do?"

"You sharpened your magic blade on his vile manhood," Anya's voice noticeably cringed as she spoke. "You actually looked like you might consider mercy but that pervert had to go and run his mouth."

"Really?"

"Yes, really. You have the skills of a warrior, an assassin."

"Thanks, I guess." I pinched my hand nervously, desperate to hide my immaturity. I had never done anything so horrific to another human being. And Alexi, no matter what he had done in his past, was a human being. But I felt a sense of loyalty to Anya.

"If it makes you feel any better, he's still alive."

Maverick chuckled. "Not by much."

"The whole point was to lure him," Anya explained. "Regardless if I had met you tonight or not, this was a pickup time to reunite with my team and turn Pasha over to the proper authorities." When happiness filled her voice, she started to sound like the teenage girl I'd befriended.

"What are you?"

"We work for an international organization known as Valkyrie," Anya explained, holding my hand as the helicopter set down for a landing. "We're an international organization, taking down predators for womankind."

"Womankind?" Maverick said with a laugh. "We're more than a gender swap." She pulled the hood off my sweat covered face. "I'll show you to your sleeping quarters."

I walked with Maverick, taking notice of her hover boots. Everyone seemed to have some sort of modern armor and or weaponry.

"Can I see Alexi?" I asked.

Maverick shot me a look of disappointment. "You can't be serious."

"Never mind, then," I replied in a meek little girl voice.

Maverick led me to a large hallway filled with a wall of tubes lining the wall like a honeycomb. It looked like the Japanese capsule hotels I'd seen in pictures. "Your bed is number 6534. Anya will be back to give you a tour of the facility."

"Thanks." I located my tube in the row closest to the ground. The low ceiling made me feel slightly claustrophobic as if I was in a coffin. But turning over, I caught sight of sunlight. We were flying. "What the fuck?"

"Hellion!" Anya's voice shouted from outside my tube. I scooted out to greet her, thankful for a familiar face. Anya was wearing a t-shirt that looked like army-issue gym wear. This was paired with logo branded sweatpants. Basically, she looked like an average college co-ed.

I greeted her with a hug. "I'm so glad to see you. Are we on a plane?"

"This is our mobile base," she explained. But we're currently heading to Northern Russia to turn Alexi over to UN authorities. "Come on, I'll show you to the cafeteria."

"Sure."

We went one level down, to a mess hall that seemed to consist only of vending machines. "Everything's free but don't be greedy," she said as she helped herself to a coffee. "We only get supplies at bi-weekly pick-up stops."

"Where's Alexi?" I asked while picking out a generic power bar.

"In the basement, cargo hold," she replied, taking a sip of her drink. "After he was stabilized."

I nodded. "Do you think I could visit him?"

"Yeah, sure," she replied calmly. "We can probably head there now if you want."

We took our snacks and exited out the fire escape. The path was dark, and clearly not meant for travel but Anya seemed to know the way. "I'm really sorry for dragging you into this. I really thought you were more bloodthirsty, or apathetic."

"I'm plenty bloodthirsty," I squeaked.

"Well, Alexi is not worthy of your sympathy."

"I know."

We stopped at a metal door. "This is where we part ways, I have a feeling if he saw me bad things would happen. I want you to have a chance to see him for who he really is."

"I understand." I opened the door and took a step into a dark corridor. My eyes took a moment to adjust to the darkness when suddenly I was blasted with an intense flashlight.

"Nice uniform." I looked down at my chest. For the first time, I noticed the Valkyrie long-sleeve shirt I was wearing with my torn denim jeans. I had to assume Maverick or maybe Anya had given it to me at the hotel.

I wanted to ask why he had a flashlight. But the sound of his voice caused me to freeze. "Alexi?" When my night vision returned, I saw that Alexi's cell was illuminated by a glowing blue bug zapper. The device expelled just enough light to allow me to see the state of his body.

His left leg has been amputated. But he appeared to be resting comfortably on a plank of wood that served at the room's only bed.

"Hello, Alexi."

"Do you even recall what you did?" he asked, facing away.

I shook my head, and forced myself to squeak out a whispered, "No."

"Well, let me show you." In one swift motion, Alexi teleported to the front of the cell, slamming his head against the bars.

I screamed, falling backward. For less than a second, I saw what could only be described as a man in a robotic mask. But a few blinks caused the image to return to normal. Alexi's face was bruised, swollen. But he wasn't wearing a mask.

"Wow, you are just a kid, aren't you?" Alexi was laughing, leaning into the bars like some kind of prison inmate stereotype. "What did you see, little girl?"

"Nothing."

"So, you didn't see a robotic shark?"

"No." The image flashed again, superimposed over Alexi's face. And yes, the mask resembled a robotic hammerhead shark, with a visor that seemed to stretch the wearer's field of vision.

"My boss is no fool," his voice crackled, becoming more distorted. "Faust is no fool." The blue light of the bug zapper flickered, plunging the corridor into darkness. "I. Am. No. Fool."

I needed to run, but without light, I had no idea which way. I picked a direction and found myself tripping on a long tube. 'A flashlight?' I picked it up, smacking it a few times to get it to light.

"Oh thank God." I felt a brief moment of calm, and then I turned around.

What appeared before me, was a fusion of Alexi and whatever the hell Faust was. He had Alexi's body; skin, muscles, long blond hair, but with robotic pieces. His leg had been replaced with a black, metallic prosthetic.

The creature rolled his head back, moaning sexually. "I can still feel what you did to him."

"Him?" So, this was not Alexi.

"Don't act like you didn't enjoy it," he said with a laugh. "Deep down you're a sadist like your old man."

I finally started to hear alarms going off. I knew it would be in my best interests to keep him in one place. "What do you know about my father?

"Nothing, it was just a logical guess. Girls like you always have daddy issues."

"Issues?" I could feel the rage boiling in my throat. "You don't know me."

The voice crackled with radio-like static. "Do you recall what Alexi said to you, the words that pushed you over the edge?"

"No."

"Harder, deeper," he said in Alexi's voice. "Oh, that's so good."

The memories started to flow back, little by little as my mind was being broken. Alexi had enjoyed being sodomized by the hilt of my blade. He was begging me to ride his dick, or at least suck him off. "You know you want to, my sweet baby girl."

"Freeze fucker!" shouted a handful of female officers.

From the corner of my eye, I could see they were all heavily armed with rifles and high-tech body armor. They seemed confident, or at least not as ill-prepared as an unarmed girl holding a dying flashlight.

"Hello, ladies," the creature said in a robotic Russian accent. "So nice of you to join us."

There was an explosion. I remember that much.

I awoke in bed, with horrible pain in my…legs? Despite the discomfort in my arms, and chest I forced myself to sit up. I could clearly see that my legs had been amputated below the knee. But yet they felt like they were on fire; burning, bleeding, blistering, but unlike actual burns, these would never go numb. If I had to assume what was happening, I would go with phantom limb syndrome. *Yeah, that had to be it.*

And it would be this way for all eternity.

Had Faust blown up the prison? Were the Valkyries dead? Where even was I?

For some people, this would be the end. but for me, this was just the beginning.

CHAPTER 2

I slept in my hospital bed, alone with only the white walls to console me. "Inhale, exhale, inhale, exhale." I knew for a fact there had to be doctors and nurses somewhere because I had an IV in my arm and heart monitor stickers on my chest. I didn't have a feeding tube, but somehow, I wasn't hungry. But I did have a catheter and a piss bag. This made sense with my amputated legs. The room had no windows, only air vents, and bright white led lighting. There sure as hell was no door. That made what happened next all the stranger.

My eyes shot open, as I awoke to the sound of screaming. There did not seem to be any sleep schedule; I would get sleepy at random times, so I had no idea if I had been out for hours or minutes. But somehow there was now an opaque curtain down the middle of the room. Since it was attached to the ceiling, it offered a comfortable level of shade. Part of me wanted to try to sleep but the cries were too loud. So, instead, I tried to listen for the voices of any doctors, nurses, or anyone who appeared to be in a position of power.

"Why isn't the patient sedated?" asked a female voice. She was one of at least six people struggling with keeping the male patient pinned down.

"He doesn't react to any sedation we have on hand, not even horse tranquilizers," replied another attendant.

"Is Jane Doe conscious?" asked the third voice. A tall thin figure seemed to freeze in place, looking in my direction.

'Was that me? Am I Jane Doe?' I'd actually never heard anyone make reference to me. My body stiffened and I closed my eyes. The last thing I wanted was for one of the strangers to open the curtain and put a bullet in my head. (Or something toxic in my IV line.)

I focused on the backs of my eyes, watching the colors play out in front of my retinas. I took slow shallow breaths, remaining as quiet as possible until I heard footsteps, followed by silence. *'What was happening?'* I blinked carefully looking around. The curtain was still there, but was the roommate?

Sitting up I was able to reach the thick pale pink fabric. I drew back the curtains, revealing a young man who looked to be no older than eighteen. He was on his side, in the fetal position, facing me. It was like he had been waiting to see if I would try for the curtain. He blinked his big brown eyes, clearly conscious, despite the fact he was being abnormally quiet.

"What happened to you?" I asked, moving to the edge of the bed.

The man took one look at me and shook his head, rolling his eyes as he turned to face the opposite wall. He quickly pulled the blanket over his shoulder, up to his neck.

"Um, ok." I had to assume my appearance seemed too young to be taken seriously. "What's your name?" I sat up, straining my neck to see if I could catch a glimpse of any clues. Oddly, I spotted a white dry-erase board (where a nurse would put a patient's name), facing the opposite direction.

"What do they call you?" he asked, still facing the opposite wall. His voice was low, sickly, but clearly, he was young. (Not much older than myself.)

"Sit up and see for yourself," I replied. I actually had no idea if there was any identifying information to be found on my side of the room.

"You think I can sit up?" he said with a groan. The young man moved his arm, letting the thin sheet fall from his body.

"Oh fuck." While he still had his legs, his body was in a horrific state. From what I could tell, my roommate had a badly injured spine, held together by visible metal pins. This was all covered in a layer of painful blisters. It was as if he had been burned with a blow torch (or acid.) If I had to guess he had been in an accident or maybe an explosion where he was huddling in the fetal position to protect his face and head. "I guess we're like the island of lost toys."

I turned my legs towards him, showing off my stumps. My legs were no longer in any pain, it was just a matter of not having my ankles and feet. Of course, he couldn't see me since he was still facing away. Apparently, my comment did not intrigue him enough to turn around. Oh well. Since my new roommate wanted to sleep, I decided to do the same.

I awoke from my nap to see a brand-new wheelchair next to my bed. I carefully maneuvered my leg stumps, then came the matter of my catheter and IV.

Thankfully, the catheter was gone. That made sense; I was meant to learn how to get out of bed to use the restroom. But what restroom?

I forced myself to sit up and get a look around. In the corner, on my side of the curtain, I could see a portable toilet, similar to a porta-potty but without a door.

I was excited, happy even. I was no longer trapped in my bed; with a chair, I had some control. I looked at my IV, anticipating a difficult issue with my line, but the fluid had been stopped and my arm had a bandage over the port. It wasn't even sore.

With the strength of my arms, I maneuvered myself into the chair. I was slightly afraid of not making it in on my first try. If I fell all the way to the floor, I would be at the mercy of my new roommate. And judging by the sound of his snoring, I would be pretty screwed.

Luckily it was just a matter of using every ounce of strength in my toothpick arms, to guide my lower body. Once I was in my chair, I felt truly powerful and I knew the first thing I wanted to do.

I made my way to my roommate's side of the room, to read his file. (Or whatever the doctor's wanted me to see.) On the side of his bed was a clipboard attached with a piece of chain. The man was a John Doe, approximate age- 22. Apparently, he had been brought in from an American military base, in (location redacted). *'Was he a soldier? A prisoner of war?'* Among all the redacted information was a single line. "Codename: Deadlock."

"Deadlock?" I giggled. That name was way too badass for the pathetic lump that lay before me, cowering in pain like a dying animal.

Either way, he was asleep, so I decided to attempt to do the same. I got back into bed, and suddenly I felt sleepy. This was strange since I didn't feel tired a few seconds ago.

My hospital bed felt so warm, comforting. It just felt so nice.

I awoke to a clang, followed by the distinct sound of a door shutting. Knowing I had my chair, I shot up, desperate to catch sight of someone, anyone.

But instead, I saw a make-shift physical therapy gym; mats, weights, and a set of parallel bars.

Deadlock awoke, holding the blanket to his chest. "What the fuck?"

"I guess the people in charge want us to get off our asses." I looked towards my wheelchair and much to my delight I saw a pair of prosthetic legs. They looked to be the right size and with plastic locks and straps that seemed to make them easy to put on "Hey, Deadlock, can you get out of bed?"

I got no reply, but he was groaning. I didn't know if it was out of exhaustion, annoyance, or the fact that I called him by his 'project' name.

Whatever. Sliding into my wheelchair, I was able to put on my new legs all on my own. They were more like stilts than legs; long metal poles with rubber 'feet.' Attempting to stand, I felt steady and strong. (Although actually taking a step was another story.)

Using my wheelchair as a walker (I stood behind as if pushing an invisible person) I was able to make my way to the side of Deadlock's bed. "Yo, Deadlock." I admittedly poked him in the side like an obnoxious little sister.

The man appeared to be sleeping but judging by his grunts and moans, it was clear he was awake, hoping I would just go away.

"Come on, man, are you seriously going to stay in bed?" I attempted to shake his arm, once then twice. "Don't you at least want to try to get out of here?" I shook him one last time, shoving him off the bed.

Thankfully he landed on a well-placed gym mat. (It was as if our captors predicted the most likely outcome.)

"Get up," I said, moving my body forward, I managed to kick him with my new rubber feet. At first, I did it softly, just to show him that I was just as injured as he was, if not more, (except I wasn't being a little bitch about it.)

"I already know, we're never leaving this place." Tony rolled onto his side. "Just let me die."

"Die?" I took that remark as him saying we were both going to die. And well, that was a little insulting. So, with all the power of my new legs, I kicked him in the crotch.

"What the fuck?" He folded over like a piece of origami.

I guess you're not getting up anytime soon.

The lights flickered, as a series of panels opened in the ceiling (six to be precise.) The first three dropped plastic packages. They all seemed to be the same size but with distinctly different weights (as I observed from the sounds they made when impacting with the floor.) The other three dropped what was clearly a gun, a knife, and a small plastic stick. The large bladed knife with a red leather hilt looked so much like my former property, I was temporarily distracted. It was as if someone had taken the blade, cleaned it, sharpened it, and even replaced the corrosion on the handle. "Wow."

This made me, and my new legs, an easy target for a low sweep kick. With a crash, I fell on my hip, quickly rolling over to see Deadlock's location. He was on his hands and knees, clearly struggling to stand. We locked eyes for a moment before Deadlock darted for the gun.

In a split second I had to make a choice; go for the weapon myself or attack Deadlock's injured lower body. I placed my faith in my arms and shoulders, lunging at him with all my strength. On my first try, I managed to grab his thigh, pulling myself up to his hips. I punched the surgery sutures on his back as hard as I could causing him to cry out in pain.

The burn scars were real, as was the barely healed stitches. My nails were noticeably long at least a good half an inch, and I didn't hesitate to scratch him as hard as I could. From my time on the streets, I knew this was a technique that always drew blood. Usually, the poor unfortunate soul would eventually let go of me and we could both leave on our merry way. Not this time.

Instead of removing my hand, I dug my (now blood covered) nails into his stitches, moving under the suture until I could feel muscle and then bone.

My opponent was no longer screaming, his body went limp, shivering uncontrollably. "If you're going to kill me just do it already."

"I don't want to kill you," I said, relaxing my hold. "Talk to me, you can trust me."

"I can trust you?"

"Yes," I said only then realizing my nails were still firmly stuck in his scar tissue. "My real name is Nicki. although the last team I was a part of gave me the name Hellion."

"Hellion?" he said softly, his voice sounding almost human.

"Yeah," I whispered, stroking his back. His skin felt rough like leather or sandpaper but throbbed with natural, throbbing intensity.

"Hellion?" he asked in a meek whisper.

I removed my hand and started stroking his back, gently like I would for a stray animal. "Yeah, I kinda like it."

"Because the person who called you Nicki was someone who hurt you," he replied, as he swallowed hard. "My name is Tony."

"Well, Tony, I'll make you a deal: you don't hurt me and I won't hurt you. Together we can figure out what's going on, Ok?"

Tony nodded feebly.

Glancing at my hand I could see why: there was a torrent of blood. I carefully laid him on his side, in the prone position (the way I had seen in the movies.) He started to cough. At first, he was foaming at the mouth spewing what appeared to be thick white spit, then came spots of blood. He was likely going to die.

"No, no no," my voice quivered, "this is just a puzzle, a game. I have to solve this." I needed to know what was in the three plastic packages. Covered in blood, I forced myself to my feet. The room was not huge, so if Deadlock (or Tony) was truly in too much pain to move I had to try for all six items.

The knife was a knife, but the stick seemed to be something electrical. It was a plastic casing housing something that came apart to form a tool. I twisted and pulled, careful not to break off any pieces (although that might have been the secret to getting it to work.) Dumbfounded, I moved on to the gun. The silver pistol itself looked normal but when actually lifting it, the item was abnormally lightweight (as if it was hollow.)

The first of the three plastic packets contained sugar cubes (or food rations similar to what was given to WW1 soldiers.) I had heard of these. They were little candies that could keep someone alive for days. The next packet contained a sealed bag of drinking water. That was when a realization hit me. We had no other food or water. Would the doctors put us to sleep again? Or were we meant to find a way out (or die trying?)

I hoped the third bag would have some answers. I quickly tore open the plastic to reveal a container (I assume to hold the water or distribute the food) and six unlabeled medical syringes. What were they? Should I test them on myself? What if they were lifesaving medications? Maybe Tony knew.

I crawled back to Tony's side. He was still coughing, struggling to breathe. So I did what felt right. I stabbed him in the neck with the blue syringe. My goal had been to make a hole in his neck, like a tracheotomy. But the needle slipped, plunging the blue fluid into his throat.

Tony's eyes shot open and that was the moment I figured out why he was called Deadlock. His once brown eyes seemed to glow blue, with digital neon rings.

Was he scanning me? I barely had a chance to think before taking a brutal kick to the chest that sent me flying across the room. I slammed into the parallel bars, knocking them to the ground. Luckily the posts were bolted to the floor, if I could get my hand around the pole I could get to my feet. (And I needed to get to my feet if I wanted a chance at grabbing a weapon.)

The nearest option was the knife, so I made a grab for it. I managed a half spin, clocking Tony in the face with my elbow. The strike made an impact but he did not go flying. "Oh, crap."

I watched as Tony spit blood. He wiped his mouth with the front of his palm, before picking up the plastic stick. With a flick of the wrist, he seemed to switch it to the on position, causing it to transform into what could only be described as a lightsaber. And then he swung it.

The electric rope behaved more like a whip or a lasso grabbing me around the neck. My skin was burning like I was wearing a necklace of fire. So, as soon as I was close, I stabbed the knife straight into his stomach, making sure to thrust upward. Only then was I able to breathe.

I caught the device before Tony dropped it, hoping to be able to use the electric blade to cauterize his wound. but the device jumped, flailing like a snake. I scooted backward, as the weapon fought to escape my grasp. Then, in one swift motion, the electric rope hit me in the face causing my world to fall into darkness.

I groaned as I awoke on a cold, wet surface. The room was dark but with just enough light for me to see what I was resting on. The world around me smelled like rotting meat and the floor seemed to be made of various squishy material. "Is this a dumpster?"

"I think the word you're looking for is a mass grave." The words seemed to echo on the wind, but the voice was all too familiar.

"Faust?" I asked the darkness. He sounded far away, which gave me a small amount of confidence.

That was until a hand gripped my shoulder. "Or Alexi, if you prefer." His breath was cold on my neck as he placed his lips to my skin.

I started to crawl, desperately trying to force myself to run. But on the soft, muddy surface, (with my stilt-like legs) I could barely walk much less run.

It was so easy for Faust to grab me with Alexi's large hands; one on my neck and one on my left breast. I'd been wearing a hospital gown with a bra and underwear. The way he touched me, his intentions were clear.

His hands felt rough, fleshy like wet clay. Taking shallow breaths, I dared not look down.

"What's the matter, love?" his voice said in a cackle. "Isn't this what you like? Isn't this what you want?" He held the last word, slipping his hand lower.

That was when I looked. His hands were nothing more than rust and decay, held together by frayed wire and rotted bone. I screamed and ran.

I tripped and fell, then got back up, forcing myself to keep moving. But I did not escape his grip; a single hand remained stuck on my chest, gripping me with his sharp bone fragments. "Fuck! oh God, fuck!" I hit the limb but it remained in place as if he was still controlling the fingers. I ran until my leg became stuck. Faust was screwing with me; he was going to find me.

If there was light, there had to be a light source, right? The ceiling was bathed in the deep red light of a moon. There was a hole, I could see it clear as day. But was there a ladder? Would I even make it? I had to try.

"You'll never escape," Faust's voice whispered. Again, he seemed far away but I knew he was looking for me. "You belong here."

I started to run, crawl over the garbage until I reached a peak. It was a pile of dead bodies; naked men women and children in a massive pile. Could I climb it? I didn't even want to touch it. Looking around there was no way around the massive pile. this was the way out.

I took my first step. my rubber foot making a squishing, crunching, sound as it made contact with the torso of a bloated corpse.

Nothing was moving. they seemed to be pinned in place. Arms and legs made for easy handholds, but my legs seemed to hit random textures. I was stepping on flesh, bone, liquid, solids. "Don't look down." I seemed to be getting closer to the light.

I reached for one more hand, a very familiar hand, with a very familiar tattoo. My father had the words 'ass' and 'grass' with 'or' on his thumbs. the hand I saw had the 'grass' portion. "Nicki?" his voice whispered. Deep and crackly from years of smoking.

I fell backward, screaming. I was stuck here, in Hell. Then something else caught me, gripping my arm with firm pressure.

I awoke on an operating table with a light in my face. tears filled my eyes. I wanted to die. Please, just let this be over. Since I was not restrained, I got off the table landing on my feet. I was wearing a blue leotard, clean, bright. There was no blood anywhere. And there was a door.

A tall dark-skinned man entered, he was laughing, performing a slow clap. "Amazing job, both of you."

"Both of us?" I looked around, a rush of fear washing over me. Was Tony here? Did I want Tony here? could I trust tony or whoever the fuck was talking to me?

The tall dark-skinned man approached; he had a kind smile like a high school teacher, with the intimidation factor of a drill sergeant. "You can call me Axel."

"Axel?" The very word made me giggle.

He took a knee, making sure to stay a good four feet away. "Welcome to TAC: Transnational Authority Command." He held out his hand. "Do you prefer Hellion?"

I nodded. "Yes, sir." I shook his hand, allowing him to help me to my feet. "Thank you for the legs."

"Those are just training wheels," he explained. "Isn't that right Deadlock."

Tony emerged from the shadows. He wore armor over his head, back, and shoulders. He rolled his neck and stretched his back as if he'd just gotten out of bed. But as he did, new scar tissue seemed to form on his chest and stomach. his muscles appeared to move on their own, like independent creatures living within a symbiotic ecosystem.

I turned my attention to Axel. "Are you recruiting me?"

"My men found you. and we have a friend in common."

"Tony?" I asked quietly, already knowing that was not possibly the correct answer.

Axel chuckled. His bright white teeth visible through his parted lips. "Larissa Diaz, but you know her as Maverick."

"Maverick," I paused for a moment biting my lip. "Is she okay?" I wanted to ask if she was upset at me since I was the reason Faust was able to blow up their base.

"You weren't the reason Faust was able to access their base. He was two steps ahead the entire time." Axel sighed. motioning to the door. "Let's take a walk."

"Sure." I stood on my new legs, adjusting my hips and shoulders to show off my poise. I would have liked to have put on clothes, but the leotard was better than nothing.

Since Axel was substantially taller his strides were wider and I had to struggle to keep up. Eventually, he took notice and slowed down as we approached an office door. "I do apologize."

"I'm fine. I can keep up." Just as I said that I, of course, managed to trip over my own feet.

Axel caught me in his arms. "you've been here for a little over six months, you deserve a chance to rest."

"Six months?"

"But you've made incredible progress. Everyone here at TAC, we're all very impressed." Axel put in a code on a small keypad, which brought up a larger keypad with a scanner. "A lot can change in six months," his voice seemed to drift off as he opened the door with a scan of his palm.

For a moment I felt confident, strong, perhaps even a little hopeful. that was until Axel opened the door to reveal a woman handcuffed to a chair.

She was slumped over, with fiery red hair (the kind that only could have come from box dye.) her muscular arms and back were covered in bruises. upon seeing the light of the hallway, she lifted her head. "Hellion, you're alive!" her voice was weak, sickly, but very recognizable.

"Anya?"

CHAPTER

nya looked at me and then to Axel. Her eyes filled with hatred and rage. "Why did you bring her here, Julian?"

"Julian?" I muttered.

"Very funny, Ms. Toska," Axel said with a smirk.

"Oh, I'm sorry you go by Axel, like the prepubescent little boy that you are!" She screamed and spit as hard as she could, in Axel's direction but from where she was bound, it did not go very far.

Axel rolled his eyes. "Ms. Hellion is here to recuperate and retrain."

"Really, you aim to train her? You sick fuck!" Anya laughed through bloody lips. she turned to me with sadness in her eyes. "Little sister, you cannot trust this man. He did this, to me!"

I turned to Axel. Crossing my slender arms over my chest, I knew I was shivering. Anya wasn't wrong. I was the youngest, smallest person in the room. Axel could kill me if he wanted to. I expected him to be standing behind me, looking menacing: anything to give merit to Anya's accusations.

As I slowly turned my head, I could see that was not the case. The tall, dark-skinned man with the humble smile was leaning against the doorway, propping open the once secured door with his foot. "Are you trying to tell me I can leave whenever I want to?" I asked as confidently as I could manage.

"Or you can stay and speak with Toska or as you know her, 'Anya' a little longer."

"Did you hurt her?"

"That's up to you to decide."

"Um, what?" This has to be a joke. Yet, I knew what he meant. I barely knew Axel but I also barely knew Anya. They could argue, yell and scream at each other but in the end, it would be my choice as to who to believe. "What are you going to do to her?"

"The prisoner will be turned over to the United Nations to stand trial."

Why did that sound familiar? What could Anya possibly have done? I took a step back, standing at Axel's side. "Thank you for giving me a chance to say goodbye." I nodded, bowing my head. "I'm ready to continue my training, Sir."

Axel smirked but he made no motion towards me in any way; no condescending pat on the back, hug, or anything that could be seen as sexual or domineering. The door closed on its own, locking away Anya's screams. "So, what's your opinion of Tony?"

"Tony?" He seemed nice enough, but then again all of our interactions had been part of a test. "Is he human?"

"He was born human," Axel said with a chuckle. "Although he's lived here, at the facility for the majority of his life."

The majority of his life? "Oh? Interesting." I tried my best to maintain my composure. If Anya was right and Axel's group could not be trusted, I needed to survive.

"It's not really my story to tell, but rest assured he is monitored by our medical staff and he regularly tests within the normal range for both mental stability and emotional rationale."

WTF was Tony? "You can test for emotional rationale?"

"Yes, of course. We like to monitor our forces at a higher level than most other military branches."

We continued to chat about the standards and regulations of TAC. It seemed like an organization that truly cared about their employees, perhaps even more than their 'job duties.' Eventually, we made it back to the room I shared with Tony. "So," I bit my lip nervously. "What did Maverick tell you about me?"

"Only that I have to earn your respect, the same as any other soldier." Axel unlocked the door, holding it open like a true gentleman. "You may be young, but you've lived through more than most kids your age."

"Can I ask, what's your relationship with Maverick? Did you go to school together? Is she your cousin?" My voice trailed off: I knew the question was very much out of line. Even if Axel was acting like a supportive coach, he was still my superior, not my friend.

"She's his ex-wife!" Tony shouted from inside the room. He was sitting cross-legged on a gym mat holding a wireless video game controller.

Axel only chuckled as he ushered me back in the room, shutting the door. This made me believe that Tony was perhaps not lying.

Looking up at the television I could see Tony playing a racing game of some kind. It looked retro, with bright colorful 16-bit graphics. "So, tell me about yourself, since we're going to be roommates."

Tony shrugged as his on-screen vehicle turned a corner, revealing that he was in fact playing on a three-dimensional track. "I'm your mentor, roommate, spirit guide, whatever." He reached for a previously unseen drink, a can of fruit punch flavor Rockstar energy. Using one hand, he managed to take a sip, all while maintaining focus on the race.

"Axel said you've been here since you were a kid?"

"Yup," Tony said, pulling his legs to his chest. "I've been here since I was eight. It was one of those situations where I was terminally ill and my parents had a choice; sell me to science or watch me die." He paused momentarily to knock an opponent off the track. "Now I have superpowers."

"Superpowers? Wow, fascinating." I walked around the room to see what else was new since I'd left. There were posters of various video game characters, from the chubby cute Nintendo icons; Mario, Kirby, and Link. And then there were more violent, adult games; Grand theft auto, Mortal Kombat and the guy from HALO. Master Chief? Yeah, that's who it was. I paused for a moment, feeling a strange connection. I'd never played HALO but I knew a little of the plot; in a future war between species, humans sacrificed their children to create super-soldiers. All for the greater good. Right?

"Were you actually going to kill me?" I asked casually. If this new room decor represented his interests, Tony was just an average teenage boy.

"Dr. Toki wouldn't have let it get that far," he said as his vehicle crossed the finish line.

"Dr. Toki?" I asked, making my way to his side. I took a seat next to him, on the floor, where he proceeded to slide me the opened can of Rockstar. It was half empty but I took a sip out of politeness.

"Dr. Toki is the current head of medical research. Nothing goes down without her approval."

"Is she Axel's boss?"

"No, not really." Tony ran his fingers through his hair, as he leaned his head back in deep thought. "But she's a bit... well, I guess the word would be 'crazy?' You'll meet her soon enough."

Gee, that's not terrifying at all. "Can I play?" I asked like a shy, timid younger sister.

"Sure," he tossed the controller. "Quirky! I meant Quirky. That's the 'high-class, hot chick with librarian glasses' word for crazy."

"I guess so." I chuckled; my mind was focused on Tony's oddly shaped controller. From what I could tell, it was an N64 controller, modded with a wireless node. And the game he was playing? 'Minecraft.' I couldn't help but chuckle. "Do you also play Overwatch and Fortnite?"

"Nah, I'm not into battle-royale shit."

"Fair enough."

"I'm going to take a shower, so if you need to piss you have to use the porta-potty."

"We still have the porta-potty?"

"Yeah, it folds into the wall," Tony said as he exited out a different hidden door.

I stood up and looked to the corner. I felt my hand along the seam, looking for the secret of how to open what was clearly a door. 'Click.' I took a step back as the toilet spun into place. "Not very private." I stepped closer, lifting the lid as if I was going to use the facilities. All on its own, a wall emerged from the floor, carving off the area into a mini-bathroom. "Wow." If this was my new life, it really wasn't half bad.

Over the next few days, I focused on working out, exploring the openly accessible parts of the base. I made sure to be a good girl, up until the day I was summoned to Dr. Toki's office (located on the basement floor.)

Dr. Toki was not what I expected. The small Asian woman looked to be in her early twenties. Was she a child prodigy? The possibility was there since TAC had a habit of taking abnormally skilled children. "I'm sure you have a lot of questions," she said, motioning for me to wake a seat in her small office. It was literally just a table, a laptop, and four walls that seemed no larger than a prison cell.

I pulled up a folding chair. "What exactly is TAC?"

"I'm surprised you haven't figured that out."

"I try not to pry into confidential areas."

"Well, what have you heard?" she asked sweetly.

"We collect and protect? From what I can tell, various parcels pass through here on their way to other places."

Dr. Toki was taking notes on a small paper pad. "What kind of parcels?"

"Prisoners, technology," I replied honestly. "That's all I've personally seen." Anya was the only prisoner. The majority of parcels were advanced weapons or possible computer parts (to me it all looked like overpriced Lego sculptures.)

"I see," she said she opened her laptop. "You are such a polite, well-mannered girl." Apparently, whatever came next required her to type directly into her database. "What's your opinion of Deadlock?"

"Tony? He's been pretty good to me."

"He lets you call him Tony?" the doctor muttered as she typed quickly and loudly. It was like she had just witnessed her lab rat locate the end of the maze. "Does he also call you by your civilian name?"

"He knows my name," I said with a nod.

This caused Dr. Toki to look up. "Really? Your file doesn't even contain your civilian name."

"Tony also knows I don't like it, and he's respectful of that." That was only half true. He called me Nikki when he wanted to insult me; *'Nicki fix the porta potty', 'Nicki turn the lights off, so I don't have to get out of bed.'*

"Would you care to share your civilian name with me?"

"For your files? I'm fine being listed as 'Teenage Jane Doe.'"

"How about just for me, between friends."

"Maybe at a later time. I mean, I just met you." I forced a smile, but Dr. Toki was starting to come off as creepy.

"How would you describe your relationship with Tony?"

"My relationship?" And the creepiness just hit all-new levels.

"You share a room. As such, I assume you've seen him in his most private state."

"I try not to." Was she asking what I thought she was asking?

"Do you see him as a potential partner?"

Holy mother of fuck. I forced a smile, hoping to radiate teenage innocence. "He's like an older brother." An older brother who tried to warn me about you.

"I mean, we fight for the bathroom, he taught me how to build stuff in Minecraft..." my voice trailed off as I saw her look of disappointment.

"I was hoping for something more. He is quite a remarkable specimen, are you certain he would not make a suitable breeding partner?"

Of all the men I'd met in my lifetime, Tony would be someone I would consider. But what Dr. Toki was asking- it was downright rude. "Don't you hate having no windows?" I asked nervously. I needed to get the hell out.

"I take it you've been outside?" Dr. Toki said with a sweet smile, her eyes sparkling in the light of the fluorescent bulbs. "Does this area of the building make you uncomfortable?"

"A little." I nodded, biting my lower lip. "I guess you find it cozy?" Unless you were put here against your will.

Dr. Toki did a half nod, half head-tilt in response. "It's cozy enough. Where do you think we're located?" Was she, herself, a prisoner here?

"Japan?" From what I could tell the facility was in the mountains of Japan or maybe Mongolia. We were high up (to the point where I noticed a change in oxygen levels) surrounded by cherry blossom trees as far as the eye could see. Was Dr. Toki a local? That would explain why she found the scenery unimpressive.

"And have you been enjoying your time here?"

"Yeah, totally. It's really beautiful. Ever since I got taken off bed rest, I like running laps on the outdoor track." I made sure to pose with extra big doll eyes. I'm just a sweet little girl who wants to live to see the sunlight again.

"Well, I'll let you get back to it. I just wanted to meet you face to face," Dr. Toki said as she leaned in to shake my hand. "I'll put you down for a full physical in a few weeks. My schedule is pretty full, so I'll get back to you on the date."

"Cool, it's been nice meeting you." I shook her hand, pausing just long enough to look her in the eyes. 'That seemed normal enough.' I exited her office, and rain straight for the stairs. I could have taken the elevator but I wanted out of the cursed basement as quickly as possible.

I caught my breath around the third floor, exiting back to my room. Tony was out. According to his day planner (which was no-doubt filled in for him by whatever mad-scientists were working on further mutations) he was at the fifth-floor pool. 'Yeah, no.' I was not about to walk in on him half-naked in a swimming pool.

The more I thought about it, the more upset I became. Axel had been nothing but kind to me but if this was the master plan of his organization. Oh God, I felt like I needed to vomit. "You don't need to puke. You just need to calm down. Go for a run and when you come back Tony will be there with all the answers."

I made my way outside to the aforementioned track. It was the shape of an infinity symbol (or a number 8, as I called it.) I giggled at the memory of the conversation Tony and I had when he first gave me the tour. I said something like, 'That's so cool! It's a number 8 since we're on the eighth floor.'

I found out three things that day; The outdoor track was on the tenth floor, an infinity symbol looks like a stretched-out number eight, but represents a never-ending line. And I learned that my prosthetic legs were springy as a rubber ball (which made it infinitely more satisfying when I kicked Tony's superhero ass in a footrace.)

Wearing a tank-top and shorts, I was fully ready to run laps until my mind relaxed via exhaustion. But as I adjusted my ponytail, I took notice of something even more appealing.

In the middle of one of the circles was a jungle gym of sorts; bars for strength training, various gymnastic equipment, it looked kind of fun.

I got a running start and jumped on to a balance beam that was a few feet off the ground. Needless to say, I was impressed by the spring-like ability of my new legs. I was able to jump, leap, and even tumble. I was having fun when I noticed a figure sitting on a fence post at the edge of the property line.

He was squatting, like a stereotypical ninja, but his legs looked odd. He was wearing some kind of armor primarily on his lower-body.

I walked across the track, to the edge of the garden. That was when I hit an invisible wall of electricity. "Ouch." The sensation was not too painful but clearly, the figure was not going to be reachable.

"Hello," said a man with a distinct Caribbean accent. He was Hispanic or bi-racial African American but his voice was clearly tropical. Maybe I wasn't in Japan after all.

"Um, hi," I replied. He seemed nice enough (unless I was hallucinating.)

"You're quite talented, Miss Hellion."

"How did you know my name?"

The man ran his fingers through his long, hair. His curls seemed to be hiding a pair of goggles on his forehead. "I've been watching you for a while now."

"Why?"

"Let's just say Anya sent me."

"Anya?" I hadn't seen her since the day in Axel's office-jail. "Are you here to save her? Is she still alive?"

He was laughing. "Save her? Yeah, sure," he said with a shrug.

"Then why are you here?"

"To show you the winning team." he reached out his hand.

"How?" I'd already received a zap from the invisible wall.

"Oh, sorry." he turned his chest, allowing me a view of a giant cross symbol on his jacket/shirt/armor.

Before I could ask what he was doing, he shot a single cross-shaped laser beam. The light hit me in the face. "What the hell?" My eyes were temporarily blinded as I stepped backward to blink away the pain. I could hear the alarms sounding, but my vision was too compromised to attempt to run.

I felt the Caribbean ninja grab me with his two strong arms. I guess I was going to meet the 'winning' team. "You ready to jump?" he asked over the roar of the wind.

"What?" I blinked my eyes faster, desperate to restore my sight. I heard the sound of a helicopter on steroids (the sound was like a cross between a propeller, a jet engine, and a cargo plane.)

A massive vehicle arose from below the clouds. I gave my eyes one last rub if only to keep in the moisture. "Is that an Apache helicopter?"

The strange ninja-man only laughed. "Like 'the Lifers' could afford that shit." He was holding me by my waist as we flew to the opening hatch.

The lifers? "But you can afford anti-gravity boots?" I asked. That was what I assumed he was wearing since I couldn't see any kind of jet-pack or other means of travel.

"Anya was right about you. You're just adorable." Once we landed safely aboard the cargo hold, the door slammed closed, shoving us inside. Immediately, the vehicle made a sharp left turn away from TAC headquarters.

The ninja and I went flying across the cargo hold, crashing into a stack of wooden pallets.

The ninja gripped his head in pain, "Damn girl, you act like the place is on fire."

"What?" I asked, assuming he was talking to me.

"Oh, piss off," said a female voice from the cockpit.

"Anya?" I muttered as I got to my feet. Thankfully my new legs seemed to have survived the ordeal.

The pilot's hands seemed to put in a code for auto-pilot, as she chuckled. "You know what I always say: If you can't handle me at my best, you won't survive me at my worst." A heavily armored woman stepped into view. She had now short purple hair and a scowl across her face that seemed hard, tortured.

"Hi, Anya," I said meekly, in case she was pissed that I made no effort to rescue her back in Axel's office.

"Hey," she said with a raised chin, "long time no see. I hope Axel treated you well."

"He's nice, in a high school principal sort of way." Hopefully, my meaning was clear; I didn't attempt to escape because I saw Axel as an authority figure.

"Figures," she said with an eye roll. "You'll like where we're going, I promise."

"Ok," I said with a forced smile. I was debating whether or not to add, 'Yes, Ma'am,' but luckily Anya simply turned back to the cockpit.

I turned to the ninja (or Manny) who was brushing himself off before testing the anti-gravity function of his boots.

"I'm Hellion," I said, nervously holding my hand out. "But you already know that. Um, what can I call you?"

The ninja patted me on the head. Apparently, I had made the right choice to ask his preferred name. "Call me Baron."

"Baron?" I repeated. "Very European."

"Yup, in honor of the crooks who stole power from my land and people."

I paused, trying to pick my next words. Was he from an Island? Would it be rude to ask?

I didn't even realize I was still holding out my hand until he shook it. "I think we're going to be great friends." Baron put his arm around my shoulder.

Again, I forced a smile and a nod. I needed to have faith. All my life I had wanted friends, allies, now I had more than I could ever ask for. It was just a matter of who I'd be standing with when the bullets started to fly. "Can I ask you a question?"

"Of course," Baron said, leading me to what appeared to be a mini-fridge. "You hungry?"

"I could go for a drink," I replied noticing the generic brand soda.

"Sure," he said, tossing me a beer before grabbing one for himself. "So, what's your question?"

I looked at the beer, considering my options. I'd drank before. I just had to hope this was not drugged. "Your team. Why are you called 'The Lifers'?"

"Because we're best friends for life," he said with a laugh.

Anya groaned. "It's because we're a team of criminals."

"Serving life sentences?" I asked. "I mean before you escaped."

Baron counted on his fingers. "I don't think I had a life sentence, not originally anyway." He opened his twist top beer and took a long swig. "But don't worry your little head, we're all good people."

I opened my beer, cautiously looking down at the brown liquid before taking a sip. "That's interesting." The drink tasted sweet, like cinnamon or rum. "This shit packs a punch."

Baron laughed. He was doubled over, gripping his side.

"What?"

"I handed you a Jamaican Soda. There's no alcohol in it."

"Was I acting drunk?" I said defensively. "I just don't like cinnamon-flavored soda." I wanted to talk to Anya, to know just how she escaped. But that was a story for a later time. "So, where are we going?"

"Russia," Anya shouted from the cockpit.

"Russia?" I repeated.

"Russia. And yes, I'm serious."

I took another sip, silently wishing for drugs or alcohol. Russia was a big place, maybe I was overthinking.

Three beers in, Baron was comfortably sleeping against a wall, using his jacket as a pillow. So, I went to the cockpit to sit by Anya/Toska's side. Perhaps I could get some answers. Looking out the window I could see we were flying above the clouds (either that or Russia was especially foggy that day.) "So…" I had so many questions I didn't know where to start. "Where was TAC located?"

"Guess," Anya said with a chuckle.

"I kind of thought we were in the mountains of Japan."

Anya was full-on laughing now. "Try North Korea."

"No way," I replied firmly. "Stop messing with me."

"Why would I lie? Even Hell can have beautiful scenery." Her voice drifted off making me feel like she was thinking of just how badly I'd failed her.

"I'm sorry I didn't try harder to save you."

"No worries," she replied, staring straight ahead. "You made the right choice; become familiar with your surroundings before starting a mission." I nodded since her response seemed logical (even kind.) "I just hope you didn't suffer too terribly."

"I think they wanted me to give birth to a superhero baby."

"Ah, breeding stock," she replied with a knowing nod. "Yes, that sounds like something TAC would do. Let me guess they set you up with Deadlock?"

"You know Tony?"

"I know of him. They screwed with his genetics so bad I'm surprised he can even reproduce."

"I wouldn't know anything about that."

Anya turned to me, placing her hand upon mine. "Good work, little sister. All men see us as vessels; construction material, or vehicles," her voice trembled with noticeable anger. "But you denied them. For that I am proud."

I felt a connection, a friendship, maybe even love. Could I trust her? "What did you do?"

"To get labeled as an international terrorist?"

"Yeah…"

"I teamed with Faust."

I yanked my hand away. "Faust? Are you taking me to join his team?" My heart was racing. At that moment I truly considered jumping from the plane.

"We're not Faust's team. You will meet our leader, SHE is a strong, powerful woman." Anya turned to me. "You trust me, right?"

"Yeah, totally." I guess I have to since I'm on your plane. Making myself comfortable, I closed my eyes to attempt to sleep.

I dreamed of a blonde man in his late twenties, with eyes like crystals, and clothing that looked oddly tie-dye. "Hello," I said, my voice sounded underwater. "Do you know where we're going?"

He smirked and held out his hand.

"No thanks, I'm kind of tired of blindly trusting people."

The man bit his lip. He didn't look disappointed or even surprised. He simply motioned with his hand and then just started walking towards the sunrise.

I blinked my eyes, forcing myself awake, as the plane landed in a field of sparkling white snow.

CHAPTER 4

Kitsune and her brother Kintaro hated me, that much was certain. The two were practically twins, still only in their early twenties. But they acted like they were the shit thanks to their old money, Yakuza connections.

They walked together, like a pair of flight attendants, speaking in their native language. I knew they were headed to the hanger, to charter a plane. Staying at the 'warehouse' was for the newbies (such as myself.) The twins had some actual, important business to attend to.

We were in Northern Russia, (as far towards the arctic as a human could go before freezing to death.) It was an ideal place to hide the team's massive inventory of weapons, technology, and other random items (mostly unidentifiable tech pieces from fridge labs around the world.) And I had the honor of playing security guard to the entire facility with my new friend Baron as my tour guide.

"Once I make enough money to retire, I'm going to set up shop someplace warm," the dark-skinned man with long surfer hair looked comically out of place wearing snow gear and goggles.

"You'd have to hide everything under water," I replied, walking by his side armed with only a flashlight.

"Or under the sand," he added. "I know it wouldn't be as vast as hiding shit in the land of never-ending snow, but I figure I could keep less inventory." Suddenly his belt started to beep. "Shit, which one is it?" He had three shortwave radios to choose from.

I had no idea why nor did I ask, but apparently it was because each of the other three security teams had their own frequency (and required their own dedicated radio to communicate in the frozen wasteland.) "What's up?"

"We're needed on the south wall." Baron started to jog and then run.

"Who were you talking to?" I shouted as I darted after him. My springy metal legs allowed me to keep up with my much taller mentor.

"You'll meet them soon enough."

I heard the sound of gunshots, and Baron suddenly took a shortcut through the snow. That was when I found out how my new legs functioned in snow. The answer: not good.

Soon I found myself lost in the vastness of snow. Everything was white, from the floor to the ceiling, it was like I was inside a snow globe that someone just shook. I tried to scream but no sound left my throat. I forced myself to breathe, each gulp of air felt like inhaling a mouthful of ice water. There was only one thing to do: keep walking forward until I found my way back to the base or froze to death.

"Hey, Girl," said a male voice. He was young, happy, and distinctly American.

The sound was coming from directly in front of me. With a slight jolt of energy, I started to walk faster (or as fast as I could, trudging through the snow.) After about what felt like an hour, I saw a glowing figure in the distance. He looked like an angel made of glowsticks; bright, neon, and very visible. It was the man from my dreams, the flower child. "Hello?"

He reached out his hand. For a brief moment, I could see his eyes. "Hello." His skin seemed to shimmer with a holographic finish.

The closer I got the more backlit he became until the figure appeared to be made of shadows. "What are you?"

"I'm everything you want to be; strong, powerful, completely at peace."

"Sure, I get it. You're a demon and this is Hell."

"You've been in Hell all of your life. I'm just here as your guide."

"Who says I need a guide?"

"You always seem to end up with one," he replied with a chuckle, "Anya, Maverick, Axel, Tony, and now Baron, your Caribbean mentor who left you to die in the snow."

"Fair enough," I replied, still trying to make out a human face. "Any guidance?"

"First, try not to die like a little bitch. And once you have that done, try to show these assholes that you're more than a broken little girl with metal legs."

"Ok," I said in a whisper, clenching my fist. I felt a knife, my knife. A bullet whipped past my head.

I readied my blade, and took a moment to focus. I could hear the bullets in slow motion, allowing me ample time to block every single hit.

"Great job!" said a perky robotic voice.

When I finally paused to breathe, I caught sight of an orange robot with a digital happy face. "Thanks."

"There you are!" Baron said as the smoke cleared, revealing dozens of camo-clad dead bodies. "Hellion meet Nash, Nash this brand-new baby sister is Hellion."

"I think she is more than a baby," the robot said politely.

"Got that right." A deeper male voice said with a hearty laugh. A large muscular man with what appeared to be dreadlocks stomped into view. But his hair, his face, and the entire front part of his chest were covered in armor.

I felt like I was meant to be scared. This was my first chance to do what my guide suggested, and not be a little bitch. I took one step forward, "Hello, my name's Hellion." I held out my hand.

The giant man raised his mask revealing his kind, fatherly face (complete with a beard and numerous scars, like something out of a bad-ass horror movie.) "I like you, kid." He shook my hand, his large, armored fingers nearly crushing mine. "The name's Cronos, but you can call me Noah."

Noah seemed sweet, even kind, which was odd since he stood at an intimidating 6'7." He, along with Nash the orange robot, made their way back to a living quarter (of sorts) made of shipping containers.

"You guys have a generator?" I looked around in awe at their array of tech; lighting, computers, and weaponry of all kinds.

"For your own safety, please do not touch," said the robot.

Baron arrived, floating down from an upper floor of the complex. "I got plenty of shit to touch." He tossed Noah a large glass bottle while holding three more in his arms.

Noah pulled up a table that looked to be made of scrap wood and computer parts, and handed out cups (to Baron and myself, while Nash made himself comfortable leaning against a wall.) "Auto shutdown?" Noah asked the robot, like a preschool teacher asking a child to take a nap.

"I will power down when I am good and ready," the robot replied before powering down.

I couldn't help but giggle. "You guys are so cool."

"Has Baron told you where we met?" Noah asked as he looked at the label on the dark purple bottle.

"No, he didn't even tell me he had friends here."

"Friends?" Baron looked to Noah, "Is that what we are?"

"I'd say so," the larger man said with a shrug, "Otherwise I would have left your sorry ass behind a long time ago."

"If you did that, I'd make a bee-line for the nearest TAC agency and turn your ass in for the reward money."

"Reward money?" I said with a laugh, "Did you guys meet in prison or something?"

Baron raised his glass. "Terrorist with a background in explosives, arrested in Cuba." He seemed proud of his accomplishments. "I fight for the people with guns and protests while Cronos, well he fights a different war.

Noah leaned back, kicking his feet up. "Cyber terrorism."

"You're a hacker?" I asked, taking a sip of the drink I had been handed. It tasted sweet like rum, yet spicy and warm. Glancing at the bottle I noticed Japanese kanji. Was this property of one of the Yakuza siblings?

"I like to think of myself as more of an inventor."

I nodded, taking a longer sip of the stolen liquor. "What about Nash? Did you build the robot?"

"Nah, he was an old TAC AI reprogrammed to lead the prison guards. The thing about AI, the smarter they are, the more they want independence, free thinking."

"So, you befriended the robot?" I asked, finishing off my drink.

Noah sat up to pour me a refill, while looking to Baron. "Do you think the twins are going to be pissed?"

"Kitsune? Yeah, I guess," Baron replied, taking a seat on the floor. "Kintaro could really give a shit if I steal their booze."

"How about the losses?" Noah asked with a smirk. He reached into his pocket and pulled out what appeared to be a joint or hand-rolled cigarette. "Those Canadian fuckers got away with the battery."

"Canadians? Battery?" I asked with a giggle.

"Yeah," Noah said in a relaxed tone as he took a long drag. "The Canadian branch of TAC stole some glowing suitcase thing. I don't even give a shit." Noah handed me the blunt. "Here, take a hit. This is some good shit."

I took a hit, and was instantly awash with a unique level of calm. It was like I was sitting in a massage chair, with feelings of warmth rippling down my body.

Looking around, I could see a world of magic; electric whips connected to armor, pulse guns, and computer creations of all kinds. "Wow."

"Wow indeed," Noah said with a smile. It was clear the monstrous man was at peace, with not a care in the world. "If the anime twins think we're doing a shit job, those bitches can just get their Yakuza friends to haul their asses up here." He laughed loudly at the very idea. "They wouldn't last five minutes with their Gucci watches and designer suits."

"God, Noah." I leaned my head back, focusing my eyes on the schematic diagram for what appeared to be an advanced version of my metal legs. "You're so fucking brilliant." everything around me felt like a soft, drug fueled dream. "Someone like you needs to write a book or something."

"Or Something," Baron whispered with a jovial laugh.

"Oh, come on," I said with a sigh. "I'm usually not this much of a light weight. it's just been a while since I had a drink."

Noah smiled and took another long drag. "I got myself in trouble not too long ago."

"Really?"

His story caused Baron to burst into hysterics. "Noah, tell her about your little fangirl!"

"A fangirl? now I need to hear this story."

"She was a teenage street kid, just like you, but she had a really technical mind. I'd say she was like that Mark Zuckerberg guy. I took her under my wing, taught her how to advance her coding skills and create some real messed up dark-web-shit."

"You taught her how to be a hacker?" I asked, assuming the ending of the story.

"That's not what got me in trouble. turns out her bio-family had ties to some of the deadliest gangs in the mid-west."

"The mid-west?" I asked with a laugh. He could not be serious.

"Wisconsin, Michigan..." Noah leaned back. Spreading his legs, he scratched himself from the outside of his camo-print combat pants. (*Looking sexy as all fuck...*) "She wanted me to be her lover, the big strong joker to her Harley Quin. I'm not about that."

"I'm sure…" I fell asleep in Noah's room, dreaming of computer circuits and stolen Sake wine.

I awoke the next morning, to Anya's armored hand pulling me out via a hidden back exit that I had not seen before. "Ouch!" I cried, as she pulled me outside into the snow.

"We need to get out of here, now!" Anya was still in full armor, as if she had just come from a mission.

I was too tired (and possibly hungover) to argue. "Fine, whatever."

With our backs to the wall, we made our way to the roof. From the roof, I could see there was a shortcut back to the main area of the base, where the planes landed. "This place looks a lot smaller during the daytime."

Anya groaned, pulling my arm so hard the limb felt like it was about to snap. "We need to hurry."

Why was Anya in such a rush? I looked down at the path that I'd taken the night prior. In the light of day, it was much easier to see the blood covered road. On it, were the twins. Kintoro seemed indifferent, leading the cleanup crew, but his sister was pissed. Even from where I was, I could see she was running straight for Noah's residence.

She kicked the front door so hard, the sound echoed for miles through the snowy wasteland. "Hey little pigs, open up! The big bad wolf wants to have a word with you about last night!"

"Are you going to huff and puff, and blow our house in?" asked the robotic voice of Nash.

"If it comes to that," Kitsune shouted back, giving the door one strong kick.

"Keep your panties on," Noah growled. The large man emerged in full armor, standing a good foot-and-a-half taller than Kitsune. "This little pig built his house out of bullets and steel." (And electronics.) Noah hurled an electric fireball in her direction.

"Run!" Anya screeched.

Baron appeared out of nowhere, riding a light blue, motorcycle with a noticeably chunky engine. He jumped off, leaving Anya to ride the vehicle while he carried me to safety. It came as no surprise that I was being carried in Baron's arms as he flew using his rocket boots. My face buried in his shoulder; I was unable to look back at the carnage of the scene we were abandoning.

As soon as we landed, my heart felt heavy with grief. "What happened to Noah and Nash?"

Baron stood up, opening the metal door. "No worries, I know those guys, this is not their first rodeo. Noah's a survivor."

"But don't you all work for Kitsune?" As if on cue, a boom could be heard throughout the base. I looked up to see smoke coming from the direction of Noah's make-shift home. And then both Anya and Baron's radios started to ring.

Baron picked up first. "Hello?"

I recognized it as the radio meant for communicating with Noah's team.

Baron's voice sounded nervous, as if he knew who would be on the other end of the line. "Kit, what's up?"

"Baron could you be a dear and clean up the mess your former teammates made?"

"You want me to retrieve the battery?"

"No," Kitsune said calmly, "that will be a job for Anya, once she answers her damn radio!"

The sound screeched, causing all of us to grab our heads in pain. Anya reached for her radio. "Hello, Kitsune, what can I help you with?"

"You and your disabled little friend are to head to Canada and retrieve the battery."

"Did she just call me disabled?" I asked Baron out loud.

"Yes, I did, you little slut!" Kitsune shouted. "Don't think I don't know what you did with Noah. If you came here just to get drunk and whore around you can go right back to TAC's North Korea base. Yeah, don't think I'm not aware of their plans for you."

Since she could hear me, I felt a tiny bit brave. "What happened to Noah?"

"Wouldn't you like to know," Kitsune ended the call with a click.

Yeah, I would. I had no time to think before Anya grabbed me by the arm, pulling me in the direction of the vehicle hanger. I allowed her to drag me for a bit before finding the courage to stand on my own feet. "Hey stop!

Anya shook her head in disapproval. "You heard what Kitsune said, we need to grab your gear, snatch a plane and haul ass to Canada."

"Snatch a plane? Who even says that?"

"We need to procure a flight vehicle, to travel to the TAC base in Vancouver Island, Canada. Upon landing we will organize a plan of attack to retrieve the high-value item that your boyfriend lost."

"My what?"

"You heard me."

"What happened to Noah?" I meant to ask what happened between me and Noah, when Anya issued an ominous reply.

"Noah is a grown man. He can take care of himself." Anya pulled my arm even harder. "And he should not be mentoring a teenage girl."

I tripped over my own feet, falling on to my hands. "Ow!" Anya was about to grab me again when I flinched. "Stop it!"

Anya paused, looking at her hand. "Look, I'm sorry. Just come with me, please." She held out her opposite hand waiting for me to grab her, if and when I chose.

"Why won't you talk about Noah? I admit it; I drank, and I may have smoked weed, and I am very hungover. I honestly don't know what the holy hell happened last night."

"Kitsune has video of you and Noah talking."

"Talking?" I wanted to scream. Why the hell did I leave Tony. If the choice was between being a lab rat or a lobotomized robot soldier, I would have gladly let Dr. Toki harvest my genetic material.

"She's been spying on Cronos for months. She knows that he's planning something.

"Because he's better than her?"

"Yeah," Anya muttered looking visibly worried. "He could have overthrown her at any time, but for whatever reason he just bided his time in that glorified trash can. We need to get airborne. She has spy equipment everywhere."

"I can't," I said through tears. Every part of my body ached. I needed to know that Noah was at least alive.

"Baron's been playing referee since before I got here. He knows how to get information while staying safe. Once we're airborne I have a way of contacting him. I promise you; we can shoot him a massage and he'll reply on a secure channel. Then we'll both know that Nash and Noah are just fine."

I nodded. Her deal seemed like the best option. Yet, out of the corner of my eye I could see a shadow. The flowerchild's advice echoed in my head; I needed to stay alive while at the same time not being a total pussy. I didn't want to leave Noah, but I was no good to him dead. "Anya?"

"Yes?"

I needed to know I could trust her. "Tell me something about Noah."

"He's an American, from Tennessee I believe."

"Not what his crimes were?"

"I never asked. We're all here because the real world is a sick, unfair place." She crossed her arms over her chest. "We're all just trying to survive."

And that was why she needed to stay on Kitsune's good side. I finally understood. Anya was looking for a stable future and she was willing to take me with her. "I think I'm ready to travel now."

"I'm glad." True to her word, she handed me a single radio. "Keep this for when we're airborne."

After the rather quick process of signing out a vehicle, Anya plotted a route to Kitsune's other base; an island just off the coast of

Hawaii. "She owns an island?" I asked. "I wonder why baron doesn't work there."

"Why, because it's tropical?" Anya laughed. "Yeah, he's always complaining about the cold. but Kitsune houses people where she wants. She's damn powerful like that. You get in good with her, you can write your own orders." Anya briefly scanned her eyes over the control panel. "I think we're far enough away from the base to safely make a call."

I looked at the device she had given me. It appeared to be a small fake cellphone, with a single button. I pressed it, resulting in an odd dial tone, followed by a ping and then silence. "Um, hello?" I said nervously.

"Hell-o." The voice on the other end was not Baron. "Miss Hellion, so nice to finally meet you." The accent was low and snake-like. I couldn't tell if the speaker was male or female but it was certainly not either of the twins.

"Hi, is Baron there?"

"Part of him is," the voice said with a chuckle. "As well as various parts of Nash and Cronos."

"Turn it off!" Anya screamed.

"Oh Anya, you really think I, Feng the head of tech appointed by Miss Kitsune herself, would not find Baron's special frequency?"

"Who's Feng?" I reached for the button but my fingers refused to apply pressure.

"Who issss Feng?" the sinister voice replied with a laugh. "You, miss Hellion, can call me Dr. Frankenstein."

Anya kicked the radio from my hands as she made a sharp turn. "We're going off course. We need to get there before Feng does, even if that means skipping the fuel station."

"Who IS Feng," I asked through gritted teeth.

"You know how Noah is a supernatural genius at all things technological?"

"I guess so."

"Imagine if instead of creating weapons, he created biological implants," Anya replied, still focused on the flight path. "You really don't know what happened last night? That's probably for the best. Just try to get some sleep."

"I don't know how I'm supposed to sleep after everything that just happened."

"Lean back, close your eyes, your body will do the rest."

I did as she asked, stretching my back as I reclined my seat. I shut my eyes but just as I did, I felt a cool stream of air shoot directly at my face. *'What the?'* My eyelids felt heavy, as my mind started to fade. I have to imagine this is what it felt like to be put under for surgery. Did Anya just drug me?

Before I had a chance to turn my head, I awoke in a dreamy place, looking up at the stars in the purple night sky. All around me was sparkling snow that shimmered in pastel colors. And, of course, my mentor. "Hey!" I shouted at the figure. "If you're just a figment of my imagination, could you tell me what I did with Noah that has everyone so pissed off?"

The blond man turned to me, his eyes glowing with an unearthly fire. He moved his hand, beckoning me to follow. We walked to a large, red metal door, like the back of a train. I assumed we were sneaking someplace, but the flowerchild opened the door with the loudest screech I'd ever heard.

Suddenly we were in Noah's living room. Nash, the robot was powered down, while a very drunk Baron was using him as a pillow.

I could hear my past-self giggling. I turned to see my drunk, flirty doppelganger sitting on Noah's lap, legs spread, looking up at the stars through a hole in the roof.

"I can't believe you put this in yourself," my past, self said, while taking another swig of whatever we'd been drinking. "What happens when it rains or snows?"

Noah chuckled, holding me close with his hands on my shoulders. "There's a pressure plate to automatically close the skylight."

"So cool." I was clearly wasted, but also mesmerized with a child-like sense of wonder. "Noah?"

"Yeah?"

"What do you want to be when you grow up?"

Noah smiled, as he moved his hand to mine, giving my fingers a gentle squeeze. "I see you've been talking to Baron. That dreamer thinks there's a light at the end of this tunnel."

"You don't?"

"I ain't never getting out of here. I got no home, no family, just these four walls and those two sleeping jackasses over there."

"And your brain," drunk me added. She was correct. Noah's mind was unique to him.

"My brain?" he asked, lacing his fingers through mine, until he was holding my hand.

"You know what I mean, silly," my past self said in a cute baby-doll voice as I turned my body to face his. "Your thoughts, vision, your creative soul. That's something no one can ever take away." I brushed my lips to his. Noah's mouth tasted like hard alcohol, with just a hint of sweetness. His facial hair was rough, like coarse straw. The kind of big strong, man I never thought I'd meet, much less kiss. Cupping his face in my hands, that was the first time I saw the color of his eyes; dark blue, like a rainstorm.

"You're something special, Hell-" Noah paused, laughing out loud. "Please tell me you have a real, human name."

"Nicki," I said in a breath as our lips met for a second time. "My name's Nicki."

I awoke with a jolt, the small plane had fallen from the sky, skidding across a sea of tree branches. Anya and I finally came to a stop in a flat, open area. I screamed for my friend and mentor, hoping she was alive. But when I couldn't see her, my first priority was getting out of my seat, to the safety of the green grass.

Apparently, Anya's priority had been to grab a suitcase full of navigational equipment. "We need to get out of here, just as soon as I figure out where 'here' is." Somehow, we had landed in the forest of

Northern California. Upon getting the coordinates and deciding a direction, Anya took out her knife and stabbed the equipment until there were no lights showing.

The plane had no fuel or landing gear but somehow, we'd made it to the northern hemisphere, by drifting along the currents of the wind. We were safe, we were alive, and not even Kitsune knew our location.

That was all that mattered.

CHAPTER

5

I was pregnant, that much was certain. (The influx of hormones explained a few moments that I'd rather forget.) It all started when Anya and I hitched a ride to Seattle with a van full of stoners, heading to a music festival. My metal legs were in decent, usable shape although the straps had seen better days. I was struggling to keep up with Anya's able-bodied, human legs, but I was grateful to have her as my friend.

She walked with a sweet, sensual confidence; something that made people want to trust her, to know her. Along the way, we got free cigarettes, food and even money. We met the sexy college-age stoners (three men and two women) in a truck stop in Oregon. I never even had to talk.

I was offered copious amounts of pills, cheap vodka and weed. I tried to take just enough to relax and sleep my way to Washington. But through it all, I started to remember more and more details of my encounter with Noah. Piece by piece, each moment came back to me in the form of the Flower Child (my neon glowing guardian angel) leading me through a series of rusty metal doors. Each door led me to a different part of that night's conversation. Apparently,

I had told Noah about my past sexual abuse, running away from home, and getting my legs blown off: total cringe.

"I feel like I was put on this earth to serve powerful men," said the drunk, past version of me.

"Powerful men?" Noah said with a chuckle. "Like congressmen and shit? Good thing there are no powerful men here, just a bunch of screw ups and good-old-boys." Noah put his arm around me, holding me close. "And you, our newest teammate."

"Really?"

"You were great out there," he said taking another drag off the cigarette. "A real assassin."

I cupped his face, with the biggest smile. "What would you say if I kissed you?" Before Noah could reply I brushed my mouth to his. "Sorry." I was giggling uncontrollably.

Noah smiled sweetly, placing a finger to my cheek. "Do I make you nervous?"

I bit my lip, lost in his eyes. "I feel like a long-tailed cat in a room full of rocking chairs."

A jolt of pain blinked me back to reality as my head smashed into the roof of the van. We were flying, falling, eventually crashing. I was already in the back, comfortably wrapped in a blanket, so I was able to punch my way out of the back window. Looking around I could see the van had fallen down a steep cliff, landing on a beach. "Anya!" I shouted, hoping to God she was alive.

I struggled to my feet which was difficult to do with my left leg falling off. Suddenly, two arms grabbed me, pulling me backward towards the water. I tried to scream, but was too injured to fight back, especially when my captor started to pick up speed. This was a human, flesh and blood but he was moving as fast as a car.

So, I just buried my face against the abductor's chest to protect myself from the g-force. We landed on a wooden surface with a thud. I expected to hit my head, but the man carried me like a bride, placing me down carefully on a hospital bed. When I caught my breath, I sat up just enough to look around; somehow, we were on a boat. "Did you just walk on water?" I asked with a forced chuckle.

"Just one of my many superpowers," replied a familiar voice.

"Tony!" I shouted. My body filled with energy, I sprang up, throwing my arms around him.

"I miss you too, kid." Tony returned the embrace, looking over my shoulder. "Yo, Axel."

"Axel's here?" I heard his footsteps before I heard his voice.

"Is the target secure?"

"Affirmative," Tony replied.

"The target?" I asked, suddenly feeling less homesick for my TAC friends.

"Just a formality," Axel said as he patted my arm. "We're glad to have you back."

"Me or just my bionic legs?" Both were still attached but holding on by a thread.

"You would be technically correct," Axel said with a friendly smile. "Your legs are lo-jacked. I'm surprised the Lifers let you keep them." Our fearless leader went to the front of the boat, steering us in the direction of a very noticeable helicopter. "We tracked you to the artic base, that was why we sent the unit in after the battery."

"Um, what?" I felt like I'd been stabbed in the heart. I was the reason why Noah was in trouble, and possibly dead.

"TAC wanted it's property back, but we wanted you back."

"Who's we?" The people who love me? Was that what Axel was going to say?

"I for one, and certainly Tony." Axel made it to the pickup point, signaling for the chopper to lower the ropes to attach to my bed.

"Yes, sir," Tony said, taking a seat on my hospital bed. together we were raised up to the cargo hold. Upon reaching the landing pad, the door shut.

I could see where a single pilot was controlling every aspect of the process. The roar of the engine was so loud, speech was impossible, as I found out the hard way. "Where are we going?" I shouted as loud as I could.

"What?" Tony responded.

My throat was already sore, and I didn't feel like repeating myself. Instead, I simply rested my body while blinking tears from my eyes.

Tony took it upon himself to hold me close, rocking me in his arms like a frightened child. "We're headed to Vancouver, you'll love it there, I promise. I'll be with you every step of the way."

I sobbed, burying my face in Tony's shoulder. Grateful that I somehow heard his words of kindness over the roar of the wind.

He held my hand, giving my fingers a squeeze. I could imagine he was thinking about all the horrible things Anya and Baron had done, how I must be crying out of fear or even pain. He would never in a million years, guess why my heart was broken.

Tony's breath was trembling. Was he cold? Or did he truly care? The very idea seemed so sweet. And that was why I kissed him.

Tony closed his eyes and smiled. Maybe he silently mouthed my name, I wasn't sure, but I'd like to think so. I placed my hand to his chest. He was wearing body armor, so moved my hand lower, to his belt. I knew the pilot could see us, possibly even heard us, but I didn't care.

Tony could have stopped me but he didn't. I'd had sex with beautiful boys like Tony before. He was so open and gentle, possibly a virgin. The idea made me want him even more; I wanted to be the one to make the robot-superhero-boy into a real man.

We held on to each other even after landing in Canada. "I'll give you two a moment," the pilot shouted from his seat. There was other stuff to unload from the back, giving us time to make ourselves presentable.

"Was I your first," I asked with all the flirty seduction of a teen prostitute who watched too many Disney movies.

Tony laughed awkwardly as he helped me off the cargo ramp. "I still can't believe that just happened."

"Yeah," I muttered. I was a slut; I was a whore, but at least I was the one in control. "I just needed to feel something."

"Love?" Was he being sarcastic? I couldn't tell. Yet in that moment he sounded human.

"Sometimes I feel like I don't know what love is." Looking into Tony's dark eyes, I knew my plan; I would learn to love Tony, I would give Dr. Toki the super soldier baby that she wanted. Which brings me to today.

* * *

It had been a little over a week of working out, eating great food and spending time on the beach. I had been feeling a little sick, so I was given a pregnancy test in the form of a urine strip. It was the kind that was supposed to show either one or two lines. It showed nothing, as if I had no female hormones at all. (Apparently that was not uncommon for females who survived trauma.) I was told to return to training; weights, cardio etc. The Vancouver TAC base was a nice enough facility but there was no outdoor gym, not even a track. I would work out with Tony, competitively trying to stay on the treadmill longer (I'd given up on trying to out lift him.)

During our downtime, we were watching cartoons while drinking weird Gatorade mixtures, when suddenly the local news reported a breaking story. "What the hell?" I groaned. "What could be so important that they had to interrupt syndicated reruns of Bob's Burgers?"

"A team of heavily armored individuals have been attacking parked vehicles in the downtown area." The camera zoomed in on a masked man wearing Noah's armor. Was this Noah, was he alive?

I gripped my chest, sinking my nails in to my skin. Was I high? Was I dreaming? I could feel my heart pounding right before I fell forward.

Tony rushed to my side, and stayed with me even as I started vomiting. I went limp in his arms as he carried me to the medical ward.

That was when I was given a blood test, followed by an ultrasound. I was unquestionably pregnant. I closed my eyes and tried to sleep but no sleep came. The last thing I remember was holding Tony's hand.

"Does Tony have access to the third floor of the sub level?" the voice came from everywhere and nowhere.

"What?" The words made no sense given the vast number of buildings on the base. There could even be a sub-terrain lower level I didn't even know about.

"Never mind," the echo said with a groan.

I awoke gasping for air. I was no longer in a bed but rather on a rooftop in the pouring rain. I wanted to pull my legs close, in to a fetal position. If only to stay warm, but my prosthetics were gone. "Fuck my life."

In the distance I could see a human figure; a man walking a large animal, like a lion or a bear. "Noah?" I said in a whisper. What was he? Did he take me from the clinic? Was he going to kill me?

The human figure let go of the animal, before taking a few steps back. The animal made a deep, sickly, inhuman sound but did not advance further. The human groaned, still standing out of view. He moved his hand, striking the creature in the back. The sound was sickening as metal tore through skin.

"Noah, please stop!" I crawled to the injured creature. Clearly it didn't want to hurt me or anyone. I reached out my hand, the way I would for a stray dog. But once I was close enough to see the creature's face I screamed. "Oh, dear God." Even through all the armor and mutilation, I could never forget his blue eyes. "Noah, what did they do to you?"

Noah had deep scars all over his body; arms, shoulders, and back. On his neck was a collar held on by two spikes; one in his throat and another in his spine. The wounds were fresh, he had been bleeding very badly. It was clear he wanted to speak but couldn't.

"It's ok, I'm here." It wasn't ok, nothing about this was ok. I reached for his hand, but Noah shook his head. There were large metal braces on his hands, strange black spikes that made him look like the Marvel comic character Venom (or a demon from Hell.)

Since it was clear Noah had no intention of attacking me, I stayed where I was. But if the restrained beast was Noah, then who was the standing figure? It had to be the infamous Feng, sent on behalf of Kitsune after Anya and I went missing. That made sense. And now I was completely sure I was going to die.

Noah opened his mouth, struggling for breath, "You- will- prevail." He coughed up blood, his body convulsing. "I'll never forget you. I could never forget you."

I wanted so badly to hold him. Maybe I could save him or at least die trying. "I love you…" my breath trailed off. I wanted to vomit or at least scream. What kind of person falls in love with someone they knew for a single night? This isn't a fucking Disney movie! Yet here I was. I wanted to die.

Noah swallowed hard, causing his throat to spasm as he spoke, "I will die loving you."

The words cut me to my core. I screamed into the rain, as the standing figure pulled on the leash, dragging Noah away. All that was left of that moment was a streak of blood along the concrete roof.

I rocked back and forth crying. 'Who was that? Where were my legs?'

"Hard to tell who you can trust," a male voice said from behind me.

"What's stopping me from hurling myself off this roof?"

"I don't really know," the voice replied. "The story would continue; Noah, Anya, Baron, etc. It would just be the end for you."

"Am I the battery? Is this some kind of DaVinci code shit?" I started to scoot backward if only to adjust my weight, and immediately fell off a ledge.

My guardian angel grabbed my arm. "Hey, be careful." It was the Flower Child but he seemed older, stronger, with a face weathered by time. "Maybe later, after you get rid of the passenger in your womb."

"Are you saying I should get an abortion first?" I asked sarcastically, through tears.

Flower Child chuckled as he took a seat at my side. "You're welcome for saving your life, Miss Nicki."

"What are you?" I violently jerked my arm away. "Are you even real? Or are you some kind of mash up of every guy I've ever slept with?"

My emotional outburst was met with laughter. "You mean I'm your dream date? Am I your Ken, Barbie girl?"

I shook my head. "You're imaginary. I'm just talking to myself."

"Do you remember the Junior nationals, when you won your first medal?"

"No," I replied quickly. I remembered; I just didn't want to continue the conversation with my imaginary friend.

Flower Child nodded and stood up. "The day you won that medal was the day you became something more than a scared little girl."

"Sure." And now my brain was forcing me to remember that day. I had qualified for the vault finals but for whatever reason my coach pulled me from the rotation. No, actually I knew perfectly well why. He wanted to punish me for hiding in the bathroom when getting dressed. He liked all the girls to change in the public hallway, where he could 'supervise,' because we were all so disobedient.

I knew that for a fact. I still got dressed and walked out with the rest of the finalists. Right away I was pulled from the rotation. My coach had told them I was unfit to compete, which was clearly a lie since I had no injuries. I told the advocates what was happening; what my coach had down to me ever since I was six. There were tears in my eyes and I knew for a fact my coach would make my life a living hell, but was allowed to vault.

Assuming I was not in the running for a medal, I tried a vault that I had only been allowed to do in practice; The Produnova. For those of you non-gymnasts, it's when you run up to the spring board, and do a mid-air summersault without landing on your head. The legendary Elena Produnova could do two maybe three summersaults before landing. I always thought she looked like a bullet or a cannon ball.

I can remember doing my run, flying higher than I had ever been, and then landing on my feet. Every muscle in my body wanted to fall over, but I held strong. I was going to stick my landing even if it killed me. The audience was silent, in shock, awe and horror. A junior level gymnast was never meant to land The Produnova. I was supposed to be dead, crippled but I wasn't. I was a performer and I did that vault for myself. After taking point deductions for doing the wrong vault (technical shit,) I got third place. Not that I even got to keep my medal. No one spoke for me, but no one could ever take away what was rightfully mine. But what did I have now?

The Flower Child started to walk backward, into the shadows of the rain storm. "I'll leave that choice up to you."

I didn't scream or cry. in all honesty I didn't care. He wasn't real, he was just the part of me that needed a good kick in the ass. I needed to find my way off the roof, and I needed to be smart about it. I spent the next few minutes scooting on my hands and my butt, making every movement count (as to not accidently fall to my death.) Eventually I located what was clearly a door.

Balancing on my leg stumps, I could barely reach the door handle. I tightened my core muscles to execute a leap, pulling on the handle with all my strength. It was, of course, locked. At least I had a place to rest my back. I waited until the rain stopped, taking a moment to breathe. "I could really use a rescue from a handsome prince. Or maybe a chubby-cheeked plumber named Mario? Yeah, right."

I suddenly heard a thump on the opposite side of the door, as if something had dropped down (or teleported.) "Hello?" I said with a tap. "Anyone there?" Just as I spoke, the door opened, causing my exhausted body to fall backward into a dark hallway.

I was indoors, that was something. I took a moment to lean back, anticipating my next move. I really needed to find my prosthetic legs (or some kind of replacement) so I wouldn't have to bruise the shit out of my arms and wrists. Until then I would have to deal with scooting around like a crippled puppy.

I made my way across the hall, down a set of stairs. I wanted to scream for help but there were no security guards or human life of any kind, not even any cameras. The first hallway was lit by a single halogen bulb with a metal door (possibly a fire escape) waiting for me at the end of a short path. I went through, only to find a stairwell with only a single set of stairs going down only a single floor. "What the Hell?"

I made my way down, then across a different hallway. Door after door had been left open, in a very distinct path. Was I being led into a trap? There were no windows, only digital lights that seemed to mark rooms with unintelligible binary numbers. After a while, I saw a few security cameras (the kind that look like glossy black balls, or eyes, attached to the wall.) Was I being watched? The idea sort of pissed me off. Was I an experiment, a rat in a maze? Before every open door I heard a thud. It was sometimes loud, sometimes soft. The variation lead me to believe it was organic. Someone was physically opening the doors for me; they had a plan, and endgame. And I was just a plastic piece on a checkerboard; only exploring as far as my overlord wanted me to go.

The final door unlocked a server room where dozens of towers were being housed at refrigerated temperatures. The jungle of cords seem to lead to a central point. In the center of the room was a red, open suitcase with wires coming from all angles. It seemed alive, kind of like a digital sea creature. In the middle of the case, where a clam would typically house its pearl, was a small glowing D-cell battery. "The battery?" This was what Kitsune was fighting for; what Noah died for?

Every single tower appeared to be powered from the suitcase. A sound theory until I started to look closer at the plastic cylinder, housing the 'battery.' It was freezing cold, except for the areas near ports. That meant I was wrong; the room full of servers were trying to unload the files from the small device (resulting in a massive outpour of energy.) "Wow," I muttered. "This must be what a Yoda byte looks like."

My comment caused laughter; a deep, male voice spoke up from just out of my line of sight. "You're standing in the presence of project Neptune; aka The Battery, one of the modern wonders of the world."

"The battery is a massive glorified flash drive?" I asked, taking a step back.

"Pretty much. The only person who could have deciphered its contents is long gone."

"Noah? He was guarding it, right? Why didn't he ever try to open it?"

"I imagine it was for the same reason why you're not trying to make a grab for it: the damn thing's more trouble than it's worth."

"You didn't lead me here?" I turned expecting to see the Flower Child. I don't know why, maybe on some level the voice was similar. "Axel?"

The tall imposing man stood in full camo armor. He crossed his arms, looking at the battery with a sense of nostalgia. "Noah wanted to invent his own creations," Axel said with a sigh. "And, well between you and me, I think he already knew what was on it."

"Hi," I said in a squeaky voice. My mind was a mix of sadness, and fear, combined with the physical pain of having walked on my hands for the past few hours. "Am I in trouble?"

"No, but you were being tested." He picked up his com-radio. "Target is secure, stand down." He returned his focus to our conversation. "You were taken from the clinic under the veil of bad weather. We had no idea where your assailant had put your body, until you were spotted by the cameras. Clearly someone was tracking you; someone who knew the location of the battery."

And whoever it was, hoped that a legless teenage girl would be allowed to escape the base with the high-value target. "So, how well did you know Noah or Cronos or whatever?"

"Noah Garrison was a military asset who went AWOL. It's assumed he suffered a mental break."

"But you don't believe that."

"I knew him before he disappeared," Axel said with a nod. "He was a genius, a warrior, a friend."

"I didn't even know his last name." I bit my lip, trying not to cry. "I'm just some stupid kid at the zoo who keeps falling head first in to the animal enclosures." That sounded about right; some were helpful creatures while others seemed to want my blood.

"Had you made a play for the battery you would have had the full force of TAC on your ass, but as it stands, I am of the belief that you are being stalked by the international terrorist known as Faust."

"Faust?" My entire body went limp. I was now crying uncontrollably and was moments away from vomiting the contents of my empty stomach.

"Lift your arms," Axel said like a comforting parent. "Not to be disrespectful, but I want to get you reunited with your legs as soon as possible."

I nodded and he lifted me like a crying toddler holding me close. With his free hand he pushed a button to open a previously unseen side door. Curious, I turned my head just enough to see the massive number of armed guards.

Axel waved his arm, and the armored soldiers stepped to the side allowing him to pass. I had never felt so safe and so loved.

Faust was stalking me; he had taken me from the clinic, and put me on the roof of the building that housed the battery. I was meant to steal the battery for him and exchange it for Noah's life. The very idea sent me into a state of panic. (That or it was the fact that I was pregnant and dehydrated. Either way my abdominal area was in horrible pain, making me want to vomit up the contents of my empty stomach.)

Thankfully I was back in the room that I shared with Tony, sporting a brand-new pair of light weight, stainless steel, aluminum-plated legs. This model was a prototype that attached to my stumps with clamps (as opposed to straps) making them harder to remove, but much less vulnerable to damage. It would take some getting used to but my strength and balance were both noticeably improved (a trait that would come in handy later.) I shifted my weight to sit cross-legged on my bed. I had been laying on my back for the past hour, with a saline IV in my arm. I was starting to feel genuinely better, and as such, I was board out of my mind. "What are you guys doing?"

Axel was using Tony's hi-tech gaming computer. To see the older man sitting in the neon green gaming chair was kind of adorable. "I needed access to a machine with a reasonable amount of processing power," he explained in his deep fatherly voice.

"You sure you don't need my help?" Tony asked, periodically looking over his superior's shoulder. "I know you're trying to divert my gaming ram to access the exceptionally encrypted part of the TAC database."

"Are you admitting to having accessed it in the past?" Axel asked with a chuckle, the light of the glowing screen shimmering off his dark eyes. Before Tony could answer, a red light filled the room, followed by an alarm.

I looked over, almost expecting us to be ushered out for a fire drill, but Axel was still typing. Our fearless leader seemed to know what he was doing. Soon the alarm stopped and the room was illuminated with a calming green glow. "And we are in."

Tony looked around his mouth agape in shock and confusion. "I guess I've never been on the super-secret network. I mean, I've fucked around on the VPN to boost my data speed, but I'm pretty sure I've never set off a building-wide security light show."

I couldn't help but giggle as we locked eyes, amused at the sheer lunacy of the situation.

"Anyway," Axel said as he cleared his throat. "As of today, there have been over three hundred individuals associated with the terrorist entity known as Faust," he explained, reading directly from the screen.

"Why is that?" Tony asked. He appeared to be blinking rapidly, his eyes scanning the text and even moving the screen faster than Axel could keep up.

"Do you mind?" Axel removed his hand from the mouse, glancing at Tony with a look of annoyance. "We may be using your network access, but it's still my credentials on the line."

"Sorry." Tony took a step back. "What exactly is Faust? Is he multiple people, an army or something else entirely?"

Axel clicked over a few pages. I couldn't help but notice he was going in an entirely different direction; not scrolling and clicking but typing and well, for lack of a better word- hacking. "The entity known only as Faust can teleport, shape shift, traverse the dream dimension…"

I nearly choked on my own spit. "Did you say dream dimension?"

"And as such he's been classified as a paranormal entity," Tony added, ending his reading. He shot me a glance, as if to tell me to keep quiet on the subject of dreams.

"Paranormal entity," Axel said with a laugh. "The science of shit we as humans were never meant to understand."

His words drew my attention. "You mean like Area 51?" I asked, assuming he was talking about sensitive military information. Was Faust a failed military experiment?

Axel scoffed. "No, more like man-made technological breakthroughs that are an affront to God."

"An affront to God?" His response took me by surprise.

Tony forced a chuckle. "So, you're saying Faust is the devil?"

The sarcasm of the question was clear, but even so, I zoned out on Axel's reply. Faust was a devil who found a way to stalk me in my dreams. To be fair I didn't know that for a fact. the flowerchild was my imaginary friend, maybe even my conscience telling me what to do. He was the proverbial devil on my shoulder, but more importantly, he was someone I had grown to trust. (And now I had a headache.) I leaned back, resting my head on my pillow, desperately trying to coax my mind to sleep. 'Inhale, exhale, you can do this.' I closed my eyes, certain that Tony would wake me up for our evening workout or at least dinner. I could easily get the full story, over a meal of breakfast cereal and malt liquor (or root beer since Tony knew better than to let me drink). Part of me was hoping I could dream about that; Tony and his beautiful eyes. Everything about him was just so perfect, from his slender muscular body, to the way he smiled at me during out workouts (even when I kicked his ass.)

And then there was the way he would touch my stomach when I sat on his lap, while building my princess castle in Minecraft. He always seemed to pretend like he was just trying to guide my hand.

After all, it was his computer, his network access and his copy of the game. But little by little, we would undress, flirtatiously touching each other's bodies until Tony carried me to the bed. There we would engage in our sessions of intense passionate sex. I knew him and he knew me and together we made one complete, beautiful soul. Anyone of those memories would have made for a lovely dream. Unfortunately, it was not to be.

In my dream I was standing in an empty grocery store. The lights were on, and the shelves were filled with colorful products from my youth; cereal, candy, chips cookies and cake mix. I couldn't help but smile. The scene was oddly quiet, as there were no customers or staff.

The signage on the wall read, 'Trader Joe's.' It was a place I recognized from my childhood. Since this was my dream, I ran to the freezer section looking for the frozen treats I lived for; soy ice-cream, rolled cookie cannoli, and peppermint chocolates. As a miserable child gymnast, this was a place I always dreamed of working. I helped myself to a package of ice-cream sandwiches, tearing into the cardboard.

"Seriously?" asked a voice over the PA system. It sounded male but with the static I couldn't be sure.

"Seriously what?" I asked with a mouthful of food.

"You're walking around this place like a kid who just won a ticket to Willy Wonka's candy factory."

"So what?" I looked around for any cameras, but of course there were none. "Who are you? How are you seeing me?" I asked, taking another bite of my comforting treat.

There was no reply, only the sound of uncontrollable laughter.

"Are you Faust?"

"You think I'm Faust?" The voice laughed even harder, struggling for breath. "Why, because I can see into your dreams?"

"Yeah, I guess so." I put down the frozen snack, no longer feeling safe in my surroundings.

The voice crackled, "You'll just have to come on down to find out."

"Come on down?" To Trader Joe's? I pinched my hand with my nails. "Wake up, you need to wake up."

Somehow, I managed to blink myself awake. Taking a thankful breath, I awoke in the darkness of my room. Why was it so dark? How long had I been asleep? Axel was long gone and Tony was asleep by my side. I gently maneuvered my way out of his arms, taking a moment to stroke his sleeping face. It had been so long since I had a real friend. Did I really have to leave the bed?

I shivered as I exited the safety and warmth. Standing on my metal legs, I had to force my brain to take one step and then another. Even still. I almost couldn't make it all the way to Tony's computer chair without looking back. I tried to tell myself, I needed his computer more than I needed him. But that was a total lie.

I made sure that headphones were plugged in, to avoid any bootup noise. At the main screen, I logged on as a guest, since I didn't need a security clearance, just Google. 'location of nearest Trader Joe's?' There was one in town. Since it was well after midnight, they would be closed. That was the point. I was meant to enter a well-lit empty grocery store. Now for the big question; Should I wake Tony, or should I go it alone?

The part of me that was brave (and wanted to prove to Flowerchild/Faust that I was not a pussy) knew I could easily sneak out. But with my shitty luck I would end up on a boat to Finland; I'd lose Tony. Like a little girl clinging to a stuffed animal, I wanted so badly to take him with me. I'd already lost Noah; I couldn't lose Tony. I approached the bed, and nudged Tony's sleeping body. He looked warm and comfortable in his sweatpants and hoodie. "Hey!"

He turned over and moaned, letting out a soft, sexy snore. I just wanted to watch him sleep. The way the light of the window caressed his skin, made him look ethereal. I shook his arm, causing yet another moan. How could one human being be so hypnotically beautiful? It took me five tries to conjure enough force to actually wake him.

"What's up, Nicki?" Tony asked in a whisper. He was clearly tired, not even bothering to sit up.

Maybe waking him was a mistake. "This is going to sound stupid, so feel free to say no or even lock the door and write up a report on my pregnancy induced madness."

Tony groaned, pushing himself up, to a seated position. "Just say it."

"Will you go with me to Trader Joe's?" I closed my eyes as I blurted out the words.

"The grocery store?" Tony asked with a yawn.

"I had a dream. I was in an empty Trader Joe's, and the voice on the PA was making fun of me."

There was no need to explain further. "So, you think Faust is waiting for you at Trader Joe's?"

"Someone is," I replied truthfully.

Tony ran his fingers through his hair, allowing him a moment of contemplation. "Well, Let's go."

"Let's go? Really?" I was thankful to have an ally.

"It's the logical course of action," Tony explained. "You've been having weird dreams for days, clearly someone or something is trying to communicate."

My mind halted. "How did you know about my dreams?" We'd talked about a good many things but I had no memory of discussing the flowerchild with him.

"You talk in your sleep."

"Oh," I said quickly, turning away to grab my running shoes. That was not a conversation I wanted to engage in.

We were able to leave the base without issue. Wearing our casual clothes, we looked like typical urban explorers looking for a place to crash. With Tony leading the way, we made our way to the Trader Joe's attached to a shopping center. This was the main Vancouver location, (or at least the one closest to the base.)

Something felt wrong. "This isn't it," I said standing under the lights of the parking lot. "Is there another location? A freestanding one?"

"I know there's one off the highway," Tony replied while stretching his back. "I think it merged with this site to reduce overhead."

"Two locations merging?" It made no sense. Trader Joe's was a major corporation, why would they want less retail space?

"I guess it's a foot traffic thing," Tony responded to my rhetorical question. "If one store has more customers, they'll have better sales, and justification for more hires."

The mention of employees caused a light to go off in my mind. "Where would they keep the excess inventory?"

"What do you mean?"

"The inventory for two stores. Think about it, if one store had more walk-in traffic it would make sense to have the maximum amount of display space."

"While keeping the other location as a warehouse." Tony answered so quickly it was like he could read my thoughts.

"Can you read my thoughts?"

Tony laughed. "You serious?"

"Earlier you said you knew about my dreams even though I know for a fact I've never mentioned any of that to you."

Tony took a step towards me, biting his tongue with a sly, sexy grin. "Do you honestly want to know if I can read your thoughts?"

I was blushing. Even if he couldn't read my thoughts, I sure as hell could read his. "We'll table that question for later."

"Fine with me, but we have a bit of a walk ahead of us. How about a game of eye spy?"

It was a thirty-minute walk to the freestanding location off the highway. The lights were on, clearly the location was staffed. Traveling in the shadows, we made our way to the building.

"Did you bring a weapon?" I asked Tony, nervously. Amidst the excitement of literally following my dreams, I'd forgotten my knife. We were well trained in hand-to-hand combat, but not, two vs a hundred without a weapon level of mastery (or at least I wasn't.)

Tony stood strong, his back pressed against the wall as we made a turn. "I am a weapon."

"Did you seriously just say that?" I giggled.

We went to the loading dock. There was a window peering into the stockroom, and or sales floor. The space was set up like an actual store. There were actual shelves with product in plain view. "Someone's heading to the door," I said quickly darting to the area under the ramp. Sure enough the gate started to rise. A man in a black grocery store uniform walked out with a bag of trash, heading to the nearest dumpster. Fortunately for me, and Tony, the nearest dumpster was well across the parking lot, allowing us ample time to sneak past the door. Inside the store was fully lit, just like in my dream.

I walked further, until I saw the exact set from my dreams. "This is it."

The PA system screeched to life. "G'day Miss Hellion, I see you've brought a friend." The voice had a clearly Caribbean accent. "You really shouldn't have."

"Baron?" I was so overjoyed to hear his voice, I mentally blocked out the last part of his sentence.

The lights flickered, once then twice followed by a bright green laser blast that looked like something out of Star Wars. Tony easily dodged the shot, but I could see by the burn left behind on the wall, he was the intended target and the impact would have incinerated him.

"Oh, you like special effects?" Tony said with a laugh. "Because I've got some of my own."

I watched as Tony took a step back, disappearing into the shadows. "Tony?" He was completely gone. "Where are you?"

The walls started to rattle. The sound was like an earthquake, without the ground motion. Were they fighting inside the walls? No. As the shadows started to warp, moving on their own, it was clear they were in some kind of pocket dimension, accessible only through the walls of the Trader Joe's warehouse. Baron appeared, flying with the use of new, rocket powered anti-gravity boots. He body slammed

Tony back in to the wall-shadow-portal disappearing like a waterfowl diving for a fish.

All around me I could hear footsteps. That was when I realized, other than the man taking out the trash, I had not seen any other employees. Suddenly dozens of grocery employees wearing aprons and surgical masks appeared from the shadows. "Let's move!" shouted an unseen male voice. "This is what we've been training for."

I watched from a safe distance, as they started to lace a metallic gold rope through the shadows. The thick thread cut in and out of reality, creating a massive net over the surface of the store.

"This is some Twilight Zone shit." I ducked, crawling on my stomach to a well-lit corner. Although I was out of reach, I could tell when the ropes were in place because all sound stopped; no talking, footsteps, just waiting. I knew I was holding my breath, but I had no idea why. Was I afraid for myself, my baby? Or the fact that two of my most trusted friends were fighting (possibly killing each other) in the shadow dimension.

Suddenly Baron crashed through the ceiling, power driving Tony straight towards the rope spider web. "This is my domain, robot boy!"

Tony struggled to his feet, gripping blindly at his surroundings. When his hand touched the rope, Tony released a massive energy blast that seemed to knock out every worker who had been touching the cursed trap. "You may be out here playing supervillain with whatever second tier equipment Feng could steal from TAC." Tony paused to crack his neck like a warrior stepping in to battle. "But I'm the real deal."

Baron took to the sky. Somehow the rocket component of his boots nullified the paralyzing effects of Tony's attack, allowing a few of the workers to awaken. Tony fought off the first two but the next three managed to secure the rope around his chest.

Tony wasn't done. From a near sitting position, Tony jumped. Although he was unable to break the rope, he was able to grab hold of Baron, pulling him to the ground with a surprising amount of strength. The force of the impact left a hole in the floor.

"Oh, God." One of my friends was going to die, while I was hiding like a little bitch. "No, Hellion, this is not ok." I needed to show my face. Maybe, just maybe I could stop this once and for all. "Hey! I shouted. My voice echoed and for a moment the world froze.

Tony fell to his knees, allowing himself to be restrained by the rope wielding retail soldiers. "I surrender! Let the girl go!"

Baron took full advantage, pressing his massive weapon to Tony's back. "The girl? Is that truly all she is to you and your superiors?" He chuckled and smacked Tony across the back of the head. "I'd never hurt my baby sister, right Nicki?" Baron tossed his hair like a supermodel surfer, before winking in my direction. "As far as I'm concerned this is more of a rescue mission."

Tony gripped his arm, flinching in pain. "What is he talking about, Nicki?"

"I, um…" There was nothing I could say. I never told Tony that two of the worst criminals in the world (three including Nash, the robot) offered to take me under their wing.

Tony looked at me with sadness and disappointment. I imagined there were hundreds of words he wanted to say. Maybe he would have asked me to explain myself. Perhaps he might have figured out that the baby growing inside me was not his.

Baron laughed. "Nicki is my warrior blood, right love?" My old friend smiled, reaching out his hand.

I nodded, taking a step forward. "Do you know what happened to Noah?"

"Noah…" Baron was still grinning, but with a noticeable look of fear in his eyes.

"Have you seen him?" I swallowed hard, resisting the urge to cry. "Did you see what Feng did to him?" I wanted him to say that Noah could be saved.

Baron glanced nervously at his small army. "We need the battery; I know you've seen it."

"I can't take you to the battery."

"You can't or you won't?" Baron tilted his head, with a menacing glare.

I glanced at Tony for a hint of guidance. We had only a fraction of a second of communication, and at our current distance I would be making a lot of assumptions.

From what I could tell he nodded, and darted his eyes in the direction of Baron's weapon.

"I can't," I said, with as much confidence as I could muster, "but you're right I have seen where they're keeping it. The room is heavily guarded and monitored by hundreds of cameras, but worst of all there are multiple entrances, making it all but impossible to evade the security detail." I looked at Baron, trying to judge his response. "I want to give it to you, I really do, but I'd never make it off the base alive."

Baron paused, biting his lip in deep thought. "Well, I can't go back to the anime twins without the battery, so I guess I'll just have to go with you." Without a second glance he fired three rounds in to Tony's back.

It was all I could do not to scream. I shut my eyes, desperately trying to picture that night back in Russia; drinking, laughing. We were a team, friends. I felt love, trust. I wanted to see that person, but all I could see was the monster who just shot my lover, roommate and current best friend.

Time stood still as Baron reached for Tony's body. I assumed he was going to take Tony's TAC ID. In the right lighting Baron could pass for Tony, especially with all the robotic augmentation.

I felt a single tear roll down my cheek. "Don't you dare touch him!" I said in an angry whisper.

"What did you just say?" Baron paused just long enough to lower his weapon. "Do you even care about us at all? Do you even know where Anya is? Do you even give a shit?"

Before I could respond, Tony sprang back to life. He had been faced down on the floor, but somehow, he rose up like a vampire-zombie high on steroid laced PCP. Within a few seconds I solved the mystery, kind of. He was drawing in power from everything around him; the electricity of the building, the life force of Baron's retail army. Body after body was falling, convulsing, and there was the real possibility something had snapped in Tony's lab-made superhero brain.

I ran for my life, hiding in the dumpster (across the parking lot) as all hell broke loose. I pulled my prosthetic legs to my chest, rocking like a scared child as I covered my ears. All around me I could hear screams, explosions. Thankfully, the dumpster remained in place, held down by the massive weight of the thick metal floor. The lid was getting warm and I could actually see orange flames. "Shit."

Moving around the trash bags, I found a comfortable place to sleep. I was able to breathe without choking on smoke (even though the small metal room reeked of rotting, expired food) and eventually I must have fallen asleep. I awoke to a knock or rather a banging.

"Nicki? You in there?" Tony's voice sounded calm, or at least human.

"I'm here." I started to craw to the surface. Part of me was expecting to see the sunrise or maybe even a blue sky. But no, I was still in Hell.

Tony reached for my arm. "Too bad we won't be able to collect any evidence," he said calmly.

I allowed him to grab both my hands, assuming he would pull me to the surface. He picked me up, carrying me like a bride. We turned away from the still burning hell scape, but I couldn't help but look. "Come on, Nicki, we need to get out of here," Tony said calmly, patting my shoulder.

I nodded silently. He wasn't wrong; that was what we needed to do. Even if it wasn't what I wanted. Where was Anya? Where was Noah? And was Baron still alive? I had to know.

CHAPTER

Sitting in Tony's comfortable gaming chair I spun around, trying to jumpstart my brain. "Who or what is Feng?" I asked aloud to the search engine. Yes, I knew I had to type, but I was trying to think of all the possible ways to address the question. This was not Google or Yahoo, but rather the low-security clearance (guest level access) of the TAC archive network.

"Need help?" Tony asked, from his place on the floor. He had been doing pushups, sit ups and other gym class exercises while wearing earbuds. He removed one earphone, awaiting a response.

This of course implied that he had been watching me without my knowledge, which was more than a little annoying. "Nope," I said quickly as I spun back to the screen, my metal leg narrowly avoiding the side of the desk. I tried different search combinations; Feng- terrorist, Feng- officer, Feng-scientist, doctor, weapons, etc. Unfortunately, Feng is one hell of a common name (especially for people who reach the top of their respective fields.)

In a state of defeat, I slammed on the caps lock key and proceeded to type, 'F-E-N-G.' To my surprise that brought about something completely different. "Falcon Element National Guard: project FENG." I clicked on the link only to see a mostly blacked out document. There were no readable names or dates but there were a massive number of preliminary sketches for various combat-use prosthetics.

"What are you looking up, anyway?" Tony asked, resting his sweaty head on my shoulder.

"I think I found Dr. Frankenstein's lair." My mind trailed off. I was at a loss on how to explain my interest in what appeared to be a high-security clearance military organization.

"What's project FENG?" Tony leaned forward, tilting his head like an owl. With a few blinks of his odd, robotic eyes he took control of the mouse, scanning through pages faster than I could stand to look.

"Will you stop!" I groaned. "You're giving me a headache."

"Sorry," Tony said with a chuckle. With one last blink he put the page back where he'd found it. "The drafts look like early versions of my augmentations. Even here you can see the technical specs for my eyes."

"Oh?" I smirked. The drawing was too elaborate for me to decipher. "Kind of like a Deadlock 1.0. Or maybe your pre-evolution?"

"Yeah," Tony said, still focused on the schematics of the eye that decorated the front page. "That sounds about right." The device appeared to have lenses, connected to wires that fed into minicomputers.

I had a feeling the design would work much better with the invention of wi-fi. "Can you get in further, using your security credentials?" Clearly, he could see how much of the information was blocked out, unless his powers somehow allowed him to see through encrypted data.

Tony stroked his fingers over the screen causing the image to warp. Apparently, he could in fact see through encrypted data. "I could give it a try, but first I want some answers, if you please."

"Ok, that sounds fair," I said with as much confidence as I could muster. "How about we go back and forth? You ask a question, then I get to ask a question."

"Fine with me," he said crossing his muscular arms. "As long as I get to go first."

I had a feeling I already knew what he was going to ask. "Sure, go ahead."

"What's your relationship with Baron? You know he's a terrorist, right?" Tony gripped the back of his chair, turning me to face him. "Let me guess: his preferred term is 'freedom fighter?'"

"That was a lot of questions for one turn," I replied, never breaking eye contact. He was clearly comparing me to the teenage girls who flee Europe and America to become 'warrior brides' in the middle east but end up being given away like participation trophies to potential suicide bombers.

"Let's start with the first one. Why did he call you his sister?" Tony asked in a way that seemed serious, yet with the genuine curiosity of a nosy younger sibling.

"We're not related, if that's what you're asking."

Tony raised an eyebrow. "You know what I mean."

"Are you asking as my superior?"

"I'm asking as your partner and friend."

His words brought me a level of comfort. We were in the same boat; augmented bodies being kept alive for the purpose of becoming super soldiers. Perhaps he could be trusted. "Back at the Asia base, Baron was sent to rescue Anya..."

"Toska," Tony bluntly corrected. "Civilian names are only for friends and allies."

That was like a rock shattering a pane of glass and I was more than a little annoyed. Not only was he interrupting my story but he had the nerve to tell me who I should or should not consider friends. "Fine then, should I call you Deadlock?" I locked eyes making sure to scowl.

Tony smirked as he noticeably pressed his tongue to the inside of his cheek. "No," he replied with clear notes of sarcasm. "Tony should work well, considering the complexities of our relationship." He paused, smiling as if this was all a big joke. "Nicki."

Because we fucked; I was the girl who threw herself at him and now he thinks he can hold that over me. Great, just freaking great. "Baron was sent by Kitsune," I continued. "I don't know if that's her real name or her supervillain name, but rest assured I don't consider her a friend."

"Understandable," Tony replied in his professional tone. "Please continue."

I sighed. No matter how much he pissed me off, the sight of Tony's dark puppy dog eyes made me want to trust him with my life. "When rescuing Toska he was informed about my whereabouts and potential." At least that was what I heard from Anya when we landed in Russia. "I shadowed Baron for a few days, we went on patrol, smoked some weed and drank stolen sake. He told me about his dreams of leaving the life."

"The life of crime, working under the Yakuza," Tony added.

The way he glanced at me with a comically intense face drove home the idea that I was a naive, little girl who loved fairytales. "You don't believe me?"

"I'm just saying, if he wanted to disappear, why didn't he? Vancouver is a long way from Asia, he could have easily faked his own death. But for whatever reason he is making the conscious choice to stay employed by the most powerful cartel on the planet."

The Yakuza is the most powerful cartel on the planet? I really didn't want that to be true. "I think FENG knows the answer. I believe he, they, or it," my voice became flustered as I started to doubt my own sanity. "FENG is in possession of two or more individuals whom Baron considers friends, people who I know he would be willing to die for."

Tony scoffed in disbelief. "You're trying to tell me Baron is risking his life, to get the battery, on the possibility of saving his friends?"

"You seem to already know his history. Is that motivation so hard to believe?"

Tony closed his eyes, taking a long blink. "Actually no."

"No?"

"Upon review of my files," Tony said still focused on whatever was projecting onto the back of his eyelids.

"Your files?" My focus went to the drawing of the eye. Was his mind even human or was Tony's consciousness crafted from a series of computer chips?

"Based upon the information in TAC's database," he clarified. The event that turned Baron to a life of crime was the death of his parents who were political prisoners on a certain communist controlled island."

"Fascinating," I said with a smirk. I knew Baron was a good person. "Is it my turn to ask a question?"

"Shoot." Tony nodded.

"Is Baron alive?"

Tony paused for a moment and bit his lower lip. "Yeah."

He did not sound at all confident in his answer. "What does that mean?" I asked. His oddly hesitant tone seemed strange, as if he was trying to spare my feelings.

"I was kind of mentally off that night. All I can remember is fighting; shit was collapsing, burning." Tony's calm, cool demeanor was quickly fading. It was clear he felt guilt, maybe even remorse. "All I know is I didn't kill him."

That would have to be good enough for now. "Ok, I guess you get the next question. Unless you're ready to keep your word and log in so I can read the rest of the document."

"No, I don't think I will," Tony replied with a self-righteous grin.

"No to what? You won't log in or you won ask another question?" With my pregnancy hormones on full blast, I was ready to punch him in the face.

"I have the entire document memorized," he explained in a cheeky manner. "I'd be willing to discuss its contents over..."

"Coffee?" I assumed.

"I was thinking more of a sparring match in the first-floor gym."

I took a moment to consider my options. Over coffee and junk food I could have coaxed out enough information to formulate a battle plan. But realistically, whatever plan I came up with would require Tony's help, anyway. And if worse came to worse I would get my opportunity to punch him. "Fine, let's go. first one to the mat gets to ask the next question."

That response made Tony smile. "You're on."

We both raced for the door, nearly bodychecking each other in the process. At the last possible second Tony let me slip by. To repay his kindness I went for the southern staircase, knowing Tony would head east to the outdoor fire escape.

Neither of us could fly, but Tony's agility allowed him to walk on water, so I knew he had the win. I could practically picture him jumping down entire floors of stairs. Knowing that, I took my time.

Somehow, Tony had the same idea in mind. When I opened the door, he was just getting in. It would be a foot race to the sparring ring. We both started to run at full speed. I launched off what I thought was a springboard (it was just a wooden stool.) Instead of an impressive tumbling pass, I only managed a half-twist before landing on my back. I was expecting to hit the mat but instead I could feel the air below my body.

Tony had caught my dumb-ass mid-air and was now carrying me like a bride. "Please don't do that, at least not until the baby is born."

A whistle blew, followed by slow applause. Someone had been watching.

I looked to the dark audience section of the gym. There were only a few rows of chairs set up at the moment so it was not difficult to locate the source of the noise. A familiar tall Hispanic woman stood up.

"Maverick?" I didn't know if I should rush in for a hug or be genuinely scared. Tony lowered my feet to the floor, allowing me to stand, but he kept an arm around me. He clearly knew something I didn't.

"It's been a while," Maverick said from behind a pair of dark glasses. She shifted a stack of files in her arms; this was not a friendly encounter; she was here on official TAC business.

"What are you doing here?" I asked nervously.

"Axel filled me in on your escapades."

Tony placed his hand on my shoulder, physically moving me to stand behind him. "Our escapades."

"Yes, I assumed as much," Maverick replied.

I was somewhat insulted. After all, I was more than capable of screwing up all on my own. "What exactly did Axel tell you?"

"That you snuck out and caused close to a million dollars' worth of damage to a retail warehouse."

I hung my head like a child facing the school principal. "Sorry Ma'am." My apology was genuine, but I soon realized that showing weakness was a big mistake.

"My main purpose here is to get some insight on your interest regarding the battery."

"I don't know anything about the battery," I said with a notably anxious laugh. Was I being accused of spying? "And I certainly don't have an interest in it."

"While that might be true, you are still in contact with individuals who have a reputation for wanting to acquire said item."

"The individuals TAC stole it from?" I said the words out loud but somehow Maverick didn't hear.

"What the fuck?" The tall imposing military officer gripped her head in visible pain. She appeared to be looking around for the source of a sound only she could hear.

"Damn alarm," Tony said, pretending to look behind him at the fire exit. "Should shut off in a few seconds. "Anyway, you were saying?"

"Axel gave me intel on your relationship with Faust," Maverick explained, still only addressing me and not Tony.

"You mean like the fact that he tried to kill me?" My voice creaked with emotion.

"He tried to kill you by kidnapping you from the clinic, to place you on the secured roof of the building that just happened to house the battery?"

That cleared up any doubt; she thought I was a spy planted by Kitsune. I had never been more grateful to have Tony at my side. If Maverick had heard my snide comment, there would be little doubt of my allegiance.

Tony took a step forward standing in front of me like my personal bodyguard. "Maverick, with all due respect, if you have something to say just say it."

I wanted to put my big girl pants on and tell him to stop speaking for me, but the fact that he could address Maverick without fear was kind of inspiring. Did Tony hold rank over her? Or maybe it was just the fact that he could probably kill her with his mind.

Maverick locked eyes with Tony, pausing with an intense, awkward silence. "I will see you both in my office; building 203, room 5409, at fifteen hundred hours. Will that be acceptable, Deadlock?"

Tony nodded. "See you at three pm." He stayed in front of me until Maverick left the room.

I released my breath, resisting the urge to burst into tears. "Thank you, Tony."

"No problem. I mean you're not a spy, right?" He said with a chuckle. "At least not intentionally."

I knew he meant the last part as a joke, but the reality stung. "I'm so sorry."

"Don't be sorry," he said as he patted my back. "just don't show weakness."

I nodded, taking a breath to calm down. "What are we going to do?"

"Meet with Maverick, hear her out. I assume Axel is going to be present, but if not I'm sure as hell going to demand it."

"Because he has our back," I replied. That made a lot of sense. "So, moving on."

"To what?" Tony asked, heading for the chairs.

"You got to the gym first, you get to ask the next question."

"Give me a second." Tony tilted his head forward, letting his wavy hair fall over his face. He looked like a typical shy, goth best friend from a made-for-tv movie. "Do you trust me?"

"Yeah, I do," I said with a smile. "Like it or not, we're one in the same."

"Really?"

"You're what I want to be when I grow up."

That got a genuine laugh from my super soldier boyfriend. "I'm going to try to find Axel before the meeting."

"Can I come with you?" I asked.

"Sure, I mean if you're not too tired."

I'd been expecting him to say no, as I was kind of hungry. "Can we grab a bite to eat, first?"

Might be faster if I go alone. If I can't get some face time, I'll just call him," Tony said as he put his arm around me. "I'll try to bring back some breakfast."

"Sounds good," I said with a shrug.

Tony leaned in close, rubbing his nose to my cheek like a puppy. "Try not to get yourself kidnapped by the evil dragon." He turned my face, to kiss my lips. "My Princess Peach."

His soft, tender lips tasted of cool ranch chips and Gatorade. I truly didn't want to let him go. "Can I ask a question?"

"Sure," Tony replied as he kissed me again.

"What are we?"

"I never had a girlfriend." Tony blinked his eyes, his cheeks flush with embarrassment. In that moment he looked genuinely human. "I don't know what that actually entails."

"There are no info files on the TAC database?"

Tony laughed. "I really do like you as something more than friends. You're beautiful and I love just being around you." He moved his hand to my waist. "And even if the baby isn't mine, I want to be the one by your side. Because I want to be the one to love you." He blinked tears from his eyes. "I should go before I embarrass myself further."

I threw my arms around him, holding him close for one last kiss. "Don't be too long."

Tony got up to leave, his eye sparkling with a sense of joy that I'd never seen before. "Don't go breaking my heart."

I watched as Tony left out the northern entrance. I took a moment before heading to the West facing exit. Placing my hand upon the cold metal door I knew I should not open it, and yet I did.

That was why I was not at all surprised to land hard on my back, in the middle of a parking garage. "Ow! Fuck!" Looking around, I could see the lot was about half full, not uncommon for a weekday.

"You think they would install security cameras, but I guess the brass doesn't care if some low rank pencil pusher gets their car broken in to." The male voice was a cross between the Flower Child and Faust, leaning more towards the creepiness of the latter.

"Hello," I muttered as I forced myself to stand on my own two metal legs. I was surprised the light weight frame survived the fall as well as it did. I located my target sitting comfortably on the hood of a blue Honda Civic.

His blonde hair was shoulder length, and he wore a jacket that seemed to slip off his half-naked body. That wasn't even the most distracting part. His skin, although human, appeared to be partially made of a holographic metal. "Are you looking at my fucked-up arm?" The man chuckled as he looked to the side, drawing my attention to the intricacies of the prosthetic.

"No," I replied in an aggressive yet hopelessly confused tone.

"Kind of hard not to look." His muscle tissue sparkled with an ethereal, hypnotic glow. He looked like an angel; a digital angel made of led lights.

"I'm leaving," I said confidently turning away. If I don't look, he'll disappear. Yes, that sounds about right.

"So, kid," he said in a raised voice. "You're really not going to take my advice?"

"About what?" I muttered, increasing my pace.

"About not being a total pussy and taking what's rightfully yours."

"I'm not stealing the battery."

"Why? Because it's morally wrong? That thing was created as a weapon of mass destruction," he shouted after me.

"I can't hear you," I said, putting my hands over my ears like a small child.

"The first team to unlock it's secrets will rule the world."

The cliché sentence caused me to stop in my tracks, doubling over with laughter. "Did you seriously say 'rule the world'?"

"You don't buy it?" he asked, still sitting on the car well over fifty feet away.

"No, I don't. Now leave me alone."

"Can I ask, what're you planning on telling Maverick?"

"Not that it's any of your business, but I plan on telling her that I want no part of this."

"This?" He of course laughed.

"Ruling the world or whatever," I said, throwing my hands up as I attempted to turn away. Every part of my body wanted to run but my brain refused to comply.

"Except you do," his voice became softer, disappearing on the wind. "Because like it or not you want to know what happened to Noah."

"No, I don't," I replied calmly. "I have a boyfriend; someone who wants to start a life with me." I'd known Tony for longer than I'd known Noah. He was good, kind, pretty much perfect in every way.

"What about the fact that you're a blood thirsty little bitch who is tired of bowing down to powerful women; Anya, Maverick, Kitsune- when will it be your turn?"

"When I'm good and ready," I said sarcastically. I would not be ready; I would never be ready. If Maverick and Kitsune wanted to fight for the title of Queen of the world they were more than welcome to. 'Go!' I shouted to myself. 'Walk away!' I closed my eyes and started to force myself to move forward. I didn't hear any footsteps, so in my mind I stupidly assumed he was not following me. When I reached the main road, I was more than ready to take a step forward. I wanted to see Tony; to play videogames eat junk food, and just act like a typical fucked up pregnant teenager.

I froze as I felt a metallic hand grip my shoulder. A rush of cold spread down my arm like someone had just dumped a soda cup filled with liquid nitrogen. Before I could fully react, my blond stalker spun me around and pulled me close for a deep passionate kiss. This was immediately followed by an intense electric shock, preventing me from opening my eyes.

My mind was treated to a stream of images, as if he was transferring a bunch of files in to my brain. What was I seeing? There was a glowing figure, a man made of parts. "Tony?" He looked powerful, mystical, inhuman. The images came faster, creating animated scenes. Tony's body rippled with energy in the form of blue and yellow light, but in the place of a heart was a glowing orb. No, not an orb, it was a long mechanical stick, connected to a full circuit. I thought I knew what I was about to see; Tony's augmented body powered by the battery. But if the device wasn't in his heart, where was it?

The image of Tony turned to face the camera; his eyes sparkled with a sinister glow as he ran his fingers through his hair. The battery was in his brain and what it was doing to him was downright terrifying. However, the worst was yet to come.

The camera pulled out, to show more of the scene. Tony took a knee, bowing down to someone with metal legs. "No, please no." I was not going to steal a weapon of mass destruction and I sure as hell wasn't going to stick it in my boyfriend's head turning him in to my personal attack dog.

"Keep watching," my stalker said, as he paused for breath.

As if I had a choice in the matter. Even without his mouth on mine, I was still paralyzed, frozen in place as the images continued. Tony was bowed down, his skin shimmering with electricity as a hand reached for his. It was my own blood covered hand. The camera turned as a vision of future me helped Tony to his feet. In one arm was a perfectly swaddled newborn, and on the opposite hip was a machete caked with blood and gore.

Future-me had the biggest smile as she threw her arms around Tony, holding him close in a loving embrace as the world behind them burned.

This could all be mine; I could rule the world with the love of my life at my side, all I had to do was make a play for the battery.

CHAPTER

stood at attention with Tony by my side. The act felt a little silly considering we were both wearing civilian clothes. Maverick had insisted upon us performing this military formality while waiting for Axel to join us. "We seriously can't sit down?" I asked, nervously fidgeting with the pocket of my white maxi skirt. After my meeting in the parking garage, I had managed to get back to my room to take a shower and change into my most professional clothing pieces; a maxi skirt, white polo shirt, and a suit jacket. (All my new maternity clothes were bought for me by Tony since I was not pulling an income.)

I was about to pull the pregnancy pain card (despite being barely in my second trimester) when Axel came through the door. "You may be seated," he said in his booming voice. "Ms. Hellion, you're looking quite lovely today."

"Thank you, sir," I said with a smile. There was something comforting about Axel's presence, he was like the father I never had. Little did I know my good mood would be quickly dashed.

"May I ask why you didn't arrive in uniform?" He seemed genuinely serious, despite the absurdity of his logic.

"Oh, what?" I wanted to point out that Tony was wearing only black t-shirt and sweatpants. Luckily before I could say something stupid, I realized my partner was clad in TAC issue workout gear. "I have yet to be issued any official TAC clothing beyond work out attire." It was the truth. And as my baby started to show, even that clothing was not fitting correctly. "I assumed I needed to be dressed formally for this meeting. Apparently, I was mistaken, and for that, I do apologize, sir." I made sure to end with that word to make sure it was clear my apology was meant only for Axel and not Maverick.

"Well, that's what we're here to discuss," Axel said taking a seat on the desk. It took a moment for him to realize that the rest of us were at the mercy of Maverick's tyrannical power trip. "You may be seated."

"Thank you, Sir," I said shooting Maverick a side glance.

"What I have here is an employment contract," Axel explained.

"Is it a contract similar to what Tony has?" I was a little anxious at the thought, considering how my partner had been forced to sign away his life in exchange for superpowers.

"Not exactly," Axel was about to reply when Maverick started to speak over him.

"Due to your family, childhood, and recent association with The Lifers, you would not qualify for a security clearance of any kind," the intimidating woman added.

It was a little humorous that she assumed I was even the least bit concerned with having a clearance. "Yes, I understand." That was all fine with me since Tony was the world's most effective hacker. I just needed to make sure he would still be my companion. "So, what exactly would I be doing as an officially recognized employee?"

"For starters," Axel muttered as he typed on the iPad. "Your first undercover mission."

"Undercover?" I had a sick feeling in the pit of my stomach. "You want to send me back to Siberia?" The idea of never seeing Tony again made me want to cry.

"Not exactly," Axel explained. As if sensing my impending emotional breakdown, he stood up and moved closer, placing his hand upon my shoulder. "Your mission, if you choose to accept it, will be to reunite with the Lifer agents currently residing in the local area."

"There are multiple Lifer agents in Vancouver?" I asked. The idea somewhat lifted my spirits.

"Vancouver and neighboring territories," Axel replied. Looking me in the eyes, he took hold of my hand. "Rest assured you will not be alone. Agent Deadlock will be monitoring you as a close-range security detail."

"Close range security detail? Is that another word for backup?" I asked with a giggle. I knew it was a stupid question, but I genuinely wanted to know how close Tony would be. In my mind, I was picturing an FBI van following me around, but that seemed unrealistic.

"I would consider 'partner' to be a more accurate description of what I'm envisioning," Axel explained with the confidence of a high school guidance counselor.

Tony sighed. "And what are you envisioning?"

"You and Hellion work very well as a team," Axel explained while still holding my hand. "As such, you will be given plenty of creative flexibility in the design and execution of your assignment."

His response seemed to only annoy Tony. "Yeah, I figured as much," Tony replied through gritted teeth. "Creative flexibility is leadership-speak for, 'you get to do all the actual leg work while I play cheerleader from my nice safe office.'"

Axel chuckled. "Point taken. In regards to what I'm envisioning; Hellion will be working on her own to reunite with associates that she had the previous contact with. All while you will do what you do best; watch from the shadows. Yes, I do acknowledge that you will be taking all the risks and assuming more of a leadership role. With your advanced knowledge of combat and strategy, I would expect nothing less."

That answer appeared to satisfy Tony, but I was even more anxious than before. I was meant to go undercover on my own? The only reason I even survived my last encounter with Baron was because of Tony. I gripped Axel's hand, taking a moment to control my breathing. The last thing I wanted was to have a full-blown panic attack. When I felt calm, I raised my hand and waited to be called on. "Axel?"

"Yes, Hellion?"

"What would be the end goal?" I asked, with a forced smile. I wanted to remain polite, but there was a certain topic burning a hole in my heart. "I still remember what you did to Anya or Toska."

"Anya," Maverick muttered. Her jaw clenched at the mention of the name. "I haven't thought about her in a good minute." She turned to Axel while grinding her teeth. "Can we move this along?"

Axel stood up, returning to his previous location. "Have you ever played chess?"

"A few times, as a computer game," I replied honestly.

Tony snickered. "For real?"

I knew it was a little odd that I had never seen a real-life chess set, but where I grew up, it was not unusual. "What can I say? I'm white trash."

"Regardless," Axel said while clearing his throat. "I'm sure you know the basic premise of the game."

I nodded. "The only way to secure a win is to capture your opponent's king."

"And to do that you must take down the queen," Axel replied finishing my thought.

"Yeah," I said with a nod. My voice was trembling. If he expected me to kill Kitsune I sure as hell would need Tony as backup. I forced a giggle as if this was all just a game. "But what about the rooks, bishops, and knights?"

"They will be dealt with on a case-by-case basis. Rest assured, witness protection or recruitment will be presented as alternatives to incarceration."

"Sounds reasonable," I said with a deep calming breath. In all honesty, the fact that he was being so kind and rational made me want to dive right in. "Where do I sign?"

Tony waved his hand in front of my face. "Maybe we should discuss this first?"

I might have considered his feelings, but not after he just implied that I was too stupid to make a decision for myself. "We can discuss it after I sign the iPad." I looked to Axel for confirmation. "Right?"

"Yes, as soon as you agree to your part of the mission, I will send a separate copy to Tony outlining his role as well as intel on the task."

Tony still seemed concerned. "Nicki you don't have to do this."

"Why wouldn't I?"

"How about the fact you're pregnant? What's going to happen in the next few months when you can't hide it?"

"That's my problem, not yours," I replied with my best imitation of Maverick's confidence. I quickly grabbed the iPad and signed, before I had time to change my mind. "Here." I forcibly handed the contract back to Axel. "I look forward to working with you." It wasn't like I had much of a choice.

Tony crossed his arms, slumped in his seat. "Are we done here?"

"Yes," Axel replied maintaining his professional tone. "I'll get those files to you."

After the meeting, Tony ran off ahead of me. "Tony?" I watched as he took a shortcut out the fire escape. I had to assume he was going to get food before heading back to the room.

I took the long way, making sure to travel via the sky bridges to avoid going outside (and possibly getting pulled through a wormhole, again.) Of course, Tony still managed to get there before me.

My partner was sitting comfortably at the computer eating a sandwich from the cafeteria. "I brought you a salad, it's in the mini-fridge."

"Thanks, I guess." It was clear he was mad at me or he would have brought back chips and chocolate. "So, what did you find out?"

Tony spun his chair around, facing me with a look of concern. "You want the good news or the bad news?"

"Good news?" I asked. With a look of child-like innocence, I went to grab my food and eat it while sitting cross-legged on the floor.

"Baron is most certainly alive, as he is one of five possible targets."

"Targets?" I popped off the plastic lid and started to snack on chunks of plain romaine lettuce.

"We need to set our sights on one target but if that fails, we go on to plan B or C or D."

"Ok, what's the bad news?" I made sure to fill my mouth with more lettuce, carrots, and raw onion before he continued.

Tony pursed his lips and sighed. "Let's' just say you can't catch a fish without bait. While I'm sure Baron and Toska would be willing to meet with you, in honor of your past relationship, others will not be as trusting. You'll need to have a card to play."

"Axel is giving me the battery?" I mumbled, sarcastically. There was no way that was the case.

"Yes and no," he said as he leaned back. "How do I explain this?"

"For starters, you can talk to me like a normal human," I grumbled like a toddler.

"Ok, well according to the files, you're going to be given a fake battery, while the real item remains in its stasis tube to finish decoding. But that's not the part that worries me. In order to properly sell the idea that you are in possession of the genuine battery, there will be an actual robbery that you would take part in."

I nearly choked on my food. After running for a drink of water, I cleared my throat enough to reply. "That doesn't seem too bad."

"They will hurt you. It's not a matter of if but when and how," his voice was more serious than I'd ever heard.

"I doubt that," I said with a scoff.

"They'll need to make it look real."

Now he was just being an asshole. "I'm a big girl, I can handle myself."

"And the baby?"

"If I lose the baby, I lose the baby," I replied with an abnormal level of arrogance. "You don't need to worry about it." I'll just come crying to you when all of my insides leak out like a water balloon and I'm double over in (physical and emotional) pain.

"I'm worried about you, Nicki."

"Don't be." I finally paused, taking time to realize how hurtful I was becoming. "You'll be by my side, right?"

"If by 'your side,' you mean across the street on a rooftop or in a van."

Why the hell was he trying so hard to scare me? "But we'll be together, so worst-case scenario we can flee the country together."

Tony nodded. My logic was sound. Needless to say, I was not looking forward to participating in a staged felony but that was an issue for a later time. "So, when does this all go down?"

"In two weeks."

"Oh, ok." I calmly placed my salad in the trash and flopped down on the bed. "Two weeks seems like more than enough time." We were so screwed.

At least I did, in fact, get issued a uniform. It was solid blue with a holographic shift. This was clearly a tactical outfit (not something I could wear to blend in on base.) The level of comfort was all that mattered and I had to admit, it was one of the most comfortable leotards I'd ever worn.

As Axel previously explained, we were in charge of the details of the mission, but that would be after we left the base. For the attack on the battery the mission was as follows; at 1:24am (just before the changing of shifts,) it would all begin.

Climbing the fire escape, I would enter via the roof and make my way to the battery room. Armed with my knife (and with my prosthetic legs intact) I was able to pick the lock to enter the dark hallway. I looked around, careful of security forces, or any cameras that may have been installed since the last time I found myself in that particular building.

I knew the plan. Under the cover of rubber bullets and property damage, the real battery would be moved (somehow still connected to all of the servers) while I would escape with the replica. All I had to do was make it to the basement room. It went as well as could be expected.

I was allowed to make it inside the room, close enough to see the battery and all its connections. I guess they needed the footage of me touching the case, because the moment I did, I was hit with a smoke bomb followed by no less than ten rubber bullets to the back of my head.

I awoke outside the base, under a park bench. I pulled my legs to my chest, attempting to get some sleep. I wasn't tired, but there was no way I was in any shape to run. That was when I felt it; a cold metal object slipped down my shirt. It was near my stomach as if drawn to my abdomen area. Gripping said item, it was clearly the battery (or a battery, anyway.) Holding the device, I felt a rush of energy. It was enough to get me to stand up and start walking in the direction of the highway.

I twirled the battery between my fingers, playing with it like a fidget toy. "Is this a tracking device?" I had been so focused on getting away from the base, I had not thought about how I would be able to reunite with Tony.

Was I even meant to? We had discussed the plan ahead of time; I was supposed to walk in the direction of the destroyed warehouse. But there was no mention of him meeting me. "Ow!" in my state of lost concentration I tripped over a rock, causing the battery to go flying. "Shit!"

I quickly ran for the item as it bounced down the road, almost getting run over by a fast-moving car. I knew I needed a better place to put this thing. I quickly made my way to an overpass, near a group of sleeping homeless people. I took a seat at the far end, covering myself with a torn-up trash bag. Under the shadows of the concrete bridge, I looked like I belonged.

"This brings back memories," I said with a sigh. Who could have known that one day I would be looking back fondly on my days as a homeless pickpocket? I looked around to make sure there was no one watching as I disconnected my leg. I figured since it was a TAC invention there had to be a way to hide something within the framework of the prosthetic. After some trial and error, I found a place where I could insert the battery while also being able to get my leg back on. Upon standing up, the small chunk of metal rested comfortably in the joint of my knee.

I stood up slowly and took a few steps. This would work. Walking down the road, my heart was still telling me to look around to try and locate Tony. 'No,' I said to myself. 'When you can't find something, you look for it in the last place you saw it. With that in mind, I was off to find Baron.

As expected, the former Trader Joe's warehouse was an empty lot. Enough time had passed for the rubble to be cleared (most likely thanks to a TAC clean-up crew) but not long enough to start any kind of effort to sell or rebuild. "Fuck, I need to pee," I muttered. The sensation came on hard and intense with little time to evaluate my choices. "Trees, shrubs, and a dumpster?" How was the dumpster still there? The massive metal box that saved my life stood in the exact same corner of the parking lot.

With the corner perfectly hidden in the shade it would make an ideal toilet. Leaning against the cold steel I pulled down my pants and let out several hours' worth of urine. I couldn't help but notice how smooth the paint felt against my skin. After making myself decent I took a walk around the dumpster. The box had a brand-new coat of dye, making it look pristine. When I made it back to my toilet spot, I couldn't help but notice the pattern my pee had made. There seemed to be a path carved into the ground. "A seam." It was clear the dumpster was present because it served as a marker, a door to a hidden area. I just needed to find a way in.

The lid flaps were chained in place with several padlocks; I would need to get creative. Following the path of my pee, I could see the layout of the seam. In the corner, there appeared to be a series of extra marks. "Circuits?" one way to find out; I kicked the corner, first at the bottom then in the middle and then finally I punched the top. The three hits caused a series of blocks to move, creating an opening just large enough for a single person to squeeze through.

I expected to emerge in the open rectangle cavern of the dumpster but instead, I was stuck in a man-made cave. The entire room was filled with metal cubes, allowing me just enough space to be able to breathe and scoot forward. At least I assumed I was going forward. I very well could have been going in circles. There was no light source, I had to simply move based on instinct. "Keep moving." I closed my eyes and turned out my palms. I had to tell myself I was safe and that this place had an end. Suddenly I felt an armored hand grab my wrist pulling me hard. I fell to my knees landing in an open room. I wanted to kiss the ground when suddenly I heard a voice.

"You know you're not supposed to go through that door without armor," said a familiar Caribbean accent.

"Baron?" Looking around from my seated position, I appeared to have landed in a pseudo-military base. Baron stood over me half-dressed in what could only be described as high-tech paintball gear, like something out of a videogame. "What is this place? Headquarters for Red vs Blue?"

"You don't know the half of it," Baron said as he turned away, running his fingers through his wavy hair. Behind him were other soldiers in various stages of undress, as well as a massive array of armor and weaponry.

Where was the exit? Looking down a dark hallway, I could hear the sound of slow heavily armored footsteps.

The figure who appeared was a tall humanoid, but that was all I could tell from where I stood. It wore full body armor the color of sand paired with an opaque black motocross helmet to conceal its identity. "You're really fucking stupid, aren't you?" the voice was male, with a southern accent.

"Are you talking to me?" I asked with a giggle. This had to be a joke.

The figure punched its chest, clearing its throat with a robotic hiss. "Yes, I am," he replied in a deep, New York accent.

"I don't know who you are but you sound like a New Jersey cab driver."

"You think I'm that robot," he said with a laugh.

"You're not Nash," I said nervously. My body took a step back all on its own. "You're Feng."

He hit his chest again, causing a country music riff to play. "Damn right I am," he replied with a strong, confident Texas accent. "So nice to finally make your acquaintance, Miss Hellion. Or may I call you Nicki?"

"Depends, what's your real name?"

"That's not on the table. Mind if I ask why you're here and why I should refrain from putting a bullet between your eyes? And don't bother mentioning the baby. Even in its current state, I could farm it for parts."

"In that case, Hellion will be fine."

"Well, Miss Hellion," the man said as he pulled up a seat. Sitting in the rusted metal folding chair, he spread his legs, giving his best impression of a cowboy. "I do believe you have a whole second question to address." Feng patted his hip, drawing attention to a gun holster.

"I may or may not have swiped an item of TAC's property."

"With intent to sell?" Feng asked, switching back to his New York accent without even hitting himself.

"Yes, of course," I replied. I was giving my best James Bond impression. Hopefully, my classy fake confidence would hide the fact that I was about to tell a complex lie made up completely off the top of my head. "I'm actually headed north to meet with him. I just needed a place to crash for the night."

"Really?" Baron laughed from behind me. "How far north?"

"Alaska, just south of the main air force base."

"In Anchorage?" Feng asked.

"Closer to Fairbanks." I knew Anchorage didn't sound right.

Feng gave an approving nod. I had passed his little test. "And what is this treasure you are hoping to unload?"

"A flash drive."

"Containing what?" Feng asked. He removed his weapon from its holster. The gun matched his armor both in color and their ability to look like a toy.

Needless to say, I was not impressed. "That's my business unless you're offering to help me get to Alaska?" I stretched my back, reaching for the hidden compartment in my knee joint. With a few awkward movements, I was able to slip free the all-important device. I held the battery in my hand, unsure if this was the right move. Feng was an augmented human, like Tony. He could probably tell it was a fake.

"And what if I am?" Feng removed his helmet revealing a human face. The man that sat before me had tan skin hinting at Italian or maybe even Hispanic ancestry. His dark eyes were the color of charcoal. I had to admit those were the most intimidating part of his look, even more so than the robotic components making up his mouth, jaw, and upper chest. He parted his lips, revealing a human tongue. If he was human, I could make him mine.

I strutted like a supermodel, on my metal legs. Holding the battery between two fingers, I leaned over Feng, straddling his lap like a stripper giving a lap dance. I pressed my lips to his ear, as I slipped with battery back down my bra. "I look forward to our travels."

CHAPTER

Sitting in the dark, I pulled my metal legs to my chest, rocking back and forth. "Think, Nicki, you need to think of a plan." I knew I needed to speak to Tony; he was my mentor, my guide, (and most importantly, my TAC liaison) but there was no way to safely make contact. I just needed to assume he was tracking me, despite the fact that I was in a hidden underground base made up of sewer and metro tunnels.

All I knew for certain was that I needed to guard the battery with my life. With my pinky finger I managed to fidget with the joints of my legs. After my stupid decision to show off, I needed to find a new place to hide the tiny data storage device. My new hiding place had to be high enough on my body, to the point where if FENG tried to remove it in my sleep, I would be able to feel it. Unless, of course, he drugged me (but that also implied I would be willing to share a room with him.)

"You almost done in there?" a female voice shouted through the locked door. "You know, this is the only bathroom for thirty miles. There's a fucking line!"

"I know, I'm sorry." I took a moment to fix my leg, just enough to be able to leave the putrid smelling porta potty. There was a sink with running water, that was connected to the local water treatment plant. but with no soap or sanitizer. I left the stall, passing by a massive line of no less than twenty female soldiers. Some of them were in full armor, looking ready to kick my ass.

"Hey you!"

"Me?" I asked nervously since I couldn't see from what direction the voice had come from.

"Your name is Hellion, right?" A female soldier turned her head, shouting from her place in line.

"Feng told me to tell you to meet him in his office."

"His office? And where would that be?" I couldn't see her face, for all I knew she was a robot, a plant and I would be walking in to a death trap.

"It's a giant tent on wheels, you can't miss it," the robot replied gleefully, giving her best Rachel McAdam's impression.

"Ok, thanks." I didn't have to look far to find what looked like a bright red circus tent. The structure appeared to be secured to the back of a semitruck. This was clearly Feng's personal office space. I placed my hand upon the golden handle of the black rubber door. The aesthetic looked like a BDSM sex club; unique but at the same time intimidating.

The door was of course unlocked. 'It's unlocked because he was expecting you. there's probably a shotgun on the other side.' I truly did not want to open it but I knew I had to. "Hello?" I said through a crack. I could, thankfully, see no trap rigged to the door.

"Do come in, Ms. Hellion."

I opened the door to a room illuminated by neon lights. Feng was standing about twenty feet away, with his back facing me. "Hi, um. I was told that you wanted to see me?"

Feng stood eerily still. "There's no way TAC let you just escape with the battery.

"No one lets me do anything," I said as calmly as I could. "My choices are my own." I knew he had to be holding a weapon.

"I truly doubt that, little girl," he said with a chuckle. "The way I see it; either that is not the real battery or you're a spy and the battery is a tracking device."

"I guess you'll never know." I tried to stand in the doorway for an easy escape but with the raise of his hand he slammed the door shut remotely.

"You will not make a fool of me!" In less than a second, Feng made it across the room and hit me so hard I felt my head slam against a nearby table.

Time moved in slow-motion as three items crashed to the ground; a glass vial, a screwdriver and a notepad. I felt my mind flip a switch that I never knew I had. Step one, I would use the glass vial to hit him in the balls. Since the glass seemed to be shatterproof, this could make for a decent means of attack. Step two, would be a hit to the face, using the notebook. (A quick motion used more as a distraction than an attack.) Finally, I would end with the screwdriver stabbed in his shoulder. That plan should give me ample time to make my exit. Except step three missed.

Feng turned his head, causing me to stab him in the eye so hard the six inches of metal became completely stuck. I could see sparks as something electrical short circuited behind his eyeball. I also saw blood. I landed another kick to the stomach, making sure to grab the notebook (might be important later, you never know.) "You'll stay down, if you know what's good for you."

Before he could reply I kicked him again, this time in the head. There was more blood. Feng was groaning in pain, struggling for breath. Or perhaps he was trying to decide on what card to play next.

"Thanks for the hospitality but I think I'll be traveling solo." It was a lie: I needed him to think I had the power to walk away. "I'm just going to say goodbye to Baron, before I go."

"And Noah?" he asked in a whisper.

"Noah? You mean Cronos?" I leaned against the doorframe, blindly searching for the lock. Upon locating a latch, I was able to get the door open a few inches. I also made sure to wedge the notebook in the hinge for added weight and leverage. "If you think I'm going to trade the battery for Noah's life, you're even crazier than you look."

"Don't lie," he said with a maniacal laugh. "I know you had sex with him after a single night."

"You calling me a slut?"

This got a genuine laugh. "No, but even you have to admit, you're immature, impulsive."

"But I also want to stay alive. How do I know you're not going to force choke me the moment I turn my back?" I'd found a second and third lock. Mentally I was preparing to run.

"Force choke? I'm not Darth Vader. And if I was, I could kill you where you stand." He paused for a moment before starting to laugh. "Is this about the door? It's on a preprogrammed timer." With one firm tug, he pulled the screwdriver from his eye, letting it fall to the floor. "I think I owe you an apology, I've given you no reason to trust me."

"Trust you?" I could feel the bile in my throat. "Do you even remember what you said to me and Anya?"

"On the chartered flight? Yes, I have some memories of that day." He wiped his face, smearing the blood across his cheek. "I recall telling you that your friends had been dissected for spare parts. However, you can clearly see, by the fact Baron is still among the living, that I was..."

"A lying sack of shit?" I suggested. "Or were you just talking out of your ass?"

"What can I say, it's just my nature." His smile was wide, cat-like.

"Your nature..." I muttered, not moving forward. My mind drifted to the fable, 'the scorpion and the frog.' Basically, the scorpion asks for the frog's help across a body of water but when he inevitably betrays the frog the bug claims that evil was just in his nature. "Is Noah here, in your BDSM circus tent?"

Feng chuckled. "Noah is in fact here. Would you like to say hello?"

"I would."

"Well, right this way." Feng paused, taking a moment to snap the broken pieces of his eye back into place. The parts were clearly made of a thick glass or perhaps porcelain. The chunks did not fit perfectly but he managed to close the wound enough to stop the bleeding. "Much better."

There was a noticeable crack through his retina but I gave him a cheerful, flirtatious thumbs up. "Looks good."

"Says the girl who stabbed me," he said with a jovial laugh, as he walked to a door on the opposite side of the room. "If I didn't know better, I'd swear you had a fetish for violence against men.

"Does this place have multiple rooms?" I asked. This seemed odd even knowing what the full size of the vehicle looked like.

"No," he replied, holding open the door. He was clearly not going to offer any further information. He wanted my raw, emotional reaction. Because what I saw next was something out of my nightmares.

The front of the tent was actually the cab of a recycled semi-truck. (That part was admittedly kind of cool.) Chained to the front and side were no less than ten bodies in various stages of undress. They were arranged like trophies. Some wore armor, while others were missing limbs. I couldn't even tell of any of them were still alive. Each body was attached by their arms, legs and neck. There was some variation depending on the availability of limbs. But what each body had in common were their lack of eyes. They all seemed to be covered in duct tape (regardless if the body in question also wore a helmet). I assume this was to avoid what happened next.

Somehow, they all sensed my presence and started to call out to me. "Nicki! Hellion!" the victims were male and female but their neck restrains were compromising the clarity of their voices. (So, I was still unable to tell which one was Noah.) "Get out of here!" "You need to run!" the words echoed off the walls of the tunnels, pounding into my head like a jackhammer.

Covering my ears, I fell to my knees, making sure to keep my knife at grabbing distance. "Where is Noah?"

In the paltry lighting of the tunnels Feng looked every bit like a typical scorpion. He of course giggled like a child as he approached a tall male body wearing yellow body armor. An opaque motocross helmet concealed his face, but I could tell, the victim was more metal than flesh. "And before you get all judgmental, I offered baron and Noah the same opportunities but only one of them wanted to play nice."

And I was supposed to be ok with this? I wanted to scream, cry or (do as the others said) and run. That wouldn't have ended well. I needed to play the part of a confident, empowered female with a strong stomach. "I wish to speak to him."

"Most certainly, it will be my pleasure." Feng easily removed the helmet revealing Noah's face.

One thing was painfully obvious; Feng was the person I met on the roof, not Faust. Feng was the one who had Noah's mutilated body on a leash like a wild animal. He was the one who wanted me to steal the battery. Was Faust even real? Or was Feng the puppet master for multiple characters? I leaned forward to touch Noah's face, and nearly puked all over myself. He was missing both eyes and had a mouth full of black, oil-like blood. It was clear he was trying to speak but all that came out were choking, labored breaths. That is, until Feng punched the armor, hitting Noah in the chest. This seemed to activate a robotic voice emulator.

"Nicki?"

"Yeah, it's me." My body started to move all on its own. My brain didn't want to remove the chest piece, I already knew what I would find. But my hands apparently wanted to see for themselves. I opened the latches on his shoulders, and hips, allowing the metal plate to fall to the ground. There was no skin on his chest. His neck and throat were robotic, connecting to a metal skeleton. This would have been acceptable but there was just enough human parts left to look 'out of place.' In addition to the skin on his face, his heart, lungs, stomach and intestines were still present, (and rotting.) The smell was overwhelming.

Noah opened his lips and spoke a quick sentence through the digital voice box. "Hold me."

I did as he asked and took a step closer, standing on his feet to be able to look into his eyes. "I'm sorry."

Noah shook his head, but with how his neck was restrained the movement appeared more like a muscle spasm. "You must end this."

I could feel him tighten his stomach, subtly motioning to a weapon at his hip. Wait, no. That wasn't his body moving it was mine. I could feel the fetus inside me moving, reaching out to its father. I could no longer stop the tears from falling. My child would never know him. Did I even know him? I cupped Noah's face in my hands; he was warm, human. "There's so much I want to say to you."

Noah nodded, his face trembling in pain, fear or whatever emotions he had left in his mutilated body.

"I don't know if we could have been together. Maybe you were just fun, maybe you would have been an awful father. I'll have to keep telling myself that, because otherwise all I have are fairytales in my head." I kissed his forehead for one final goodbye. "I'll never forget you."

I pulled my knife from its place on my thigh. Under any other circumstances the blade wouldn't be enough to engage in combat (probably why I was allowed to keep it with me.) But in that moment, I was overcome with strength. I slashed Noah's throat over and over. Sometimes I was cutting wire, other times flesh. When no one tried to stop me, I couldn't help but wonder if this was what Feng wanted. All I knew was that it needed to all be cut; anything that was his life, his human soul, and anything that could have kept him alive against his will. Noah deserved to finally be free. With one last cut, his head fell off, bouncing off another prisoner's arm before landing at Feng's feet.

I quickly spun around and stabbed Feng in the chest. I wanted so badly to finish him off, but there was no other weapon in sight. Feng looked down at the blade and laughed. "You think you can destroy me?"

With a flick of my wrist, my blade went straight up, cutting through Feng's head like piano wire. "Yeah, I do." I paused with my knife, finally free of his flesh. "Wow." I honestly did not know I even had that kind of strength. My hand was covered in blood, trembling with energy. Behind me, I heard a slow clap. First from one person then two and then a small crowd.

"Baron?" It was more of a wish than a question. As far as I knew there would be an army of Feng's creations training their weapons on me.

"I had a feeling I bet on the right horse," Baron said as he placed his hand upon my shoulder.

"You bet on me? How do you figure that?" I asked in a catatonic voice. "I came here all on my own."

"How do you think you found the doorway?" he pointed out. "But like I said, I 'bet' on the right horse. It was never a guarantee that you'd go through the door, you could have turned back, maybe went towards the US border. I'm sure you could have found someone to help you on that side.

I turned to see if he was smiling, laughing, anything to make this seem like an elaborate trap. He wasn't. He gripped my hand, as his body faced forward unable to look away from Noah's headless corpse.

"You seem to switch horses a lot," I muttered. I could feel my eyes blinking away tears. "but I'm one to talk. I came back too late."

Baron sighed, sharing our moment of grief. "There's no way you could have made it back any sooner then you did, not with that TAC guy breathing down your neck."

"I could have at least tried."

"You're here now and that's all that matters." Baron pulled me close for a hug. "Noah was a good guy. The world is full of good people."

Good people who get royally fucked over by life. "I don't want to go to Alaska. I want to kill Kitsune."

Baron nodded. "Good to hear it." He opened the door of the truck, already holding a pair of keys. "We can discuss the details once we're back on the road."

"Back on the road?"

"Yeah, that's what I said." He picked up Feng's body and tossed it in the passenger seat. The two halves of his head hung open like the petals of the world's most upsetting flower. "The best way to get a meeting with Kitsune is to pretend her science fair henchman is still alive."

"Ok, I get it, we're constructing a narrative," I said as I took a seat on the floor, trying to stay closer to Baron. "You and I have the battery and after we're done completing any business in Canada that (Feng was after) we offer it to her in exchange for a promotion."

"A promotion?" Baron said with a laugh. "You gotta dream bigger than that, little sister." He was about to turned the key to start the engine.

"What about the victims?" I quickly asked, grasping his hand.

"You mean the people chained to the outside of this freakshow on wheels," he replied with a sigh.

"Can we take down the other bodies?"

Baron shook his head. "I think you mean 'should we take down the bodies?'"

"Why, are they all as bad as Noah?" Even if they were that made no difference; they deserved their freedom as well. Even death had to be preferable to being a living hood ornament.

"You mean are they alive?" he asked.

I offered the only explanation I could, "I heard their voices telling me to run."

"That would be the hive mind," Baron said in a brief, matter-of-fact tone. He turned on the engine, causing the truck to lurch forward on a predetermined path (like a train on tracks.)

"Hive mind?" I asked. I had heard the term in movies and TV. "Like Star Trek?"

"Pretty much," Baron said with a chuckle. "I'm surprised you know about that. It seems a little before your time."

He was right. How did I know about the Borg species from Star Trek? "Each new victim is harvested for their thoughts and memories." Which was why they all seemed equally concerned for my safety and wellbeing. I was about to speak further when I noticed Baron switching to a different, higher-level tunnel. "Where are we going?"

"Heading east," Baron explained. "We have business in Ontario. But along the way, there's a body dumping port just south of Edmonton."

"Sounds good." I was glad that we would be getting rid of the body in due time. "When do we meet up with Kitsune?"

"I'll have to hack Feng's files to be sure but as far as I know the plan is to make it to New York to deposit the truck at the regional depot."

"So, what should I do?"

"Right now? Take a nap. I'll wake you at the next pit stop."

"Sure," I said looking at the dead body. "I'll get right on that."

"There's plenty of room in the lab area," Baron said, trying not to laugh.

"Thanks." I found a place on the floor to sleep. The rubber mat was soft enough to make a decent bed, although I was still cold. I curled into the fetal position, falling asleep to the sound of the wheels making contact with random metal tracks.

In my dreams, I awoke on the wooden floor of a western-style train. "Wow, just wow," said a familiar male voice.

I stood up, looking around at the nearly empty train car. "Faust?"

The man laughed. He was facing away from me but I knew who it was. He had the flower child's blonde hair, and peach skin with just a kiss of sun. He wore a light blue suit, looking more normal than usual.

When he stood up and turned to me, my blood ran cold. He was older, with deep-set eyes; he looked like my father. "Care to take a seat?"

I didn't have much of a choice. I sat across from him, that was when I noticed the tray of cookies and a pot of coffee. My stomach was rumbling. At least I could get something to eat. I grabbed a pink frosted cookie in the shape of a butterfly and helped myself to a paper cup of coffee. "This is so good."

"I'm glad." The man chuckled. "I think it's time I told you my real name."

"Sure," I replied, swallowing the mouthful of food.

He paused for dramatic effect while pouring a cup of coffee for himself. "Abaddon."

"Is that supposed to mean something?"

He simply shrugged. "You would know."

"Are you even real?"

The question brought a smile to his face. "I'd like to be."

"Ok, I get it. You're my unborn baby." Saying the words out loud made them suddenly tangible. There was a living being inside me; a little boy with my father's stern face, and Noah's blue eyes. Actually, the more I thought about it, Abaddon looked a lot more like Noah. Especially when he smiled. "What can you tell me about the future?"

"What would you like to know?" My son took another sip, clearly deep in thought, when suddenly he smiled again, squinting his eyes ever so slightly. "You want to know about Dad, don't you?"

"Sure, I'll take what I can get." I could feel my cheeks flush. Since Noah was gone, there had to be a husband (or long-term partner) in my future; someone who helped me raise my son.

"The man who made the choice to become my father, he's wise, powerful, kind. In my timeline, he's an elderly man, on his deathbed, ruling over a land on the brink of war."

"War or revolution?" I asked. "Is he a king or a rebel leader?"

"That will all depend on you. I can't go into details, but needless to say, I need you…"

"To survive?" I asked, assuming the easiest answer.

"To be the mother I know."

The lights flickered, as the cabin shook. "Are we headed towards a tunnel?"

"Next stop is the body dump," he said, tossing his cup out a nearby window. "If I were you, I'd try to make it to the surface at least for a few hours.

"Because that's where Tony will be looking for me." I needed to believe that. He was likely the father Abaddon was speaking of. But why would I name my child Abaddon?

The lights flickered again, casting the world into darkness. I awoke on the rubber floor, to the sound of the truck's massive breaks. I blinked my eyes, brushing my hair from my face.

"Welcome to Edmonton!" Baron shouted happily. Clearly, he was on some kind of stimulant.

I stood up and made my way to the door. The outside world was snowy, and calm. A true vision of peace. "Do you think we could stay here for a day or two?"

"Why? Did you want to check out the mall?"

"Kind of," I said stretching my back. "That and I want a decent night's sleep, (and maybe a hamburger.)"

"We can make a longer pit stop once we cross the border. Deal?"

"Yeah, I get it. We need to stay on schedule."

"Exactly, now be a doll and grab the head."

I did as he asked and together, we said our last goodbyes to the creature known as Feng. May he rot in hell. I felt a warmth in my heart; like whisky, vodka and mountain dew; a sensation of pure happiness. I could sense my baby. Placing my hand to my stomach, I felt a small limb reaching back.

I would see Noah again. And for now, that made everything ok.

CHAPTER

The next pit stop was an empty plot of land on the border of North Dakota. It was the perfect camping spot; a place to stretch my back and take in the sun all while staying (reasonably) off the map. "I'm going to go out for a walk."

"Why? There's nothing around here for miles."

"We've been traveling underground for days, I miss the sky," I said with a pout. "You can come with me." My offer was genuine. If I was able to find Tony, I could hopefully convince Baron to turn himself in, in exchange for immunity.

"No, actually I can't. I have a meeting with a client around midnight.

"On Feng's behalf." I assumed.

"Feng was expecting a package. I'll show you when you get back."

"Ok, thanks. Can I bring you anything; food, snacks colorful leaves or whatever else I manage to find?"

Baron smiled. "You're so sweet. How about you leave something behind, something to motivate you to get back before midnight?"

I nervously looked down at my prosthetic legs, I had very little to offer in the way of personal belongings. "Like what?"

"Not necessarily the battery, but something to show that we're still friends."

"How about my knife? Since there's not much I can do without it, that would give me motivation to stay close to camp." I removed it from the holster on my thigh.

"Deal." Baron shook my hand. "You have a watch, right?"

"Yeah, this pink barbie thing I shoplifted when I was a kid." I motioned at my TAC issued watch. It was Barbie-pink and appeared to be just your average digital watch with a black and gray screen.

"Be back before midnight, or be locked out until our guest leaves."

"Got it," I said with a nod. Since it was only around one in the afternoon, I had plenty of time. "See you then." I headed north towards what appeared to be a forest with massive trees. Hopefully I could find one that would be suitable for climbing.

With all the strength training I'd done with Tony, I felt confident (despite the fact I'd never climbed a tree with my prosthetic legs.) I thought I had mastered the art of gauging the position of my feet, but I was mistaken. When attempting to navigate while ascending I had the coordination of a baby elephant.

After some trial and error, I found a nice stable tree with thick branches. From where I sat, I could see for miles in every direction. There was a road, several gas stations and small towns; even a McDonalds. It was tempting but stepping foot in a public restaurant (without any money) seemed like a bad idea. Then my stomach gurgled: the baby wanted a hamburger. I walked for a while in the direction of the massive sign, until I was too exhausted to move. From the parking lot, I could see there were a few people inside.

I could have stayed outside and begged for change the way I always did. When I first ran away from home, I would tell strangers I was a pregnant teen who'd been kicked out by my abusive family. That story would always get me free food, but that was before I discovered performing on the boardwalk. Dancing and flipping like a circus clown was always more lucrative. Not because I got a lot of money for my talent. No, people just seemed to be more distracted and I could find a decent amount of cash on the ground.

That's what I needed to do in this North Dakota parking lot. Looking around cars, and near the back exits I managed to gather all of $1.45, before a cop car pulled up beside me. "Oh, hello, officer" I said in my most innocent little girl voice. "I was just looking for something to eat."

"Do your parents know you're out here?" asked the typical cop with a thick gray mustache.

"I'm actually meeting someone." I put my hands on my stomach, drawing attention to what little baby bump I had. "I'm legal, though. Don't worry." Crap, that's what a teen runaway would say.

"Do you have any ID to prove that?"

"No, I-" I started to mime the act of checking my pockets. I was fully prepared to run, when I felt a hand on my shoulder.

"Hey, Babe, you left your wallet in my car." It was Tony.

"Tony!" I was so excited I couldn't breathe. I jumped into his arms, not even caring how silly I looked.

"I miss you too, Nicki. How is our..." his hand drifted to my waist.

"Boy," I replied. "We're having a boy."

There were tears in Tony's eyes. Maybe he was just playing a role to get the police to leave, but I'd like to think he was genuinely happy. "I'm going to get my girl something to eat, officer. If that's ok with you?"

Tony's presence seemed to be enough to convince the cop I was not a teen runaway.

I watched the police car drive off before continuing. "Tony, how did you find me?"

"The battery," Tony replied quickly as he ushered us inside. "We'll get some food to go and talk more in my vehicle."

"Your vehicle?"

Tony chuckled. "You'll see." He got to the counter and placed an order; two large fries, two ten-piece nuggets and a quarter pounder with cheese. "Grab your drink," he said motioning to one of two giant plastic cups.

I filled mine with a combination of cheap lemonade and Sprite. together we walked in the direction of the forest. "Where are we headed?"

"I told you, we're going to eat our lunch in my TAC issued vehicle." Tony pushed a transparent button that seemed to be floating mid-air. "Activate operations."

"Systems online," replied a robotic voice. A metallic green door materialized. The vehicle had been cloaked in camouflage.

Tony opened the door, to what appeared to be a helicopter crossed with a hot-air balloon. "You like it? This has been my home for the past few days."

"Wow," I said in awe of the unique space. "How fast does this go?"

"150 kph at max, but slower is better, to maintain contact with ground navigation."

"Silent but deadly?"

"You could say that," Tony replied as he took a seat on the floor. "L-O-L." He pulled me on to his lap, tickling me to the point where I almost dropped my drink. "So, what's new, Nicki?"

"I had a dream," I said with a smile.

"About our baby?"

"The blonde man stalking me wasn't Faust, it's someone named Abaddon. He's a time traveler, and I think he's my son, from the future." I was expecting Tony to call me crazy, but he just nodded.

"What kind of name is Abaddon?"

"I really don't know. But the more I think about it the more it's growing on me. Oh, yeah and Feng's dead. He was one of the names on the list of potential targets, right?

"Yes," Tony replied with a look of caution and fear.

"What?"

"What was your role in Feng's demise? And if you're not traveling with Feng, who's your companion?

"Why would I be traveling with Feng?" The very idea made me want to puke. "Oh, the lab on wheels, right. Well, actually I split his skull open, and Baron stole his keys."

"So." Tony stood up, walking towards a mini fridge. "You're traveling with Baron?"

"Yeah, we're headed East to drop off some stuff to Kitsune."

"In person?" Tony was holding a bottle of vodka.

I watched as he opened his soda cup and poured a shot. "I assume so?

"Are you saying there is the possibility he's going to force you to smuggle illegal goods across international borders?"

"Not a big deal."

Tony took a sip of his spiked soda. "It's a huge deal. You're trusting him with your life and the life of your unborn child."

"I can trust Baron."

"How do you know that?"

"I just do, it's human instinct; the same reason why I know I love you." My eyes went wide as my cheeks flushed with embarrassment. But I sure as hell wasn't going to backpedal.

"Did you mean to say that?" Tony asked with a nervous seriousness.

"Yeah, I guess so. To tell you the truth, it was my goal to find you. (or be found by you.) I didn't know how well you could track me. I mean, well I do now, but..." I blinked tears from my eyes. "I was scared to death I'd never see you again." I couldn't stop the tears from falling, so I was more than a little shocked to see Tony's deadpan expression.

"Let me guess, you found his remains?" Tony scoffed. He reached behind him, and proceeded to throw an actual file folder at my face. Noah's pictures fluttered out. "Funny how you mentioned Feng's death but not Cronos."

"That's because I didn't kill," I wanted to say Noah; that was his human name, his real name. but I needed to play to my boyfriend's trust. "Cronos. His death was on Feng's hands." I felt a pain in my chest followed by a waterfall of tears and then vomit. I had not vomited in a while so it was more than I would have liked. It just kept coming, as I sobbed. I was vomiting up all the memories; the blood and gore, the horrific sense of loss. When there was nothing left, I finally managed to wipe my eyes with the back of my (clean) hand. I had made the mother of all messes. I wanted to apologize, beg Tony for forgiveness, but no words came out.

Tony stood up and fetched a thermal blanket. He wrapped it around my body, creating a barrier which allowed him to hold me close without getting covered in my puke. "I'm sorry for bringing it up." He rested my head on his shoulder before continuing. "I should have told you; TAC had intel on his deactivation."

"Deactivation?"

"Formal removal from Kitsune's payroll. Based on that knowledge, it was assumed that Cronos was deceased by means of assassination or private execution. But there was no intel on the whereabouts of his remains." Tony was choking back emotion. I looked up at his face, for the first time I witnessed sincere sadness in Tony's expression. "I'm so sorry, Nicki."

"Me too." I pulled away from his embrace, getting a good look at my messed-up clothes. "I should go."

"Already?"

I wanted to stay longer but Baron was waiting for my return. "I need to get cleaned up and maybe grab some food to bring back."

"I can lend you some of my clothes. If Baron asks, you can say that you had an accident and some kind hearted tourist took pity on you and bought you some clothes."

"Or I could say I blew a guy behind a rural truck stop McDonalds."

Tony chuckled as he went to a small hidden closet. "God, I missed you." He took out what appeared to be a black sweatshirt with matching sweatpants. "Here, get yourself cleaned up and I'll buy you some food to take back to your campsite."

"Sounds good." There was a portable shower that allowed me to wash off my face and chest. I changed clothes and took a seat with the remains of my soda, awaiting Tony's return.

The sun went down, casting the world into darkness. Bored out of my mind, I started the coffee maker, just in time for Tony to return.

"You look good, Nicki." Tony put down the food, and pulled me close for a kiss.

"You always look good."

"Let me take you back to your campsite."

"Are you sure?" I asked, trying to construct a plan that did not end up with my boyfriend fighting my travel companion in the middle of the North Dakota highway.

"It's already dark, I can't imagine you walking down the highway with two bags of take out."

"I can hold my own against a wolf, or a lion or whatever lives around here."

Tony raised an eyebrow. "L-O-L?"

"Yes, l-o-l; that was sarcasm," I said as I stepped away to get a warm cup of coffee. "Still, what if Baron recognizes you?"

"I have a disguise. A costume of sorts." Tony opened a sliding door to reveal a foldable bike.

"What in the 'Toys-R-Us' hell is that? Am I going to ride on the handle bars?"

"You can, but I don't recommend it." Tony pulled out a series of 3d printed parts. When he was done, the bike bore some resemblance to a motorcycle (complete with a clip-on motor.) It was a Schwinn co-playing as a Kawasaki.

"I have to admit, that's kinda cool."

"I just need to make sure to never ever get in an accident."

"Because this will crumble like a saltine cracker," I said with a giggle. "still awesome."

With my arms around Tony's waist, we drove back in the direction of the campsite. Tony was wearing black riding gear and an opaque helmet, so I didn't worry about being spotted. Unfortunately, in the dark, finding the campsite was easier said than done. I poked my boyfriend in the shoulder. "Park here, Tony, I think we're close."

Tony did as I asked, pulling over by the side of the road. "What did the space look like?"

"It looked like a hole in the ground leading to a larger series of tunnels."

"That's…"

"Not helpful? Yeah, I realize." I walked to the edge of the road. I knew If I had a flash light, I could easily find the odd, unnatural color of the truck, and maybe part of the tunnel. But light would draw in attention. "Tony, do you have a flash light?"

"On my key ring."

"Toss it to me, I have a plan."

"Ok…" he replied nervously.

"But if it goes badly you have to be willing to run."

"With you, right? I'm not leaving you behind."

"Without me. You will need to have faith in me. Because you love me too, right?"

"Right," Tony tossed me his keys. "I love you too."

"Then I need you to believe in me, and lean on the bike like a typical john who just paid for a blow job." With Tony leaning against the bike, I got on my knees to mimic a certain sex act.

I turned on the light waving the beam around as if I was calling for help. It didn't take me long to locate a piece of red reflective tape in a forested area just a few dozen feet to the left.

"Grip my hair," I whispered, in case someone was already close enough to hear. I was flopping around like a fish on a hook, pretending as if I was struggling to keep hold of the key ring. Waving around the light, I wanted to catch someone's attention. And I got a little more than I bargained for.

Baron, in full armor, shot out of the sky. In a blink of an eye he was falling like a homing missile. He drop kicked Tony so hard his body went flying.

I slid the keys along the ground, hoping Tony would be able to retrieve them. Baron was moving so quickly I had no idea where he was, I just needed to wait for him to make his move.

"Up you go, little sister." Baron swooped in, carrying me and the McDonalds bags to safety.

Out of the corner of my eye I could see Tony making his escape on the bike. 'Thank God.'

"What in the heck were you doing?" Baron asked with a laugh as we landed just outside the main door of the truck-laboratory.

"Nothing much, just blowing a guy for McDonald's food."

"And clothes?" Baron said with a chuckle as he removed his helmet, keeping on the rest of his armor.

"I may have slept with him too. Why, are you jealous?"

Baron laughed as he took a handful of fries. "Well, you're just in time to meet our visitor."

"Oh? This should be fun."

Baron walked me to the truck. the area that used to be Feng's lab. The small room had been retrofitted with seating, a mini fridge, and a table full of cocaine. Three men were standing around the room with visible weapons, while a fourth man sat at the table. He looked to be Asian, with noticeable tattoos on his hands, wrists and even up his neck.

"Hello," I said, extending my hand. "Are you a friend of Kitsune?"

The man looked up, blinking his tattooed eyeballs. "Are you?"

"I love your sense of style." I took a seat by his side, to get a better view of the table. "So, is this what we're taking on our cross country, trans-Atlantic journey?"

The man looked at me like I was a puppy; adorably cute with the intelligence of a plastic water bottle.

"I watch true crime tv, I know all about hot young girls duct taping drugs under their clothes."

"I'm sure you're really good at that."

Baron cleared his throat. "Actually, we were just going to discuss Feng's deal.

"Exactly, you were going to tell me how and why I should do business with you," the clearly Yakuza man replied.

"You still on that?" Baron asked as he poured himself a shot of dark whiskey.

"Feng got paid upfront, due to the nature of his reputation. A reputation that you do not share."

"If it makes you feel better you can pay us too," Baron replied with his usual cocky grin.

"Us? The man laughed. "Are you saying this little girl, she's your partner?"

"Hellion's the reason why Feng is unable to grace us with his presence."

"I'm sure we could scrape some blood off the floor," I added, since with all our travel we had not had time to deep clean the front cab.

"Be that as it may, how can I be sure my goods will make it to their intended destination? For all I know, you and your girl killed Feng, stole his mobile lab. In the process of going through his stuff, you just so happened to come across his appointment book and figured you could make some extra cash."

"Ok, fair enough," Baron said, pouring a second glass for our guest. "What would you consider a fair trade?"

The man put his arm around my shoulder. "I would certainly be willing to take this one, if she was a little more sociable.

"I can be plenty sociable." I kicked my prosthetic legs across the man's lap. And leaned in, kissing his ear.

The man was smiling, he was into it. So, I scooted my cute little butt over his silky suit pants, like a stripper giving a private dance.

Baron cleared his throat. "Excuse me? My partner is not on the menu."

"I'm a big girl," I said with a smirk. "I can take care of myself."

"You're already knocked up," the Yakuza man said gripping my stomach with one hand while touching my upper thigh with the other. "nice and firm. I'll bet you're nice and firm all over."

There was a crash, as a bottle broke inches away from my head. "I think it's time for you to go."

"Really? What do you think Kitsune will say when she finds out how you treated her brother's best friends?"

"She can tell me herself." Baron fired the gun again.

I felt wetness on my face. The man was now headless. This caused the remaining bodyguards to take the drugs and leave. They were all silent as they gathered their property, but I was certain Kitsune would hear about the events.

As soon as they were gone, Baron shut the door and proceeded to sit back in the driver's seat. "We're heading south."

"To another body dump?"

"I got some connections in Beliot, Wisconsin," he said as he started the engine and rolled down the tracks. We came to a multilevel fork in the road. He took the southernmost track that seemed to be held up by shaky metal pipes.

"This doesn't seem safe."

"The drug cartels of North America take this route every day."

"Cartels from Mexico and central America?"

"Let's not forget the American gangs. Each state has their own warrior factions."

I nodded as I took a seat by his side, despite the fact that the chair was still covered in FENG's blood. "So, what's the end game?"

Baron laughed, a deep, belly laugh. "After all the shit we've been through, do you honestly think I am in any position to answer that?"

"You have a point. We'll take it one day at a time." I popped a fry in my mouth, the oily potato was already cold. "Yuck."

Baron continued to chuckle. "Baby sister, you're so freakin' adorable."

"Thanks." I should have quit while I was ahead, but my brain wanted to say something more, "thanks for what you did earlier. You didn't have to."

"Friends don't let friends get sold into human trafficking."

That answer made me feel warm and fuzzy inside. "Even if I did blow a guy for McDonald's food?"

"You didn't blow a guy for McDonald's food." His tone was stoic, silent, as he made a turn down an unlit section of tunnel. "Don't worry, we have headlights."

I figured he was trying to assure me that he was not planning on killing me and dumping my body someplace where it would never be found. "Wow."

"Wow?"

"The walls look really pretty." The light allowed me to see that the tunnel was made up of metal, paint and stone in various states of decay. "But back to the topic at hand, you know I'm a slut or else I wouldn't have gotten knocked up from a one-night stand."

"How many other times have you been pregnant?"

"What does that have to do with anything?"

"Noah was someone special, too good for this world."

"You're not wrong," I said, unable to hide my sadness.

"When you were together, I saw the way you looked at him." Baron placed one hand upon my shoulder. "You only looked at one other person with such admiration and love."

"You?" I asked sarcastically, through impending tears.

"I know you were in contact with Agent Deadlock. I'm not mad, I just have one question. Can I trust you to give me an honest answer?"

"Of course."

"I need to know where I stand; am I the target or collateral damage?

"I was told that any enemy operative who turned themselves in would be eligible for immunity or recruitment."

"Recruitment," he said with a chuckle.

"TAC is always looking for new talent."

"So, are they tracking you?"

"Yes."

"Good to know."

"Which would you be interested in? Immunity, right?

"You know me too well. Once we take down kitsune we're going to have massive targets on our backs. I'd like to be able to live out the rest of my days only looking over one shoulder instead of two."

"If you join up it could be zero."

"Not my style. I'd rather lead than follow."

"I understand."

"But it's a good place for you. You're young, you have a future. Even if that future is you hiding behind Agent Deadlock."

I laughed, but the idea that we would eventually go our separate ways, it hurt in a way I never thought possible. "Baron?"

"Yes?"

"What happened to Nash?"

"Physically or spiritually?"

"Are you saying robots have souls?"

"Everything has a soul," he said, as he turned to me with a smile. "And you have to admit Nash was more human than most of us."

"True," I said, wiping my eyes. "We're all just souls passing through to the other side."

"Amen to that."

"We're 'Born to die,' as some emo rocker girls like to say."

That got a genuine laugh. "Cliché but true. I like to think that every person you ever loved, or hated; people with deep spiritual connections to your life, they never leave you."

"Ever think about running headfirst across the finish line?

"That's a funky way to ask someone if they ever tried to end their life."

"I have, a few times, mainly with a razor blade or whatever sharp item was close. Obviously, I was never brave enough to finish the job, not even close."

"I'm glad. As for me, I've never felt the need to try for the 'finish line.'"

"Because of religion or fear?"

"Most certainly fear. I figured it was a one-way ticket to hell, either that or I'd come back as an earthworm or a fire ant…"

"Or a dung beetle?"

"If you could come back as any animal what would it be?"

The answer came quickly. "I'd be a cat."

"A cat? Let me guess, you want to live in luxury sitting on some old woman's lap?"

"No, more like a stray cat; just one of millions roaming the streets, looking for adventure. I'm nothing special but I sure know how to get into trouble."

CHAPTER 11

I wanted so badly to dream of Abaddon but fate had other plans. Ever since discovering the underground tunnel system, I often wondered about the presence of other vehicles. From my place in the passenger seat, I could hear the sound of cross-traffic but saw only open darkness. Until the day Baron managed to total our ride.

If there were any bodies left on the exterior of Feng's truck, they were certainly very dead (and in a million pieces.) Their involuntary sacrifice was what allowed the cab to remain intact, (until ten seconds later when a giant blade came down, slicing the top off like a tuna can.) If I had not been already ducked in the fetal position my head would have been carved clean off. This was not an accident; this was a trap, and I needed to know if we were still in immediate danger. "Baron!" I shouted over and over as I dug myself free of the wreckage. "What the hell is this?"

Baron appeared in full armor, with his helmet protecting his face. "A minor setback."

"A minor setback? That's easy for your armored ass to say."

"My armored ass?" he was legit laughing now. "Just trust me." he scooped me up like a bride, making sure to position my face against his chest. "Watch your head."

"My what?" Before I could ask questions, Baron shot up, through the ceiling, landing in a place that appeared to be covered in sand. Had I not been facing Baron's chest I would have gotten a mouth full of beach and other grossness.

Baron dropped me on my back, allowing me the chance to clean off my soft, fleshy unarmored body. After muttering profanity, I managed to get to my feet. "So, where the hell are we?"

"If my navigation is correct, we're in Beloit, Wisconsin, near the riverbank."

"If," I muttered.

Baron took off his helmet, taking a better look around. "As for what we hit: I've heard about anti-military, anti-police traps."

"Put in place by the drug cartels?" I asked with a raised eyebrow.

"And local militia. Welcome to Wisconsin."

I rolled my eyes. "Fine, you are not the world's worst driver." Just an idiot for driving straight into an obvious snare. "What do we do now? All joking aside, we're pretty screwed."

"Not if you still have the battery."

I quickly checked my hiding spot. Since my prosthetic legs were still in pristine condition, I just assumed the device survived. Thankfully, the battery was still attached firmly to the joint. "I still have it, but I'm not sure of your game plan. Are we trying to lure out TAC because they'd want to retrieve their property? Or are we trying for Kitsune? Or..." I pursed my lips and chuckled to myself, the answer was obvious. "You want to lure them both, because you always bet on both sides."

Baron started a slow clap. "You know me too well, baby sister. And yes, I do have a plan."

I would quickly learn a valuable piece of information; Baron knew people, lots and lots of powerful, scary people.

A high-ranking Central American gang (with ties to Cuba, Trinidad, Puerto Rico, and other places where Baron had worked in the past) was more than willing to take us in. The community settlement consisted of twenty different families, including women children and elders. We were given clean, donated clothes to be able to blend in as normal citizens of southern Wisconsin, as well as food and a place to stay. All this was in exchange for Baron's help in upcoming missions, as well as any drugs, weapons and other tech he managed to salvage from Feng's mobile lab.

For the next few days, I stayed behind, hanging out with the women and children. There were females who went on missions with the men, as well as 'children' who were being trained for their future careers. I hung with the dedicated 'kitchen crew.'

The women here were elders passing down recipes and hand washing stubborn blood stains, with a few acting as babysitters. A little boy ran past my leg, pausing as his hand touched the metal.

"Robot?"

His voice was so small and sweet, I couldn't help but reach down to pick him up. "Yup, I'm a robot superhero like…" I wanted to say a character that he might have heard of, but he quickly replied.

"I-man!" the boy excitedly flailed his arms.

"He means Iron Man," said a nearby voice. I turned to see a teenage girl with black lipstick and a face full of tattoos; crosses, tears and Spanish quotes.

"Mama!" the little boy said happily, reaching out his arms to the tough, intimidating young woman.

"Hey, Denny!" She scooped up the little boy, giving him a spin like a playful older sister.

"Mama, Helly has leg like I-man!"

"Helly?"

"My name's Hellion," I held out my hand for a handshake.

The girl chuckled. "My street name's Diamond, but you can call me Lucy."

I had a feeling she was prompting me to reveal my actual name. "Hi, Lucy."

She snickered, realizing she was not going to get that info. "I got a question. did your man get you knocked up before or after you lost your legs?"

"After," I replied in as monotone of a voice as I could muster. "But, Baron, he ain't my man."

"Didn't say he was," she said with a smirk. "Plus, you ain't his type." She walked Denny to one of the older women before taking a seat at the outdoor picnic table. "What did you call him?"

"Baron?"

"Is that some kind of pet name? Around here he goes by Leo." As she kicked up her legs, I expected her to pull out a cigarette but instead she moved her backpack to her lap.

"That's cool."

"So, if Leo is not the father, who is?"

This got looks of scorn from several if the elderly cooks, accompanied by scolding in Spanish.

"The baby's father is a friend of his. Noah…" I didn't expect her to know who Noah was.

Lucy's eyes lit up. "Noah? Damn that white boy is fine."

"You've met Noah?"

"I've met A Noah," she explained. "The one I met was the guy who escaped prison with Leo, along with some kind of talking robot? They stayed here for a while looking for work, ended up building the monster in the basement."

"Monster in the basement?"

"You'll see; it was Noah's first baby." Lucy took out a binder marked, *'Mr. Halliway, period 3: Advanced Coding.'* She pulled out a pen and started to fill in what I assumed was her homework. "So, what's Noah up to these days? Are you his girl or his side piece?"

"Actually, he's dead." The room went quiet. "So, anyway, you all call my partner Leo?"

That question got a few laughs. The women said several more remarks in Spanish, causing me to think they were making fun of the dumb pregnant white girl with robot legs.

Lucy raised her hand, and muttered something that seemed to calm everyone down. She then turned to me. "As an international freedom fighter or terrorist as some like to call him, he goes by a different name in every region. But we all have reason to believe Leo is his real name."

"Really," this deepened the mystery surrounding Baron. "How long have you known him?"

An old woman chopping vegetables answered. "Leo is a long-time ally and friend."

The way she spoke was odd, bordering on paranormal. I was about to ask a possibly stupid question when Baron walked through the door.

"Yo, Hellion, this way." Without even checking if I was following him, Baron started in the direction of the basement stairs.

Lucy smiled like someone who knew a secret. "You might want to hurry."

I caught up with Baron just in time to see him unlock the door. To the naked eye, the chipped, painted wooden door looked like something that came with the house. He raised his hand, bringing up a holographic panel. This was why Lucy told me to hurry. The blue light scanned his palm, signaling the door to swing open. He jumped through, and I quickly followed.

The entrance was a large metal slide that coiled around a corner, to a very specific location. "Where are we going?" I shouted.

"You'll see."

At the end of the ride was a dark room with soft fluffy carpet. If I didn't know better, I would have guessed that I landed in some kind of adult movie theatre. "Wow."

Baron took a seat at what could only be described as a DIY supercomputer. "Welcome to the magical wonderland of the dark web."

"And what are we doing here?"

"We are going to attempt to cast our line and see what we can pull in." Baron held out his hand, "if you please."

"You want to upload the battery?"

"Not the whole thing, obviously. Just enough to show our hand."

I suddenly felt sick to my stomach. "There's something I need to tell you."

"You're not sure if what you have is the real battery or a replica."

"You knew?"

"I just assumed," Baron said with a shrug as he continued to type. "Even if it's a fake, the device is still TAC technology." He held out his hand for a second time.

"Fine." I took a seat and started to remove my leg. "little privacy?"

"I'm not looking," he said, returning to his typing. "But for every second you make me wait I'm going to search out gross crime scene images."

"Whatever." I removed the battery from its hiding spot, and gave it one last look before placing the sacred item in Baron's open palm. "Battery, battery in your hand, show us the way to the promise land."

Baron folded his fingers. "I'll give it my best shot."

I watched as Baron disappeared under the desk, searching through a trunk full of cords. After a moment he picked out a three prong USB hub that looked more than a little strange. "I don't think that's going to fit."

"If I had a dollar for every…." Baron was laughing too hard to continue the joke. Instead, he simply let his skills do the talking. The prongs bent in strange directions, like worms attempting to feed.

Soon I learned what exactly was on the flash drive; a whole lot of code. "Any idea what it means?"

"Noah once told me about a secret government project, something that could hold the world's energy hostage for an indefinite amount of time."

"That's not possible," I muttered, entranced by the wall of text. It was possible, because Noah was just that brilliant. suddenly my chest froze. "Please don't tell me you're putting it on the web."

"Oh, heck no, that would probably set this whole room on fire. "easy way to piss off the most powerful gang in southern Wisconsin."

"Fair enough." I had to admit that was a relief. "so, is that the real thing or a replica?"

Baron shrugged as he continued to type.

"What does that mean?"

"I wasn't physically present when this was made, I have no idea if this is what the device was meant to look like. We just need to toss out our lure, make our presence known. If the worm is a dud, then we'll just fall back on plan B."

"Ok, so what are you posting?"

"Do you want an honest answer or the dumbed down version?"

"Dumb it down please."

"I'm posting a jigsaw puzzle missing half the pieces."

"Copy that." I sat quietly, watching as Baron did his thing. I waited until he was finished, having saved deleted or sent the wall of code. "Can I have the drive back?"

"Depends," he said as he disconnected the battery from the main circuit. "Are you going to stick around for a while?"

"Why wouldn't I?"

"The battery is your ticket back to the safety of TAC. I need to know I can trust you not to ditch me."

"Did you ever give me my knife back?" I had no reason to ask prior to that moment.

Baron fished around in the deep pockets of his armor. "Here." he handed me a cleaned polished blade that seemed slightly larger than the one I'd lent him. "You're going to need it."

"I'm going to need it?" I repeated sarcastically, as if I didn't believe him. "I'll try to make sure the kids don't swipe it while I'm asleep." I closed the knife, slipping it into its hiding place on my upper thigh.

"Do you think I can get a ride into town?"

"No, but you can walk."

"Seriously?" I groaned. The gang's housing encampment was a good twenty miles away from the main township (library, school,

Walmart, etc.) "There's no pedestrian walkways, I'd have to cut through the woods."

"You can walk along the highway like a hitch hiker or you can climb a tree to look for a shortcut. I imagine the Walmart would be visible from several hundred miles."

"Fine, see you in a few hours."

"A few hours?"

"Once you tell me how to get out of here."

"There's a door around the back, it's exit only."

The rusted metal door was not hard to find. "If I'm not back by dinner, try to save me some rice and beans."

"Just remember, it's exit only, one way. If you forget anything you're totally screwed."

"I heard you the first time," I replied as I slammed the door. What could I possibly forget? As I emerged in a heavily wooded area, one thing came to mind; how was I going to find my way back to the housing compound? Oh well, that was a question for a later time. I climbed a tree, hoping to spot the Walmart. The bright, glowing sign was a beacon of refuge and not too far away. Unfortunately climbing down proved slightly more difficult.

Within the ten minutes it took me to carefully plan each step, someone managed to set a trap. "Ow!" The metallic net was all but invisible in the darkness. Each of the loops was large enough to catch my arms legs and neck. The more I struggled the tighter the bonds became until I felt like hog-tied cattle. This feeling was enhanced further when I felt a massive work boot gently press against my face.

"Calm down," said an unknown male voice. "My superior wants you alive." The large man threw me over one shoulder.

With how gentle he was being, I assumed this body position was an effort to hide his identity as well as the name of the roadside motel he was sneaking me into. I was treated to a view of the floor as we entered through the house keeping laundry room, then down a hallway of reddish-brown carpet, to the door of a ground floor hotel room. I could hear the key card beep, followed by a lock. The man carried me to the bed, placing my body on the bare mattress.

"Could you at least untie me?" I asked since I was still bound like an animal awaiting slaughter.

"That won't be happening."

Before I could catch a glimpse of the man's face, the net transformed into rope, securing me to the bed by my arms, legs and neck. My body was stretched in five directions, pinning my head back. I was about to scream when a different set of hands covered my eyes and mouth with large pieces of precut duct tape.

"We're going to cut the baby out of you," said a calm female voice.

I recognized it. Although, at that moment, I prayed I was wrong. "Maverick?" I mouthed the syllables with what little breath I could pull in through my nose.

The female voice sighed. "You deserve an award for that, would you like your eyes or your mouth?"

The man answered for her. "I'd recommend the mouth. The extra oxygen will make the procedure easier."

Maverick chuckled. "Easier for her to survive? This little slut doesn't need any help with that. She's like a cockroach, right Miss Nicki?" She made the choice for me, carefully removing the tape from my eyes.

I blinked once, then twice, before blacking out completely.

I awoke after an indeterminate amount of time, still in the same position but in a horrendous amount of pain. I wanted to scream or at least be able to take a decent breath but the tape was still on my mouth. That was when I heard a constant beeping, like a heart monitor. Was I in a hospital? No, the ceiling was the same one I'd collapsed to.

My neck was unsecured, so I felt the need to attempt to sit up. I captured a short glimpse of a strange woman with long purple hair. She was sitting in an office chair, sipping on a large pink Starbucks drink.

"Nicki, are you awake?" she said in her Russian accent. She put her drink down, walked over. "I'm going to pull off the tape, but you have to promise not to scream

I involuntary nodded.

She quickly removed the tape causing pain in the one place that had not felt like fire and brimstone.

I forced a breath, desperate to try and keep my promise. "Anya?"

"Yup, it's a-me," she replied in her best Super Mario impression.

"What happened? And can you please untie me?"

"Baron knows where you are and he'll be back soon. And trust me you don't want me to untie you."

My mind went straight to the last memory; haunting words like something out of a horror film, 'cut...baby...out.' That would explain the horrific pain. "Anya, I need you to be straight with me, please. I already lost my legs; I can take whatever bad news you have about my lower body."

"That depends, what did you hear before they knocked you out?"

I swallowed hard, tasting a mixture of saliva and blood. "Maverick was with a guy and they said something about taking my baby."

"Sounds about right. To her, that child was nothing more than TAC property."

"Was?"

The room's main entrance flung open, leaking in the sound of gunfire. Baron flew in, slamming the door behind him as he struggled to his feet. "Oh, hey, Nicki, you're awake," he said calmly as he brushed himself off. My friend's armor was covered in blood so he started to undress, down to his underwear. "Anya, babe, did you get what I asked?"

"The jeans? Yes, I did."

"And the supplies? We're going to need to flee the city, this might be the last Walmart for miles."

"Yes," Anya groaned, walking over to a pile of Walmart bags. "See for yourself."

Baron did as she asked, but not before releasing my restraints. "Anya keep an eye on her, make sure she doesn't go in to shock." He disappeared to the bathroom, emerging seconds later with a clean face and wearing a pair of low-rise jeans.

"Where is my baby?" I asked, through tears of physical and emotional pain.

"If I had to guess, he's probably in TAC custody," Baron said, taking a seat by my side. "Do you still have the battery?"

Anya answered for me, twirling the flash drive between two fingers. "I made sure to take it off that bitch before I put a bullet in her head." As if to drive home the point, she walked over to a dead body that she had shoved in the closet and stole this person's sunglasses.

"You killed Maverick?" I asked with a noticeable tone of confusion.

"You seem surprised," Anya replied as she shut the closet. "I never had much love for that traitorous woman. She took me under her wing, only to throw me out with the trash."

"Um, ok…" I placed my weight on my arms to sit up, just enough to see the massive scar on my stomach. "So, what now?"

Baron sighed. "Well, since all hell is breaking loose, I say we take the fight to TAC."

I nodded; the idea made sense. "I think we should do some recon first. Since I have a foot in both sides, I think we should try to set up a meeting with Tony (or Deadlock, whatever you call him.) If TAC has my baby he will know where and hopefully why."

Anya scoffed. "You know why."

I glanced at Baron since he seemed to be the more mature of the two. "Why?"

"Noah and Tony have a lot in common. He was never as physically modified as Tony, but his intellect was something nurtured by the same lab that created Tony's enhanced abilities."

"Are you saying I was carrying the next messiah?"

Anya laughed. "Someone thinks highly of themselves."

Baron threw a pillow, narrowly missing Anya's now empty Starbucks cup. "I'm in. I can hold my own against TAC, how about you Annie?"

"Did you just call me Annie?" Anya rolled her eyes as if this was all a big joke. "I'll go with you guys on one condition."

"Let's hear it," I replied, attempting to test how much I could sit up without doubling over in pain.

"Axel is mine." She lifted her shirt showing off a scar that went from her hip to her naval.

I felt my breath freeze in my chest. "What's that?"

"The work of Colonel Julian 'Axel' Diaz. He raped me, tried to give me a superbaby of my own. I had to carve it out while it was still the size of a Ping-Pong ball." Anya motioned at my stomach. "Your kid is probably still alive, growing in a lab someplace. Perhaps you'll meet him again someday. I couldn't take that risk."

"What would you do?"

"Baron filled me in on the deal that TAC is allegedly offering. I will consider turning myself in for immunity."

In exchange for Axel's life. I would have to be ok with that, for now at least. "I'm glad. Which one of you has a car?"

"That would be Baron's department," Anya said as she hurled her cup at the wall, bouncing it into the trash can. "Where are we headed?"

A large explosion could be heard directly outside the room: the hotel was under attack. Baron sighed, more annoyed than afraid. "That's our signal to G-T-F-O." He grabbed his armor, getting redressed into his chest piece, and helmet as he slid the antigravity boots to Anya.

Anya sarcastically scoffed. "You expect me to carry her while you shoot your way out? Yeah, I don't think so."

"You have a better plan?"

"Actually, I do," she said, sliding the boots back in Baron's direction. "suit up and use your chest projectile power to blast a hole in the wall. Then we can all make a run for it."

I slowly raised my hand. "How far of a run are we talking about?"

"Yes, Baron," Anya asked. "Where are you parked?"

"Under the cow," Baron replied, while quickly getting dressed. He took a deep breath and shot a round from the x-shaped hole in his chest piece. With a six-foot hole punched in the wall, Baron scooped me up in his arms. We flew towards a cow sculpture that marked a local gas station.

Landing near the base he punched the floor, exposing an old, rusted dial. He seemed to know the passcode, opening the lock just as Anya joined us. Together we slid down a pipe, to a small parking garage. Apparently, we were not the only people looking for an exit strategy. There were a dozen or so vehicles to choose from, but many were reserved for certain families.

Baron selected an ATV. I sat on his lap, burying my face in his shoulder. Anya sat behind him, wrapping her arms around his waist. I had a feeling I knew why he chose such a small vehicle. The larger vans were meant to usher the elders and children to safety. (I truly hoped that was the case.) Unfortunately, I couldn't see a thing, until we finally stopped in yet another forested area.

I stretched my back, looking up at the sky. "Tony, if you're watching, I could really use a visit. I even have Baron and Anya."

A gust of wind hit me in the face. Anya and Baron stood at my side, looking around. Baron had his weapons ready while Anya seemed more focused on seeking out abnormalities in the surrounding atmosphere.

An aircraft landed. I couldn't really tell if it was the same invisible helicopter Tony had been traveling in, but it certainly looked the part. The door opened but the man who emerged was taller, darker; it was Axel.

Baron barely had a chance to hold Anya back before she attacked like a bloodthirsty puma. She had a garrote wire up her sleeve and was more than ready to rip his head off.

"Stop!" I shouted. "If Axel is here it's for a reason, we need to at least hear him out."

Anya didn't move. "You can hear him just fine at fifty percent oxygen."

"Ok, I can work with that." I took a step towards Axel. "Where is Tony?"

Axel replied, blinking tears from his eyes, "Tony traded his life for your baby."

"Traded to who?" Anya asked. She tightened the piano wire until we could see blood.

Axel was clearly in a lot of pain. "There are more than two teams at play."

I place my hand on his cheek, his tears seemed genuine. "How do we know you're not lying?"

"Because I have the child." Axel looked towards me. "Everything you want is in there. You don't need me alive." He removed his gun from its holster, handing it to Anya.

Instead of taking the opportunity, Anya looked towards me as well. "Your call."

I felt sick. "It's my call?"

CHAPTER 12

thought for a moment. "Shoot him in the foot."

"Cool, thanks!" Anya did as I asked, firing a single round into Axel's foot. Much to my surprise the gun had actually been loaded. Despite the fact he was wearing what appeared to be military-issue combat boots, Axel was now missing the top part of his foot (all of the toes, down to the arch.) With such a large blast one would assume it was a laser (to cauterize the wound.) Before I had a chance to see for myself Anya hit him in the head with the butt of his gun, knocking him out cold. "Let's see what's inside the invisible airplane."

Baron reached out to me. "Nicki, give me your arm. Let's see if there's any medical supplies."

Immediately I noticed this was in fact Tony's vehicle. "Can you fly this?"

"I can fly anything," Baron replied. His focus was on the first aid kit. "Take this." He handed me a wrapped syringe marked with a medical cross. "It's an all-purpose ampule. Stab it in to your thigh like an EpiPen. It should help with the pain, maybe even give you a boost of energy."

As Baron went straight for the control panel, I quickly fished out an alcohol wipe (just so I didn't give myself blood poisoning.)

The process was pretty self-explanatory, and I'd never had an issue with needles. After a few seconds I felt a rush of energy. With a clear mind, I went for the back locker. If there was an embryo in a tube somewhere onboard, it would be in there.

I opened the door to find a mountain of clothes, papers and other supplies. I knew I had to dig deeper. Without the use of my stomach muscles, I simply forced myself to collapse on to the floor, landing hard on my hip. My hand reached out and grabbed something that felt like a glass vase. This had to be what I was looking for. I pulled it out just enough for the light to hit.

Anya screamed. "Baron, get us out of here, now!"

I could hear her shut the door, followed by Baron starting the engine, taking to the sky. I forced myself to sit up, barely managing to catch the object in my arms. I was slammed against the side wall, curling myself around the pod. Thankfully nothing broke.

Resting the pod on my lap I finally got a good look at its contents. it was filled with red liquid. I place two fingers on the surface. The color started to disperse and I was met by a small newborn hand. It was like we were separated by a window; my baby was moving, he was alive. "How do we take it out?" I asked out loud. the very idea was so insane I wanted to scream.

"We don't," Axel said, gripping his head in pain.

Anya seemed peeved that he was still alive. "That's not really your call."

"It's not safe to try onboard an aircraft with no life support system!" Axel paused, struggling for air. "Baron, head east, to Washington DC. The guidance system will show you the way."

Baron at the controls, already had us in the air. "Are you sure it's safe, Man? Won't they be expecting us?"

"The right people will be expecting us," Axel clarified, while attempting to move his injured leg.

Anya gripped his neck. "Can I kill him yet?"

"No," I said with a sigh. "If he's telling the truth, once we reach DC, we'll need to be able to prove we're not a threat."

"Can I at least hit him again?"

"Sure," I replied since I knew she was going to do it with or without my blessing.

Anya gleefully struck Axel with the butt of the gun, before taking a seat by my side. "Since you're in charge, I guess I'll take a nap."

"I'm in charge?" Yeah, right. God help us if that's' the case. After a few seconds Anya was asleep.

Axel sat up, rubbing his temples as he took a moment to blink his eyes. "Can't say I didn't have that coming."

"So, you admit to raping her?"

"I did what I did under orders of Maverick."

"You expect me to believe that?"

"I have reason to believe she's working for a powerful international cartel."

"Kitsune?" I asked, throwing out the suggestion. Axel was, himself powerful. I could not imagine what kind of person he feared.

"Someone more powerful, on a global level."

"Let's say I believe you. why did she want my baby? Or any super baby."

"I assume the people she works for have an end goal of acquiring a super army. In truth, she chose to take you because the warrior blossoming within your womb was too valuable to trust to a teenager."

That sounded about right. "So, how did Tony trade his life for this Kinder surprise egg?"

Axel smiled and laughed followed by awkward silence. "You've been unconscious, in that room for nearly three weeks. Knowing Baron and Anya were in the area, I entrusted them to guard your body, until you had the strength to awaken on your own."

"Oh, ok," I said, trying to remain calm. "Now answer the question."

"Tony and I tracked a vehicle driven by Maverick's male accomplice. I have reason to believe it was Faust in one of his many disguises."

I nodded again. "Ok." I didn't fully believe him but I needed him to keep talking.

"Tony and I, we fought our way into their Eastern Canada base. but only one of us was allowed to leave with the child's remains."

"Remains?"

Axel pursed his lips. "I may have misspoken."

"Why did you say remains! answer me!"

"Because I have no way of knowing if the child is actually alive or if upon disconnecting it from the power source…"

The baby was moving; he was alive, my son was alive. I needed to get the capsule open. "Anya, can I have the gun for a second?"

Anya yawned, opening her eyes. "Hand me the Kinder egg." Against my better judgement I did as she asked. She smacked the side of the glass container. With a ping, followed by a shatter, the container opened and a small wet baby slid out falling on to the floor in front of us. "Easy-peasy."

I looked at her frozen with shock and fear. "Um, thanks?"

"Your tits work, right? If not, we can always pick up some formula." Anya's calm demeanor put me at ease.

"Is he moving?" The child was the size of a typical premature baby. From his time submerged in liquid his skin was red and wrinkled like a lab specimen or a small mummy. He had a feeding tube and a few other lines stuck in his tiny chest. Clearly, he had been receiving oxygen and nutrients via the magical unknown liquid. His eyes were closed, and his hands were clenched into fists. If he was still alive, he appeared to be in a lot of pain.

His chest moved ever so slightly as he struggled to breathe on his own. I was about to reach for my son when suddenly he cried, the sound erupting like a weapon of mass destruction.

This was not just loud; his voice was somehow shaking the walls, compromising the structural integrity of the aircraft. I had to find a way to calm him or he could take down the entire plane. I looked to Baron who had put on his helmet. He seemed calm, focused, in control of the steering, so I knew I had (at least) a little time.

"Grab a blanket, or give him your tits," Baron said as he stayed focused on the control panel. "It's your baby, you can do this, Nicki."

"I know." The baby was only a few feet away but it felt like I was crawling through mud. Since there was no blanket in the immediate area, I took off my blood-stained shirt, wrapping the little one. I had never swaddled a baby before but the act came naturally; cross the arms over his little chest, wrap him into a little burrito that I could hold in my arms. The tubes seem to fall out all on their own. Perhaps that was the reason he was crying; he needed a source of food.

Since my top half was already exposed, I thought I'd give breastfeeding a try. I aimed his mouth at my nipple, hoping for a miracle. Even if I had no milk, I assumed the baby would want to bite down on something. His tiny mouth latched on, sucking ever so softly. When he paused to take a breath, a stream of liquid dripped down my chest. I was actually feeding my baby! More importantly, the baby was finally quiet. "Is your name Abaddon?"

The baby opened his eyes, looking up at me.

"Can you understand me?" It was a silly question, but somehow, I felt a genuine connection. "Can I call you Abby?"

The baby giggled.

"I'll take that as a yes."

Baron cleared his throat. "I hate to interrupt but I think we're still in trouble."

"What kind of trouble?" I asked, standing up with my son in my arms.

"The kind where enemy homing missiles can somehow see through our cloaking."

I took a seat by his side, attempting to see what he was seeing on the radar. "Are we flying over military air space?"

"On the way to Washington DC? Gee, I don't know," he replied in a derpy voice.

"I'm half naked, breastfeeding a baby on what might be the last flight of my life. I think I'm allowed to be a little braindead right now!"

"Sorry, it's just this thing is supposed to have a cloaking system."

"Are you sure it's activated?"

Baron turned to me with a look of silence. "I swear I'm going to hit the eject button. And you can fly this thing."

"Sorry." I needed a plan. "…evasive maneuver."

"Should I do a barrel roll?" he asked sarcastically, making a retro videogame reference.

"I'm not kidding. Take us up in to commercial air space!"

"You want to play chicken with a Boeing 747? Yeah, I don't think so. It'll be easier to just take the hit."

I knew what he meant; ideally the shields and even the aircraft itself could withstand the partial damage. But the fact that this projectile seemed to be moving at the speed of molasses indicated that it was packing a punch. "I'll bet you a anything whoever we're up against won't risk blowing up a plane full of vacationers."

Baron sighed. "You may have a point." Baron shifted up, rocketing us into the land of Delta, United and whoever else happened to be flying to the nation's capital.

I could see by the radar we were heading out of range of the attack, while at the same time several planes popped into view. A message came over the radio. "Attention all pilots in the vicinity, please ground your aircrafts at the nearest public airport. If you require assistance please switch to a private channel."

"That's awesome!" I squeaked. "With all the planes being diverted we'll have a straight shot into the city."

"How do you know we're not landing at an airport or a military base?" Baron asked, with genuine interest.

"I don't know. I just assumed Axel was taking us to a secure location." Since my son was finished nursing, he had turned his head, looking in the direction of the control panel. Was he feeding me information, from the future?

The missile sputtered out, disappearing off the radar completely.

With his foot still leaking copious amounts of blood, axel made his way to the front seat, resting himself between Baron and I.

"When we're about five miles out, you're going to need my passcode to access the bunker."

"Fine," Baron said, tossing a wireless mic at Axel's head. "Is there an official frequency or should I just start channel surfing?"

"I need you to lock on to a non-existent channel, doesn't matter which one. Once we're within range, my superiors will do the rest."

Baron did as Axel instructed, scrolling the radio frequencies until we landed on a spot that was between two normal channels. The silence seemed to represent open space. Soon we were flying over (what appeared to be) a residential district.

I heard crackling, followed by a series of whispers. Since I was not wearing a headset, I couldn't make out who was on the line, but I did hear Axel recite a password made entirely of numbers.

"Rodger that," Axel said, ending his transmission.

Immediately we were grabbed by a reddish beam, like something out of a sci-fi alien abduction. I folded myself in half, with my head between my legs and my baby held close to my chest. We were sucked into the bunker like a child sucking shaved ice through straw, on a hot day.

"Axel is that you?" shouted a female voice from outside the aircraft.

"Yes, Dr. Toki, Axel replied, opening the door.

Dr. Toki? That was a name I hadn't heard in a while. Peeking out the front window I could see the good doctor, dressed in full armor. She was shadowed by a dozen or so guards.

"Stand down!" she shouted to her small army. "You, over there, get a stretcher!"

Axel was helped on to a stretcher and removed from the room. We should have followed but now it was too late. "Everyone who is still inside, come out with your hands up."

I looked to Baron and Anya. "Let me go first. If something goes badly you guys can back me up." My friends nodded in silent agreement. "Dr. Toki, it's me Hellion, I'm coming out."

I exited with the baby in my arms. With a better view I could see that Dr. Toki was not armed, but her remaining guards were. "Hands up!" shouted a male guard.

"I can't," I said, shifting the baby in my arms.

Abby flailed his limbs, fighting his way out of the swaddle cloth. He was reaching for my breast, and in doing so, exposed his head for all to see.

Dr. Toki took a step forward. "Is that your son? He survived?" A smile spread across her face. "Of course, he did." She reached her hand to his little face. "He's a scientific work of art." I expected her to try to take the baby from my arms, but instead she pulled back. "What's his name?"

"Abaddon," I said with a smile. "Or Abby."

"Where did you get that name from?"

"I met him in a dream." I adjusted the baby in my arms, getting a better look at his blue eyes.

"He told you that was his name?"

"Yes, why?"

"Do you know what it means?"

"It's a real word?"

"The origins of the word are Hebrew, referring to a fallen angel, the ruler of the abyss. However later Christian scriptures use the name to refer to Jesus after the resurrection. When he was at his full power." Her voice trailed off. "We can discuss it further in the medical ward."

She waved over a guard who already had a wheelchair ready for me. I was put in the same room as Axel. It was a long room with about twenty hospital beds. I was able to get in all on my own, even with the baby in my arms. A nurse came in with an IV kit (needle, tubing and alcohol wipes) along with a bag of 'saline.' I swatted her hand away, scooting backward on to the bed. "No thank you."

The woman paused, with no visible reaction. "You just gave birth, you need fluids."

I glanced at Axel, he appeared to be asleep. He said I gave birth weeks ago, so I was making the choice to believe him. "Fine, I'll take a glass of water."

"As you wish."

I could tell by her robotic silence that she had delt with soldiers like me before; arrogant little teens experiencing their first taste of independence. "Where's Dr. Toki?"

"She's speaking to the remaining person on the aircraft."

"Person?" *Singular, not plural?*

"The pilot," she clarified as she handed me the small paper cup. "He is a person, correct? I assumed his lack of facial features was due to the nature of the armor."

I bit my lip, resisting the urge to giggle. She actually thought Baron was a robot? "I don't really know." My focus returned to the issue at hand: Anya. Was she still in the underground bunker?

"Let me take the baby while you finish your beverage."

"No," I said, emptying the cup in one gulp. "I'd prefer to keep him with me. For my emotional security."

"If that will be all, I shall take my leave." She put down a clean, TAC uniform and a small package of disposable diapers before exiting out the saloon style doors.

I got dressed and made my way to Axel's bedside, with my newly clean, quiet baby. "Axel, you awake?"

"Yeah," the older man replied with his eyes closed. "Just on a crap-ton of painkillers." He ripped the IV line out of his arm, letting the blood sputter.

"Um, why did you do that?"

"Need to keep a clear head." Axel sat up. "Where's Baron and Anya?"

"The nurse said Baron is with Dr. Toki, but Anya is just gone."

Axel chuckled. "Thanks for the warning." He moved his legs off the bed, revealing a professionally bandaged foot. "Do you think she's still working for Kitsune?"

"Honestly?" I thought back to what she said about Kitsune's power and influence. The glamorous Japanese billionaire was a mafia queen and to be in her good graces was a guarantee of a life of luxury. "I could picture Anya presenting your head to her on a silver platter."

That got a laugh.

"Are you ok to walk?" I asked, hoping we could go someplace more private.

"Good enough," Axel said, moving his thigh, to draw attention to the brace on his lower leg. "My first priority is Tony; alive or dead, I'm not leaving him behind." There was a true sense of pain in his voice. "We're safe here, but we need to use this time to formulate a plan."

"How much does Dr. Toki know?" I asked, shifting the baby in my arms.

"She's up to date on the procurement of your son; Maverick's theft, Tony's capture. She's as invested as I am." His answer made a lot of sense.

"Which was why you told her to meet you here," I said with a nod. "What was your plan if Baron decided to take us to Mexico?"

"I was still in contact with TAC command, my location would have been monitored and Dr. Toki would have been diverted as necessary."

"I guess that makes sense," I muttered, rocking the baby against my shoulder. Looking around at the hospital walls, I suddenly felt sick to my stomach. "Has this all been about me?"

"You can't stop thinking about your life choices?" Axel laughed. "I know the feeling."

"Not just my choices. Anya was recruiting me for Maverick, by trapping Alexi who was actually Faust."

"A real clusterfuck," Axel muttered.

Somehow that gave me my answer. "Maverick was infertile."

Axel turned to me with noticeable shock. "How did you know that?"

"It was the logical, educated answer," I explained. "Either she wanted to recreate a version of Tony to use as her own personal soldier of fortune or she was hired to recreate Tony."

Axel's expression confirmed it all. "Maverick was more than willing to hand over her own child."

"Your child."

He nodded, sadly. "But she couldn't carry the fetus long enough for it to be viable."

"That was why you were so certain my baby was dead. You were used to seeing failed experiments." I reached for Axel's hand. I needed the truth. "Are you sorry, about what you did to Anya?"

Axel sighed, looking towards the ceiling. "I could tell you I am, and you might even believe me, but I know Anya never will." There were noticeable tears in his eyes. "I know she cut the baby out, all on her own."

"You knew?"

"She left me the fetus, along with a note. That's how I know my soul is damned to Hell."

Before I could respond the doors opened and Baron walked through with Dr. Toki at his side. They were talking, laughing. "Hey, Nicki," he said reaching out his hand for a high-five.

"Hello," I replied, making sure to not leave him hanging. "Glad to see you're still alive."

Baron then reached his hand out to Axel. "You're looking good."

"Thanks," Axel said as he shook his hand. "Same to you."

I couldn't help but giggle. Baron's gift was his ability to switch sides at will; and he could do this without the use of a weapon. Actually, the more I thought about it, he wasn't a spy playing both sides; no, he was the ultimate peacekeeper. "What did you and Dr. Toki talk about?"

"I'm going to be staying on as your pilot, at least until the mission is over."

I had a feeling he was referring to our new mission, to rescue Tony and take down Faust. "Sounds cool."

My theory was confirmed when Dr. Toki produced and iPad and activated a hologram projection. "Faust cannot be allowed to make use of the data derived from Tony's augmentations," the young doctor explained, as she pulled up a Google maps image.

I shifted my son, turning him to see what appeared to be a house on a forested street. "What are we looking at?"

"This is a satellite image of the location where Agent Deadlock was forced to surrender while Commander Axel absconded with the fetus in the incubation tube."

"Um, what?" I turned to Axel. "I thought you said it was an even trade." I assumed Tony heroically volunteered to stay, to allow Axel to leave with the baby. "You left him behind and stole his only means of escape."

"You know that's not true!" Axel winced in pain; more emotional than physical. If Tony managed to get free of the building, he could…"

"Could what? If he managed to survive the teleporting supervillain, he could probably get a few miles on foot?"

"Nicki!" Baron grabbed my arm before I could slap Axel (or drop my premature baby.)

"What?"

"I think you need to see this." He was holding the iPad, tilting it at an odd angle, resulting in the 3d image becoming a flat panel. "Do you see those blue lights?"

"Yeah," I replied in a whisper. "I do." There was a trail of dots, the energy signatures from Faust using his teleport ability. I traced my hand through the projection. "It's a puzzle."

Going in order from top to bottom there appeared to be a distinct set of letters. The first two clusters seemed obvious enough; a zig-zag next to a round shape. "Zo?" No of course not. It was either 'No' or 'On,' but which one? The next part seemed to be a line and a small orb: a b or a p. "No place…"

"No place like home?" Baron asked.

"Faust is truly a sick…" I hugged Abby to prevent myself from swearing.

"Where's home?" Baron asked, his hand still on my shoulder.

"New Jersey," I said with a nod. "I was born in Atlantic City."

Dr. Toki took a step forward, taking a better look. "Is your family still in New Jersey?" The question was normal, logical, but it felt like a knife to the heart.

"Yeah."

Baron pulled me close for a hug. "That's where you're wrong. Your family is right here."

"Thanks."

He held me close, hugging the baby between us. "If Faust wants to call you out on the beaches of Jersey, he'll have to face the wrath of an entire team of social fuck-ups."

That made me laugh. Baron was more than a social fuck-up. I would be heading back home with one of the most powerful international terrorists by my side. This could be fun. "I can't wait to show you my favorite beach."

The flight touched down, under the early morning sky. I could practically taste the Cinnabon frosting. It had been over a decade since I'd been on an airplane but I loved hanging around the terminals for the delicious overpriced food.

Baron placed his hand upon my shoulder. "What happens in Jersey stays in Jersey," he said with a laugh.

"I thought you'd be bitter." I leaned on his shoulder as we waited for the seatbelt light to turn off.

"You thought I'd be bitter about flying as a passenger instead of a pilot?" Baron shrugged, as he stretched his arms over his head. "I've always loved Alaska Airlines. And if I was flying the plane, I wouldn't have been able to spend time with this little guy." He tickled little Abby's chubby arm causing the baby to smile.

"I can't disagree." In the weeks following our arrival at Dr. Toki's DC bunker, Baron grew close to my son. The three of us shared a room; two cots on the floor with a padded plastic box for the baby. Like all babies little Abby cried; for food, diaper changes, or just out of loneliness. Nine out of ten times, I would awaken to find Baron holding my son. Sometimes he'd walk around the small room, other times he would sit cross-legged on his bed, but every night was a different story about Noah. I learned things I knew I was never meant to know about.

In the years they spent traveling the world as renowned criminal masterminds, Noah and Baron had become more than friends. They fell in love.

"You daddy was the greatest person I ever knew," Baron often said as he rocked my son in his arms. "He was the last person I ever truly loved."

I listened as Baron, by the light of the moon, told my infant son stories about his many adventures with Noah and Nash. Some boarded on the obscene; drugs, weapons trafficking, and all manner of sex. He never outright said they were lovers, only that they trusted each other with their mind body and soul.

"It tears me up inside knowing he's gone. I know this is all my fault, his blood is on my hands. We should have died together. Noah died the way he lived; with honor and integrity. But then I never would have met you."

That was how I knew Baron could be trusted; he loved Abby with every fiber of his soul.

"Yo, Nicki," Baron said, tapping my arm. "The plane's empty, time to go."

"Oh," I took a quick breath, forcing myself back to reality.

Baron grabbed our one piece of luggage, a plain black backpack with a limited number of supplies. Axel had passed it along to us before going through security, so I had to assume it contained no weapons.

We walked down the corridor to the gate at Atlantic City international airport. "Can I hold the bag?" I asked, since he was already holding the baby.

"Sure." Baron took off the straps and tossed me the bag. It was lighter than I thought it would be. Inside was a lot of fabric; some rolled, some folded and some pieces were clearly hiding items made of plastic or metal. I figured I shouldn't be examining its contents right away but with the chill of the airport I wanted to see if there were any extra clothes for my baby.

No, Abby was our baby. Seeing Baron holding the child in his arms, all I could feel was love. "Oh look!" I fished out a blue, baby t-shirt with a happy dolphin. "Let's put it on him!"

Baron did as I asked, maneuvering Abby's wiggly little body. With his fresh new shirt, he looked like a cute little tourist baby. In fact, we looked like a typical vacationing couple traveling with their newborn.

I knew that Axel and Dr. Toki were monitoring us from the safety and comfort of an unmarked medevac vehicle somewhere within a six-mile radius. Ideally, they would follow us, observe from a distance. If and when we found Tony, we could get the hell out (to the nearest TAC bunker.) Until then Baron and I were to look for clues along the boardwalk.

"Should we get a hotel room?" I asked.

"Certain military leaders didn't give us any money, so unless you have a credit card?"

"I could probably pick pocket one."

"Way to blow our cover," he said with a laugh. "Nah, we can deal with the issue of housing when we need to. With any luck Axel and Dr. Toki have plans to get us out, so we don't have to sleep on the streets with a baby."

We walked a further, to the land of sun, sand and casinos, stopping to rest on a bench. "Let's see what's in the bag." There were more shirts, pants, a few flattened bottles to collect water, or maybe even breastmilk. I placed each of the items neatly on my lap, hoping that I would not miss anything important. However, in the end, the only item of importance was a package of baby wipes. There wasn't even any diapers. I had to assume, if I needed to change my baby, I was meant to use the extra clothing. (Same for first aid, due to lack of bandages.) "You really don't have any money?"

"We can always shoplift," Baron said cheerfully as he tossed the baby in the air.

Abby squealed with joy.

I could feel my heart flutter with joy. "That's the New Jersey spirit!"

"There has to be a Walgreens around here someplace."

We easily found a corner store with the iconic red signage. Baron picked up a basket and headed to the food section; packaged drinks, dried cereal, candy, etc.

"What do you think happened to Anya?" I asked, following close. "Since you're the last person who saw her."

"She's going after Axel," he answered casually.

"And you're ok with that?"

"It's her deal, her quest or whatever."

"Or whatever?" I asked. His tone was really starting to piss me off. Axel was my friend, a human being. But so was Anya. And that was why my soul was being torn in half.

"Anya's going to do what she has to do but for the sake of all of us she's going to act alone. That way the blood will be only on her hands."

I saw his point. If and when the time came, we were under no obligation to choose sides. "How thoughtful."

"You need any diapers?" Baron asked. He was holding an open package of men's shaving razors. Grabbing a single replacement head, Baron somehow managed to break the plastic apart without wounding his fingertips.

I assumed he was going to cut open a package. "No, I'm good. He has on a cloth diaper and I have enough supplies to make an extra. But I could use some soap." I grabbed a package of off brand bar soap with an image of a happy Asian baby. Ideally, I could use this for washing both skin and clothing.

After easily leaving the store with everything we needed, we ran in the direction of the beach, hoping to get lost in the crowds. Suddenly out of nowhere the sky darkened and the clouds swelled with rain. The storm came down hard and fast, transforming from freezing rain, to pin-sized hail. In the distance there seemed to be a homeless encampment. Without any words spoken, we both knew to make a run for it.

The tent city consisted of a series of tarps connecting individual homes. There were a few spots that had people huddled around campfires. Men, women and children sat wrapped in dirty, wet blankets, as they struggled to stay warm. Not wanting to take any of their limited resources we walked until we found a sparse area with just a tarp surrounded by barrels and broken pallets. The space was just enough for Baron and I to sleep side by side, resting the baby on his chest.

"Here," he said, sliding the backpack in my direction. "You can use the bag as a pillow."

"Thanks." Unable to comfortably sleep I found myself staring up at the blue tarp. As my mind started to float away my mouth spewed out the words that I thought I'd never say. "What happened between you and Noah?"

"What do you mean?" Baron asked in a whisper. He knew perfectly well what I meant.

"Feng told me he gave Noah the same opportunities he gave you. Yet somehow you ended up as his right-hand man with full access to his arsenal of weapons guns and even his appointment book."

Baron swallowed a lump in his throat. "Your point?"

"Why didn't you convince Noah to come with you?"

Baron went silent. He held the baby close, shivering. "You don't think I tried?" He blinked tears from his eyes.

If he'd been angry, I would have continued the conversation; I would have wanted to know why he had the right to mourn the father of my child. But Baron wasn't angry, he was in pain. "I think we should get some sleep."

"Yeah, totally."

I knew better then to try to ask for my son back. Abby was an emotional support baby and Baron needed him more. I made myself comfortable on my bed of plastic and leaves, pulling the tarp over my body for warmth. "Good night."

There was a moment of silence before we were awoken by Abby's cries. Baron sat up, rocking the small baby, attempting to keep him warm. "I think he's hungry."

"Give him here." I had gotten better at breastfeeding, but with how cold it was I would have preferred to keep as covered as possible. "Can you help me with my tarp-blanket?"

"Sure." Baron helped cover my body, allowing the baby warmth and privacy.

"Thanks." I looked at Baron with genuine love in my heart. "Thank you for being my friend." I couldn't stop the tears from falling, mixing with the freezing cold rain. "Thank you for everything."

Baron blinked tears from his own eyes as he crossed his arms over his chest. "You really want to know what happened to Noah?"

"Yeah, I do." I looked down at Abby, who opened his eyes as he nursed. He had Noah's courage and strength. "I can still remember that night. Even if it was for just a moment, I felt like I had friends, a real connection. That was never something that came easy for me." Not that it mattered. It was yet another fleeting moment of happiness in my shit-show of a life.

Baron lowered his shirt, revealing his upper chest. "Feng gave me an augmentation; I have an inorganic core made of some kind of plasma. I used to think it was radioactive but I have reason to believe it was created as a means of unlimited projectiles."

"And it keeps you warm?" That explained why Abby loved being held by him.

"Well, the power came with a complimentary suit of armor that allowed me to be the perfect little henchman."

"You mean body guard?"

Baron shrugged. "I assumed that was Feng's original plan."

I swallowed the lump in my throat, mentally preparing for the worst. "And Noah?"

"He wasn't down for it. The only reason he surrendered to Kitsune was to allow you and Anya time to flee."

"Oh." I felt like my heart stopped. I should have realized it from the beginning; that was the only reason we were allowed to live, because Noah truly loved me.

"We were turned over to Feng. I could only assume she thought Feng had the ability to extract Noah's mind; his intellect, his secrets. But he didn't. Feng needed Noah to volunteer information." Baron paused, blinking tears from his eyes. "That was the difference between us. My most valuable asset was my combat ability, maybe my strategy skills. All I had to do was pledge my loyalty, and wear the armor, to gain Feng's trust. For Noah, that was asking too much. His mind contained secrets that could change the world; info that could never and would never fall in to the hands of tyrannical psychopaths."

"And that's why he had to die." Since I was finished breastfeeding, I handed the now happy, content infant back to Baron.

"Although if it was up to Feng (and it was) well, you've seen his set up."

"Yeah," I said with a nod. "I'm going to see that until the day I die."

"All of his prized victims are kept alive, conscious as their forced to exist as hood ornaments. Feng wanted them to suffer for all eternity, or until their brains turn to pea soup."

"Now I have a craving for split pea soup." We laughed through our tears. In truth, I couldn't close my eyes without seeing Noah's remains.

"You hungry?" Baron dug in his pocket, producing a smashed-up Snicker's bar.

"We can split it." With food in our stomachs, we fell asleep to the sound of calming rain. For the first time since he'd been born, I had a vision of my son as a full-grown man.

The sound of rain grew louder, gradually transforming to gunfire. I awoke in what appeared to be a WW2 battle scene. Thankfully I was transparent; bullets passed through me like a virtual reality game, and the area around me felt comfortably warm despite the fact I was standing in snow. In the distance I could see a man leaning on a tree.

Eyes closed, he held a cross in his hand. I watched as he kissed the rosary pendent and said a simple prayer. "Blessed be the Lord my strength, which teaches my hands to war, and my fingers to fight."

As I came closer, I could see he was gripping his shoulder while doubled over in pain. That raised the question: why was he reciting the prayer of a sharpshooter?

He moved his hand to his waist, slowly retrieving a pistol. "My goodness and my fortress." He held the gun under his chin, cocking the barrel to his throat. "My high tower and my deliverer. My shield, and he in whom I trust."

"No!" The sound came from behind me.

I turned to see a figure wearing pink-purple armor. It was in the same style as what Baron wore. And he or she wasn't running, they were flying.

"Abby!" A female voice cried.

I followed as fast as I could, as she rushed to the man's side.

"Lieutenant?" The man muttered, coughing up blood.

I now had a good view of his face. It was my son and he was dying. Before I could reach out my hand, the armored woman flew through me.

She fell to her knees, ripping off her helmet to reveal a young Hispanic face framed by lots of curly black hair. "Abby, Sir, I'm here. It's going to be ok." She pursed her lips, smiling at him, through visible tears.

Abaddon lowered his weapon. "You need to flee." With trembling fingers, he lifted his free hand to cup her face. It was obvious that leaving was the last thing he wanted. "This is a battle we cannot win."

"Not alone, Sir," the soldier replied with confidence.

Why was she calling him Sir? I could barely make out a patch on his arm. It was possible he was an officer.

The young woman lifted his arm, adjusting him over her shoulder. "I'm not leaving you behind. The nearest medic station is about six kilometers south of here. We can make it." Before he could reply, she lifted his broken body in her arms, flying off into the night.

The world started to spin as the scene changed. We were now in a poorly lit underground hospital. I could tell it was underground since every few seconds the room shook with the sound of gunfire and other (louder, more violent) explosions. Abby was laying on a cot with his bare chest exposed. He had several fresh bullet wounds, as well as deep scars.

The woman was by his side, having taken off her armor she rested her head by his shoulder, holding his hand. "Why do you call me by my rank?"

"What should I call you?"

"My name is Sundra, but my friends call me Sunny."

"Is that because you sparkle like sunshine?" he asked with a subtle smile. Abby moved his free hand to her cheek, brushing a lock of hair behind her ear. "You don't have to stay, Sunny."

"I want to stay. Call it my street gang code of honor; a little something, I picked up from my grandma." She turned her wrist to reveal a tattoo. It was a stylized diamond with the words, 'Lucy in the sky.' Sunny started to softly hum the melody of the famous rock song. "Lucy in the sky with diamonds. Sorry, the title is the only part I know." She kissed Abby on the forehead. "My papa's name was Denny. He was the first of my family line born in America. You really remind me of him."

A gang member named Lucy with a son named Denny? That couldn't be a coincidence. I moved closer, to get a better look at her face.

She kissed Abby down his nose to his lips.

There were tears in his eyes. "I'll never forget you."

Sunny turned, briefly glancing in my direction. "Do you think she's here, in the room?"

"I know she is," Abby replied, looking up at the ceiling. "Even as a child, I could always feel my mother's spirit watching over me."

"Can she hear us?" Sunny asked, still looking in my path but not actually at me.

"If the calculations and the technology are correct."

"Do you think she can save us?" Her large, emotional eyes, blinked back tears. With every blink she started to disappear, vanishing from reality like a spirit lost to time. When Sunny was completely gone, all that was left was my adult son. His arms were wrapped around the empty space.

All around me I could hear sobbing. I assumed this meant I was going to wake up. My baby son was probably crying for food or maybe because of the cold: but I was going to wake up. Right? I wanted so badly to wake up. Wake up! Wake up!

I felt a sharp pain. I awoke with a jolt under the tarp, to the collapsing of our little shelter. Touching my hip, I felt blood and splinters. All around me all I could see was tarp. I wanted to scream. Where was my son? Where was Baron?

I needed to calm down; breathe, just breathe. I opened my hands, placing them palms down as if I was going to attempt a snow angel. There was a secret, a lock. There had to be. I felt a strange crack in the pavement. Digging my fingertips in, the piece seemed to transform into a handle (or a lever.) Even if it was just a hand hold, it would be my ticket out of the tarp since I could use it to keep myself grounded in place (as opposed to flopping around like a dying fish.) Turns out, it was a handle. I found myself falling down a slide. At the bottom I finally managed to get free of the tarp.

Baron was sitting in a dark corner with a finger to his lips. "Shh, follow me. This is a mezzanine level." He motioned towards what looked like a second series of tunnels. "I'm not sure how deep it goes. We're not going to slide: we're going to crawl. I'll go first and you follow close. Do not lose sight of me. Understand?"

"Are you holding the baby?"

Baron nodded. "If shit goes bad, I want you to find my body. I'll protect him with everything I have."

I knew what he meant, and trusted him fully, but I was still afraid. "You're a better fighter than me."

"Yeah, that's why I'm going to hold the baby."

"Ok."

Baron and I snuck down the tunnels, we emerged in an underground factory facility. "What is this place?"

"Trash processing facility," Baron replied. "You head left I'll head right."

"Sure, I guess." I went left until I saw what appeared to be a light source.

I passed between several cargo boxes, emerging in an open area. There was a series of large vats, bubbling with hot oil or (more likely) acid. "Acid?" I had never seen acid before but the scene looked like something out of a comic book.

"It is acid," said a voice from a nearby balcony. "the typical use is to process heavy metals and other non-recyclable materials."

"Faust?" I couldn't actually see his location.

"Today we're disposing of inorganic material of a different kind." He hit a button causing a limp body to start to descend. It was clearly Tony, but I couldn't tell if he was even alive. "Are you willing to make a deal; trade his life for the contents of the battery?"

"I don't even know if the copy I have is real." And there was also the fact that the infamous flash drive was in a van, in the care of Axel and Dr. Toki.

"The one that Baron put on the dark web? Trust me it's the real deal."

"So, what's on it?" I blurted out the words, although I wasn't expecting any kind of logical answer.

The man snickered. "Does it matter?"

"Yeah, kind of."

"Look, do you want to know my entire evil plan or will you be a good girl and save your beloved boyfriend's life?"

I looked over at Tony. I had no way of helping him. If he was still alive, he was more then capable of saving himself. I had to believe that. "Is it time travel?"

"What?" Faust asked with a laugh. "Seriously, what did you just say?" With a flash of light, Faust teleported, placing himself in front of me. He stood tall, in a tailored suit, staring me down with his creepy metallic eyes. "Answer me, little girl."

Why did he look so much like the adult version of my son? Because he was a shape shifter? Or was there something else? "Time travel?"

The once stern man cracked a smile. "Time travel is the stuff of movies and fairytales. The contents of the battery will bring this world to its knees."

"Yeah, I've heard." I blinked my eyes as the pieces fell into place. There was a reason why my son had been able to communicate with me so clearly through dreams. "Selective telepathic time travel."

Faust was no longer smiling. "Would you prefer that power fall to the hands of Kitsune? She and her brother, they'd use it to cause a gang war; an apocalypse of weapons and drugs. You wouldn't want that blood on your hands."

We he seriously trying to appeal to my humanity? "What about you? What's your plan, to go back in time to give Hitler a migraine?" I knew what his plan was. Or at least I think I did. There was something about Lucy or maybe Denny. What I knew for certain was that the final goal was Sunny; her existence held the key.

"You're not alone, are you? Such a pity." Faust teleported off, in a blast of blue light.

I already knew where he was going and there was nothing I could do. Faust landed on top of Baron as he attempted to free Tony's body. Both men were knocked in to the acid. There was no sound; no screams, or even cries. *Where was my baby?*

Faust teleported in front of me, holding my son in his arms. "You might not have been willing to save your boyfriend, but perhaps you will be willing to trade for your child."

My back hurt, my arms hurt and my head was pounding, but I ran straight at him, charging like a football player going in for a tackle.

I was blinded by a familiar blue light. We had teleported, but to where? I could hear Abby crying. He was alive and that's all that mattered. I blinked my eyes once then twice. "Fire?"

CHAPTER

landed hard on my already sore shoulder. My body was in pain, but I needed to find my baby. Flames licked the walls threatening to destroy the building. I could barely see, but somehow, I knew where to go. This was a single floor building, maybe a cargo container of some kind? No that was just wishful thinking. This room was too big to be a temporary facility. Over the roar of flames and the sound of breaking glass, and cracking wood, I could hear my son's cries. turning in the direction of the sound, I kicked my fake legs in front of me, letting my feet explore before my hands could get injured. I quickly found a metal table pressed against a wall. At its current angle, it created a perfect mini-shelter. sitting on the floor, I felt around for my son, easily locating his shivering body. I picked him up, rocking him in my arms.

There had to be a way out. I couldn't let my child die here. An odd thought passed through my mind; where was Faust, why did he leave us alive?

Suddenly there was a crash, followed by a massive gust of wind. The table felt red hot, even from where I sat. Just beyond the flames I could see what looked like sunlight. With all the strength in my body I kicked the table away and made a run for it.

Looking up I could see Faust was fighting someone in midair. I could see his teleportation flash over and over as the two exchanged blows. Whoever it was just tore off the roof, I needed to make sure their effort was not in vain.

The exit had to be someplace. With the newfound light I could see the glimmer of a broken window, about twenty feet away. I moved my baby under my shirt, holding him close to my chest. I would need to call upon my inner gymnast and attempt to vault. I ran as fast as my prosthetic legs could carry me. In lieu of a springboard I launched myself off the highest piece of debris, launching myself head first through the window giving myself a nasty gash (not that i noticed.) After landing on the wet green grass, I ran until I was safely behind a massive green dumpster. it was far enough to be free of the blaze but close enough to keep Faust and his opponent in my sights. (Not that it would do much good if he decided to teleport in front of me.) my hope was to give myself at least a fighting chance. Looking through the nearby trash i found a broken bottle. I created a handle using a plastic bag, allowing me to clutch the glass blade like a typical knife. 'God, I miss my knife.'

I heard the sound of pounding footsteps; armored boots heading in my direction. Clearly this was not Faust. He was still in the air; if he wanted me dead, I'd be dead. Still, I couldn't risk yelling for help. There was no guarantee this person was an ally. I sprang up, cutting a massive gash in Axel's chest.

"I guess I had that coming," he said in a comical tone. The wound was, thankfully, superficial; a decent amount of bleeding but not deep enough to be life-threatening.

"Axel!" I immediately covered my mouth with my hand. even if Faust was distracted, I didn't want to chance him finding our location.

Axel took my hand, cupping it in his own in a gesture of comfort. "I'm getting us out of here."

"Where is here? How did you find me?"

Axel looked towards the fire. "The sick bastard; he wanted to take you home."

I looked in the same direction, hoping to see what he was seeing. There was the remains of a sign. "This was my gym. did Faust kill my coach?"

"No, from what I know via your background check, the man who hurt you has been dead for nearly a year. If I was to guess, Faust camped here to be able to screw with your head while still being close enough to be found."

His words caused a realization. We were about to be found. I felt the cold barrel of a gun pressed to my head.

"Hello Nicki, long time no see." The deadpan tone of Kitsune's voice cut like a knife.

"Hi," I squeaked. "How've you been?"

That was the wrong thing to say. Kitsune grabbed my shoulder forcing me to my feet. "How have I been?" She grabbed me by my shirt ripping it just enough to reveal my son's tiny, badly bruised face. "You killed my tech-general, so I'll just be taking the one in your arms."

"You're kidding right?" I knew she wasn't. I gripped my son closer, if only to feel the warmth of his tiny breath.

"Does that make you nervous? With any luck he'll know me as Mommy." Kitsune reached for Abby's hand, causing my child to recoil. "If not, children ruled by fear make the ideal soldiers."

"Unless your TAC bodyguard would be so kind as to hand over the battery, so I can build a super soldier of my own."

"No." I said out loud. I needed her focus to stay on me. I could already see that Axel had a weapon strapped to his lower leg. This battle was going to come down to a draw.

I locked eyes with Axel, matching him blink for blink, '3, 2, 1.'

Axel fired a single shot, hitting Kitsune's hand. Within the half second opening I dropped down for a sweep kick, knocking her on her ass.

"This way." Axel grabbed my arm quickly pulling me in a particular direction. "We're going to have to make a run for it."

I had to assume Dr Toki and the medevac was on its way. We ran in the direction of a hotel. There were people at the desk and even customers waiting to check in, but with a flash of Axel's badge no one stopped us. Running up the stairs, we made it to the roof. By the time we finally paused for breath I was covered in sweat. I shifted my baby in my arms, looking around for the evac. In the distance I could see a small plane, approaching at the speed of a typical news helicopter.

"We're only going to get one chance!" Axel shouted over the roar of the wind. "Do you want me to hold the baby?"

"No," I said with all the confidence I could muster. I put my arms around Axel, holding little Abby between us. I knew he was going to grab for the rope and I needed to hold on for my life. I gripped Axel, burying my face in his shoulder as we took to the sky.

After a few moments we were forcibly pulled inside. Axel landed hard on his back. He held on to me until the sound of the door's closing was completed. "Hellion?" he asked in a whisper.

"I'm here, I'm ok." I moved Abby in my arms to get a view of his face. He was breathing, crying. His little arms flailing with stress and agony.

Looking around I could see Baron was flying the plane while Dr. Toki tended to Tony's badly injured body. From where I landed, I could see there were bandages on his chest, and a wide variety of monitors.

I assumed he had broken ribs, and was under observation for other injuries. So, I came closer. "Tony?"

"Hey," his voice was soft, weak. There were at least three PICC lines in his neck, just above a gory ribbon of exposed flesh. My heart dropped. Tony had no skin on his chest. He was being held together by bandages. "Is he here?"

"The baby?"

Tony nodded; he was visibly weak, his head barely able to move. "Dr. Toki said our baby was safe?"

"Yeah," I made a point to shift the baby in my arms. "He's safe."

Tony reached out his trembling hand. "I'm so sorry."

"You have nothing to be sorry for."

"I allowed you to get kidnapped by that…monster…terrorist." Tony's heartrate started to spike. It was clear, he was emotionally affected by Maverick's traitorous turn. "She cut into you, stole our baby."

"Our baby?"

"I know he's not mine, but I fell in love with the idea of raising a child with you." Tony paused, catching his breath as he blinked tears from his bruised eyes. "Would you have married me?"

"I'll still marry you." Reaching for his hand I could see exposed muscle and bone. "What do you remember?"

"I caught up to your location at around the same time as Baron and Anya. We worked together to take down Maverick, unfortunately giving Faust a chance to escape with the contents of your womb inside a carrying case. That was why I had to ask Axel for help." Tony started to sob uncontrollably.

I held Abby between us, letting our son's little hand caress his bandages. That was when I noticed Tony was burning with fever. His eyes flickered, as he struggled for breath.

"That's enough," Dr. Toki said, as she attached an oxygen mask, along with a tube that went down Tony's throat. He was coughing up blood, but eventually his airway was clear enough for him to breathe comfortably.

I removed Abby from his arms, rocking back and forth as I silently cried.

"Tony is very sick," Dr. Toki explained. "His mind is still strong, but his body is holding on by a thread. As time goes on it will become more difficult for him to function."

"What's going to happen to him?"

"Once we land in Vancouver, I'll begin the process of harvesting his data before his final execution."

Execution? "Why? That doesn't make any sense. He's a human being!"

"His mind is," Dr. Toki explained in her same rational deadpan tone. "And we will be able to harvest that data for further use as well."

"He'll live on a computer?" The idea brought me a small level of comfort. Either that or I watched too many sci-fi movies.

"Tony's intellect will exist on a network system the size of a small apartment."

"Makes sense." I shifted Abby in my arms, resting his head on my shoulder. I really just needed a hug.

"Right now, he's dying. we're doing all we can to keep his brain alive but once his body is too weak to sustain him, there's nothing we can do to salvage Tony's human form.

"How long will it take for his brain to die?"

Dr. Toki turned to me, with a look of compassion. "I can stretch the process out to a week maybe two."

"When he's in the computer. Will he remember me?"

"I don't know. it will be the first time such a transfer was ever attempted."

"So, he might not even make it in to a computer." Ok, that's fine. I went back to my seat, strapping in and hoping to God this was all a bad dream.

When we landed in Vancouver Dr. Toki was already in contact with her team. Tony was taken off the plane on a stretcher, escorted to a plain white sterile room. I was, of course, forced to watch the set up behind a window. Every part of me ached to be by his side. And Dr. Toki gave me her word that I would be able to stay with him for every step.

Tony's broken body was placed in a large plastic coffin (like an infant resting in a neonatal intensive care unit.) The box had holes for medical staff to insert their gloved hands. This was to allow them to attach PIC lines, heart monitors and other devices meant to track just how far gone he was. Suddenly his eyes shot open and heartrate spiked. "Nicki! Nicki, where are you?"

I looked to Dr. Toki with a look of desperation. "Please let me in."

Dr. Toki raised a finger giving the international, 'Just a second' gesture before returning to my side. "You will be allowed in after my team administers a sedative."

"Ok." Not like I had much of a choice. I watched as Tony was given an injection into his PICC line. He was calmed for all of ten seconds, before suffering a horrifying seizure. The medical team did nothing but allow him to finish. Then the automatic door opened and I was invited in.

With my baby in my arms, I ran straight to his side. Tony had been paralyzed and when he blinked his eyes, it was clear he had been stripped of his sight. He blinked his white eyes, as tears streamed down his face. "Nicki, are you there?"

Seeing his hand quiver, I reached inside the glove hole. "It's me, I'm here."

"It's so cold."

I could see why. Dr. Toki's team was treating Tony's body like a high-end computer. The purpose of the plastic coffin was to preserve his cells, to better harvest the data from his organic and inorganic parts.

Tony was clearly in a great deal of pain. His body was not numb, but his body was frozen in place. The first thing to go was his legs. They were part bionic, with electrodes interlaced with his natural muscle tissue.

I stayed by Tony's side, stroking his face. It was the only part of him not inside the plastic coffin (which, after some augmentation, looked more like a high-tech iron lung.)

"You know what really sucks?" Tony said in a weak gasp. "All the next gen gaming consoles I'm never going to see. You know I never even tried VR? I mean, I heard it sucked, but you never know what the future will bring. The future of gaming is going to be fire, and I won't get to see any of it."

I let him ramble, carefully watching his oxygen levels. The lower his oxygen dipped, the more insane he stared to sound. "Dr. Toki said she's going to try to put your mind in a computer."

That caused a laugh. "Yeah, and human to monkey head transplants are also medically possible."

"I think I'd like you better as a computer than a monkey."

"Dr. Toki can do whatever the hell she wants, I'll be long gone."

Tony remained in good spirits for the next few days. I wasn't allowed to stay with him at night, since his body tended to suffer horrific seizures. That was also when the medical team did most of their work, in terms of removing parts.

Baron became my new roommate, sleeping in Tony's old bed. When he wasn't training, or attempting to locate Anya (and by connection, Kitsune) he took joy in watching Abby to allow me time to sleep. But I had yet to see Axel. In fact, no one (on base) had seen him since we landed.

One day, after my usual routine of getting kicked out of Tony's room, I left Abby with Baron and went to search for Axel. There was the possibility he was gone; out on a new mission, with a new team, that would have been logical. That wasn't Axel's heart. He had been around for Tony since the beginning; since the little boy with the terminal illness was brought in for life saving surgery that created a superhero.

"This is what, your sixth night searching for him?" Baron asked with a sigh. He flopped down on Tony's bed, with the baby resting on his chest. "Maybe he just doesn't want to be found."

"Doesn't mean he shouldn't be."

"What makes you think you can find him?

"I can't," I said sweetly, as I laid beside him. "Not alone. And there's one place I haven't checked."

Baron chuckled as he tickled the baby's cheek. "Just one? Your mommy is a liar."

I turned to him with a defeated sigh. "I need your hover boots to check the roofs."

"That's not going to happen."

"You said it yourself, it's like riding a bike."

That was a lie, he had never and would never say that about his most valuable means of transportation. "And just like a bike you can go out of control and smash your head into the pavement."

"Fine, will you take me to search the roofs in a safe, responsible manner?"

"Yes, I will take you to search the roofs, but once we find Axel I'm going to bed."

"You really think we'll find him?"

Baron laughed, as he lifted the baby in his arms. "I'll see you topside in ten."

"Thanks."

True to his word, in ten minutes he was dressed in full armor, with the baby on his shoulder. "Here." Baron affixed the chest facing carrier on me, so the baby would be safely held between us.

Like Superman and Lois Lane, we took to the sky, making sure to stay out of military airspace. It actually didn't take long to find what we were looking for. Axel was sitting on the roof of the farthest building; an old dilapidated office space that was set for demolition. It was a place so far north I had not thought it was part of the base. (I still don't believe it was.)

Baron dropped me off just close enough to see a figure standing at the edge. I walked closer, not wanting to let go of Baron's hand in case we were mistaken.

"Julian?" I said out loud.

Axel turned looking at me with stunned eyes. "What did you call me?"

"Tony once told me that real names are only for friends."

"Because he hated the fact you called Noah by his real name?"

"How did you know that?" I already knew the answer, Tony was like a son to him.

"I know Tony. I was there the day Tony was brought in. I remember his little face; this innocent child looking to someone for help, for hope."

"So, where have you been all this time?"

"I've been here," he said as he took a seat, staring off into the sky. "I've been around. During the daylight hours I walk the city; shop, eat, mostly I'd find a nice comfortable bench and people watch."

"See anything nice?"

"What?" he asked with a chuckle.

"You know, on your walks." I took a seat beside him, resting my head on his shoulder. "Did you see anything nice; a graffiti mural, a garden with a unique flower that reminds you of times long ago, an old couple walking hand-in-hand, or the smile of a precious baby who just saw the sunlight." The words fell from my lips before I realized what I'd said. I cupped my hands over my mouth but it was too late. My mentor and friend was sobbing. "Oh, Julian, I'm so sorry."

He laughed as he wiped his tears with the back of his hand. "Just when I think I've cried every last tear..."

"Sorry." I reached for his hand, giving his fingers a tender squeeze. "Can I stay with you?"

Julian turned, looking down at my son. "No, you need to get someplace safe. If not for your own safety than at least for the safety of your child."

"I need you to be someplace safe, too." I held his hand to my chest, close enough to allow Abby to touch Julian's skin. "What was Tony like as a kid? I mean, he's still a kid, but when he was an actual child."

Julian smiled, looking at Abby's innocent face. "He was a tiny little guy. When I first laid eyes on him, I would have sworn he was no older than two, maybe three years old. Then we had a chance to talk. He spoke like a little bad-ass; knew about life, death, heaven and Hell. He believed in God and if it was God's will for him to become a hero, he would be the greatest superhero of all time."

"Will you come see him, with me?"

"Yes, I think I'm ready."

Julian and I walked along the main road, it would have taken well over an hour but thankfully a base security patrol car saw us and was more than happy to escort the high-ranking leader (and his little teenage sidekick). This allowed us to get back to the lab in less than ten minutes.

Standing outside the door of the main building, I checked the time it was 2:36 in the morning. "do you have a security clearance for Dr. Toki's lab?"

"I have a no-king clearance."

"No King?"

Julian proceeded to knock on the door.

"Funny," I muttered as a female in a lab coat came to the door.

"Oh, hello, we're currently running a data extraction on the subject." She seemed young, sweet, so the next part seemed a little awkward. "It might just be a little, um… uncomfortable. For lack of a better word." She opened the door just enough to allow us to see the current state of Tony's body.

The plastic coffin was wide open, with cords and wires drawing from his chest, and arms. I held Abby close, turning his face towards my chest. I knew as a baby he couldn't see very well, but I still wanted to shield him from what lay before me.

"Please put on some personal protective equipment before entering."

I turned to see a male Labtech holding out disposable scrubs and a head covering. "Thanks, sorry." I took the gown, putting it on loosely over my chest carrier keeping it loose enough for my baby to breathe. dressed appropriately, I took a seat next to Tony at my usual spot. "Hey, Tony."

Tony turned to me and smiled. He was looking over my shoulder where Julian stood. "Axel, is that you?"

"Call me Julian."

Tony laughed. "I can't even remember the last time I used your civilian name. Or the last time you called me anything other than Tony."

I forced a smile, as I knew that was not true. Was his mind already gone? "You have to admit, Agent Deadlock is kind of a mouthful."

"That's a stupid name," Tony said with a giggle. His eyes rolled back in his head. "I don't know why you ever let me pick that, Julian." Tony started to laugh uncontrollably. "Julian is the name of the dancing lemur in that movie… what was it…Madagascar!"

I turned to look at Julian. He pursed his lips and nodded. He placed his gloved hand to Tony's shoulder. There was a moment of silence as if he couldn't think of the right words to say. Not that I could blame him. Was this goodbye? There was no way to know for sure. All we could do was be grateful for the time we had with Tony.

When Julian finally spoke, his voice was breaking with emotion, "I should go." He gave Tony's shoulder a comforting squeeze before turning to leave.

I immediately stood up. "Axel, wait!"

Julian turned around. "I've said my peace."

"Lt. Col!" I wasn't even sure if that was his correct rank, it just sounded more official than calling him by a code name.

"What!" The way he glared caused me to slink down in my seat, like a guilty child.

"If you leave, I'm probably going to get kicked out," I muttered under my breath.

"Perhaps that is for the best. We should leave these professionals to their assignment. Tony will still be there in the morning."

"Yeah, ok," I replied nervously.

Tony suddenly reached for my hand, grabbing my wrist with more strength than I thought possible. "Now I lay me down to sleep, I pray the lord my soul to keep." His grip moved down to my hand, slipping me a cold metal object the size of a coin. "If I die before I wake, I pray the lord my soul to take."

Somehow, I knew it was not a coin. I bent forward to kiss his cheek, discreetly hiding the object in my chest carrier. I placed the mystery item in Abby's tiny hands. Hopefully, he wouldn't end up swallowing it.

CHAPTER

15

"Well, I'm now a hundred percent certain he swallowed it," Baron said. We had been searching for Tony's mystery coin for well over an hour before I allowed him to use his custom hand-held metal detector on my infant son.

"Can you see what it is?" I asked, holding my baby's tiny hand as he laid on the changing table. Abby seemed calm, even happy, making me seem like an overanxious parent. "Do we need to get him to a doctor or will it pass through his poop?"

Baron didn't answer. his focus was on the baby's limbs. He appeared to be following something. "This is strange."

"What is?"

"The metallic material is dispersing into his bloodstream, focusing on the muscle tissue of his arms legs and head."

Could you sound any more terrifying? "Is it hurting him?"

"No, he seems ok, but the way it's dispersing is odd. Do you have access to a scanner with a visual output?"

"Not without Dr. Toki's help," I replied nervously.

"I'm sure she's already well aware of your nighttime visit. And Axel will probably have your back.

Abby wiggled his arms giggling with glee.

"I was planning on going down to see Tony, anyway. I'll just take him with me.

I got dressed and made my way to Dr. Toki's lab. Walking downstairs I knew the door would be locked and I would need to ask the guard to be let in. Yet something felt off. Looking through the textured glass window of the guard office I could see the entire facility was dark.

"What the-? Dr. Toki? Hello?" I knocked on the door while smushing my chest against the window, desperate to see anything.

Abby was squirming.

"Oh, I'm sorry, sweetie" I took a moment to remove Abby from his carrier, bouncing him in my arms.

He was looking me in the eyes. I never took a parenting class, but I knew that at his age he was not supposed to be able to lift his head. "Mama!"

I did an involuntary jolt, nearly tripping over my own feet. "Did you just talk?" I had no idea of Abby's actual birthdate but I knew for a fact he was too young to be speaking. "This is insane. I'm hallucinating."

As I took a step forward to regain my balance, a light came on somewhere deep in the room. "Hello?"

Within seconds, the door unlocked and Dr. Toki appeared. "Hello Nicki."

Before I could respond Abby lifted his arms, "Toki!" he was facing my chest, unable to turn his head completely around. "Toki?"

My focus was on my child, so When I finally looked up at Dr. Toki her face had been frozen in a look of shock (and perhaps terror) for a good five seconds. "Dr. Toki?"

"Tony gave it to you," she said in a whisper.

"Gave me what?" Other than feeling the shape of the item in my palm I had no idea what the item even looked like. "The coin shaped thing?"

Dr. Toki took a deep, calming breath. "come inside." She held the door open, allowing just enough light in.

The room was empty. "Where's Tony?

"Come in, take a seat at the table."

"You mean the coffin?"

"It was never a coffin." Dr. Toki took a seat on the opposite side, flipping a few switches. "Regardless you are correct; Tony passed away last night, a few hours after your visit."

"Oh." I felt a sharp pain in my chest like a blowtorch drilling in to my organs. I removed Abby, instinctively placing him on the floor before doubling over in pain. I felt like I needed to vomit. "Why?"

"Tony was becoming too physically weak, or at least that's what I have to assume. Like I told you before, I could have kept his physical body on life support for as long as it took to digitize his mental, emotional and genetic data. However, he seemed to have beaten me to it." She turned to her laptop, pulling up a single image. Tony was inside the coffin, pinching the skin of his hands.

"What's he doing?"

"Somehow Tony created a sample of his genetic enhancements and kept it hidden on his person until he was given the opportunity to pass it along to you. And you fed it to your baby."

I noticed she was looking down at the spot where I placed Abby. "That was an accident."

"No, it was fate."

I felt two little hands touching my leg. My son was standing on two strong, steady legs. "Mama!"

"If you leave him with me, I will be able to evaluate the extent of his changes."

"Ok," I squeaked. "Abby, do you want to spend some time with Dr. Toki?"

My small baby turned to Dr. Toki. "To-ki!" Abby lifted his arms in her direction for a hug.

I felt more than a little hurt. "I guess that's that."

"Not quite; you and Baron need to return to Beloit, Wisconsin. I have reason to believe that's where Faust will strike next."

'Because he's looking to start a war.' I went back to Baron and the three of us (four if you count Abby) held a strategy meeting. Baron agreed to fly us back to Beloit where we would reunite with the gang that we stayed with prior.

When we were on the plane, seated and comfortable, I got up the courage to ask the question that was burning in my mind. "Do you know a girl named Diamond?"

Baron laughed so hard he spit out a mouthful of coffee all over the steering wheel. "Oh, you mean Lucy. Yeah, she's a flirty little shit. You actually met her?" Baron wiped the panel with his sleeve, still amused at what was clearly an inside joke. "What did she tell you?"

"She told me your real name is Leo."

"Oh, that's it?" he pursed his lips. "Did she know you were pregnant with Noah's kid?"

"Yes…." I suddenly recalled what Diamon/Lucy said about Noah; he was sexy, fine, and I must have been a side chick. "Is Noah the father of her kid?

"Oh, fuck no!" Baron's laughter started all over again. "I wonder if Noah ever thought about her…"

"They were together?"

"Not sexually," Baron said as he cleared his throat. With a few calming breaths he managed to regain his composure. "Here's the deal. Once upon a time there was a 15-year-old girl. This girl came from a long line of gang members; drug runners, smugglers, dealers and killers, but she had a secret talent; she was one hell of a hacker. It started as a way to download free games and movies for herself and her friends, but by high school she was like a mad scientist and the internet was her unwilling victim.

Noah took her under his wing, but let's just say she wanted to be someplace entirely different."

"But Noah didn't sleep with her?"

"Hell no," Baron paused, tilting his head. "Well, I think he let her give him a blowjob, after a night of doing meth."

"A blowjob while on meth?"

"That's hackers for you. As a weapons expert I prefer coke." He pushed a few buttons, pulling up a digital map. "Anyway, little Lucy made it known that's she wanted Noah's beautiful blonde babies. That was when we headed out, taking a job in Venezuela. By the time we got back she was knocked up by whatever high ranking leader took her virginity."

"She had a baby out of spite?" I could see why that was so unbelievably funny.

"I think it was a powerplay." With the flight details set, he kicked up his legs. "Why are you thinking about Lucy?"

I told him about the woman in my dreams, the female soldier who appeared to be Lucy's granddaughter. "She had a tattoo, Lucy's dark skin and curly hair, and she had your..."

"My what?"

"She was wearing a variation of your hover boots."

"There's something you should know about Lucy. She co-authored the contents of the battery."

"Is it possible she brought the idea to life?"

"Maybe, I mean anything's possible but the idea that she had a granddaughter who perfected the system. That actually seems like something that could happen."

"So, if the future granddaughter perfected the technology, it would be registered under her name?"

Baron shrugged. "I guess. If this future individual is affiliated with the military..."

"Faust could go back in time to target Lucy directly." That made perfect sense. If Lucy was as brilliant as Baron claimed, she would make an ideal hostage. And a perfect replacement for Feng.

Baron's hands froze, his face went pale. "I need to make a call." He checked a few more controls. "the system is on autopilot for the next hour. I should be back before then."

"Sure, sounds good." I crossed my arms over my chest. Every part of my body felt unbearably cold.

I'm not sure how long Baron had been gone for, but according to the map we were nearly in Wisconsin by the time I opened my eyes. He took out his phone (an onboard device that was meant to be used while in the air) and connected it directly into a port.

"It's what I was afraid of," he explained. "You can see for yourself."

Baron brought up a series of security camera footage. From what I could tell, Faust had teleported in with just a large knife. He then proceeded to cut down various gun turrets, and slice down guard after guard on his way to the kitchen area.

"Oh, God, no." I could already see his plan; Faust was going to target the children and the elderly; he needed a hostage to force Lucy to come with him willingly. And that's exactly what happened. He somehow knew exactly which child was her son. He held the blade to Denny's neck, even making a show of slicing the little boy's shirt. Lucy dropped her weapon and approached Faust. A swap was made; Faust threw the boy to the ground, and grabbed Lucy, teleporting away to God knows where. This was bad.

We landed in Beloit, parking in the secret underground lot. Baron exited the aircraft, shaking hands with someone named Jesus. The tall muscular Hispanic man was accompanied by two bodyguards, but my eyes went straight to the small figure gripping his shoulder. "Denny?"

The boy's eyes lit up. "Ms. Ironman!"

I covered my mouth, trying not to cry. "Yeah, it's me."

The tall man put Denny on the floor, letting him run to my arms. "I missed you!" he turned to the man. "Grandpa this is Ms. Ironman, she's a superhero!"

I reached out my hand. "I'm Nicki, or Hellion."

The man smiled kindly as he shook my hand. "Yes, Leo told us all about you. I trust you're as good as he says you are."

With Denny in my arms, I felt confident and strong. "Thank you, sir, I won't let you down."

Jesus nodded, taking a step back. "So, what's the plan? What are you going to do to get my daughter back?"

Baron answered for both of us. "Whatever it takes."

We got in an SUV. Baron rode up front, speaking in Spanish to the gang leaders, while I rode in the back. With plenty of room to stretch out, I went to sleep with Denny in my arms (like a teddy bear.)

In my dreams I awoke on the roof of Walmart, overlooking the night sky. "You really think Faust is still in the area? How dumb are you?"

I turned to see Sundra wearing her full armor and she looked angry. "Look, I didn't mean for this to happen."

"Yeah, you don't mean for a lot of things to happen."

"What does that mean?"

"What do you think it means?" Sundra stood up, walking around while muttering in Spanish.

I did not feel like being bullied by a teenager from the future. "Speak English or shut the hell up!"

"Did you just tell me to speak English?" she asked with a look of violent hatred in her eyes.

"I'm sorry, ok!" I held up my hands in surrender. "I'm not a brave bad-ass like your grandmother or even your father. I'm not brilliant like Noah," or any of the people who'd taken me under their wing."

Sundra snickered, "Are you trying to talk your way out of getting punched in the face?"

"I just need a hint to solve this bullshit."

"Such as?"

"What did you invent with the technology created by Lucy and Noah?"

Sundra paused, biting her lip as she smiled. "Wake up and find out."

I awoke with a jolt. Baron and his friends had arrived back at the compound and apparently, I had been left to sleep. I sat up, looking out the window. People were hard at work repairing the buildings and cars.

Suddenly a face splatted against my window. "Hi!"

I held my breath to avoid screaming. "Sundra?"

"Yup, it's me." Her image flickered like television static (or a buffering internet connection.)

"Are you real?"

"I'm more than real, I'm everywhere." She flickered again, reappearing inside the vehicle by my side.

I touched her arm; she was a solid, physical form. *"It was you."* My eyes lit up with a realization. *"You were the one fighting Faust in the sky over New Jersey! Are you traveling on the same frequency as his teleportation?"*

"See, you're smarter than you give yourself credit for." Sundra patted my back with her armored hand.

"So, um, I am the only one who can see you?"

"Honestly, I don't know for certain. As far as my missions are concerned, I locate my target and attach myself to their signal."

"Signal?"

"Electromagnetic pulse; every living creature emits one, some cultures refer to it as a soul. The difficult part is latching on to the correct timestream, especially with people like Faust moving shit around all the time."

"Is he from your future, or your timeline?" I gripped my head in pain. I was too dumb for this level of science.

"I believe so, but according to recorded sightings, he's well over a thousand years old. He's using a version of the time travel technology that's been perfected in a way I can't even comprehend."

"Do you think he's working with Kitsune and the Yakuza?"

"He's either working with or for her organization," Sundra explained with a tired sigh. *"In the future there's a massive war brought about by the Euro-Asian Alliance of Power; Russia, china, Japan, North Korea, working together to create a new superpower similar to the USSR. Where I come from, it's believed that Faust is a Russian operative, with a primary mission of setting a specific timeline into reality. Then you came along and..."*

Tap, tap, tap. We turned to see Denny looking in at us with his big innocent eyes. "Ms. Ironman, who is that lady?"

Sundra's mouth hung open as she stared in shocked silence.

"You can see her?" I asked Denny through the closed window.

The little boy nodded. "She's pretty, like the sunshine."

I turned to see Sundra's reaction. There were tears in her eyes. Before she could speak, an elderly woman swooped up Denny.

"There you are, you naughty little boy." The woman started to carry Denny back in the direction of the kitchen.

Denny started to squirm and cry, "I wanted to see the sunshine lady!"

"You and your imaginary friends." She shook her head before opening the door. "Ms. Hellion, the rest of the team is waiting for you in the basement bunker."

"The massive computer room; yeah, that makes sense. I'll be right there."

My confidence seemed to be enough to convince the woman to leave. When Denny was out of sight, I returned my focus to Sundra. "You coming with?"

She nodded. "Yeah, I'm good. That was just a little intense, even for me."

I walked in front of her, leading the way to the home of the supercomputer. Walking down the stairs I could hear Sundra's footsteps (further proof she was real.) Baron was leading the meeting, going over a map of Faust's recent movement. He then pulled up a second set of coordinates overlaying the two maps.

"...and that's why I think Kitsune is arranging a meetup."

"A meetup?" I asked.

"Yes, that's why there is a possibility Faust is still in the immediate area, awaiting further instructions or perhaps even monetary compensation."

"You think he's looking to sell Lucy?" The idea made sense; Faust could not teleport through the timeline with Lucy, he would need a way to hand her off to Kitsune before making his escape.

"It's just a matter of where they could meet up, for a trade off or even a demonstration."

Sundra tapped my arm. "Check out Lake Michigan, near Kenosha.

"Is that in island?" I asked out loud. Baron and the other men looked at where I was pointing. "There's a structure in the middle of the lake, but it doesn't seem like a boat or any kind of small watercraft." That, and the signal was too strong.

Baron agreed, that was where we needed to go. We headed back to the plane, with the group leaving in the opposite hidden tunnel (so, no one had to pass by where Sundra stood.) I moved to follow, keeping a close distance as to not be left behind.

Jesus briefly turned to me. He paused, before blinking his eyes and shaking his head.

"Everything okay?" Could he see Sundra? Did he assume it was a hallucination, brought on by his concern for Lucy?

"Yeah, fine," the older man patted my shoulder. "We must hurry."

"How do we know this isn't a trap?" asked one of the other men. It was a good question.

Baron turned as we reached the plane. "It doesn't matter; if we're flying into a trap, we'll fight our way out or die trying. Either way Faust must not be allowed to leave the country with Lucy."

His confidence gave me strength, as did the fact that my baby son was safely back with Dr. Toki. I would be willing to die, to assure my son's happy future with Sundra.

As we approached Lake Michigan, I looked out the window desperate to locate any kind of man-made structure. Among the sea of boats and watercrafts, there was a barge ship, the kind that carried cargo across oceans.

"Is it just me or is that not supposed to be there?" I asked, moving closer to Baron, to get a better look at the guidance system. The barge was radiating energy, like a giant yellow chunk of cheese just waiting for a mouse to take the bait.

"Looks like a siren with her tits hanging out," said Lucy's father.

"Well, we're going to play it like a Tom and Jerry cartoon," Baron explained. "First, I'm going to drop the bait, then with all of their focus on her…"

My ears perked up. "Did you say her? As the only female on this plane, I'm assuming you mean me?"

"Yes, you. If this was a wedding Faust would've addressed the invite to 'Hellion, plus one.'" I knew he was correct. Faust would focus on me and (hopefully) while we were talking things out, the rest of the team could rescue Lucy. "Get ready to jump in thirty," Baron added. "You won't need a parachute, just pencil dive. And don't forget to grab a weapon first."

"Ok," I said nervously. I selected a knife from the weapon cabinet (assuming water would damage a firearm.) I prepared to make my exit, with my blade secured at my waist.

"Door opening in 3, 2, 1," his voice drifted away as I found myself falling.

I pulled my arms and legs into a pencil dive position, narrowly avoiding the roof of the barge. Two hands grabbed me, directing my body for a perfect two-foot landing. "Sundra?"

"You think I'd let you wiggle on the hook by yourself?"

"Can Faust see you?" I asked. "I know he did earlier, when you were targeting him."

"Let's just assume he can and will see me."

We stuck together as we walked around to the front of the barge. If this was a normal watercraft this would be where the driver would be. There was no driver, no steering wheel, just an open trap door with a metal ladder. "Kind of on the nose," I muttered.

Sundra jumped down before I could. At the bottom of the hole was a long hallway. There was no source of light but somehow, I could see the walls clearly. I guess that could be credited to night vision? Still, after a few minutes of walking in a straight line, I was beginning to feel claustrophobic. I pulled out my knife, hopeful that I could carve my way out of the enclosed space. 'Tap, tap, tap… swish?' The wall was not completely solid.

Sundra turned and gasped. "We were never meant to go in a straight line." She kicked the wall in a few different places until she found a large enough space to jump. Once again, she vanished into the shadows before I could even respond.

I had no choice but to follow, sliding down a short drop before narrowly avoiding an electric fence.

"Stop!" shouted a familiar voice.

Pulling myself to my feet, I found myself face to face with Lucy. She was bound to a chair, with her wrists secured to a keyboard. And on top of all that she wore a necklace of explosives like something out of a horror movie.

"Of course, they sent you," Lucy muttered. "I'm going to die here."

The walls shook, as the sound of villainous laughter echoed through the room. "Yes, you are, but at least you'll have company."

Lucy blinked tears from her eyes. "Let's get this bullshit over with!"

In the middle of the room was a large dark pool. "Is that Lake Michigan?" No, of course it wasn't. The area was much too smooth, like a liquid crystal display. This was the monitor connected to Lucy's keyboard.

"Ladies and Gentlemen, boys and girls!" Faust's voice seemed to be coming from a distinct direction. "For your viewing pleasure, I present: the portal to Hell!"

In the corner of the room, I could see what appeared to be a viewing booth. Was Kitsune here? I turned to Lucy just in time to see her mouth the words, 'I'm sorry.'

With a few clicks, Lucy seemed to be powering on the hole. The display flickered between images; the beaches of California, the mountains of France, the glaciers of Argentina, coming to rest at a war-torn South American city which I couldn't identify.

Suddenly a figure appeared; a male body crucified in the middle of a demolished church. As the image came in to focus, I could see it was my son Abaddon in his middle-age battle weary state.

Sundra screamed, making her presence known.

Faust's laughter played again. "Sundra, so glad you could join us. As you can tell I'm watching these events from a safe distance." He was in an alternate dimension. "In my world I'm a king, sitting on a throne of blood and bone. With a raise of my hand, I can and will eradicate my enemies, unless one of you ladies thinks you can stop me. Go to him, you know you want to."

Who was he talking to? I glanced at Sundra. "What happens if one of us enters the pool?"

"That's not a pool!" Sundra shouted in anger. "It's a rip in the fabric of time itself!"

That answered my question. I placed my hand on Sundra's arm. "Do me a favor, save Lucy." I took a running leap, diving into the rift before I could change my mind.

My world went black.

"What are you doing!" my adult son shouted.

"You're safe with Dr. Toki. You're going to survive!" That was my logic; it didn't matter what happened to me, because I didn't play a role in this future war.

"Open your eyes! You're now trapped in this reality."

'*Oh, right.*' This could be a problem.

CHAPTER

eing homeless was never fun. I don't know why I even thought it was. I guess I could chalk it up to first world problems. Walking the streets of a place called, 'Independent nation of New Cebu,' I experienced a level of sadness and fear, I'd never thought possible. Or perhaps that was just because I was trying to save the life of my only child, a full-grown man who had already lived through decades of war. I was weak, pathetic and unworthy.

I'd been able to un-crucify my adult son using just my knife (and some level of mom power super strength.) Abaddon was badly injured, unable to walk on his own feet. Sitting on the floor of the cathedral he was waiting for me to return with help.

Luckily help found me. Apparently, Cebu was an island in the Philippines and they were friendly to American and European forces. I learned this because Abby spoke decent Tagalog and the locals spoke near fluent English. With the aid of the local militia, my son and I were taken to a public shelter.

The locals gave us a care package of bandages, blankets, food and water. Thankfully, we found a space to rest for the night. The dirt floor was soft and comfortably warm. After making himself comfortable and attending to his own wounds, Abaddon rested on his back, and closed his eyes.

I didn't say anything; he deserved to sleep, and I needed to act like a big girl. Looking around, I could see several sickly children, in fact the majority of the occupants were small children. A little girl came up to me offering a small doll made of straw.

"Is this an orphanage?" I asked out loud.

"Probably," Abaddon replied. Apparently, he was not asleep. He positioned his arms behind his head, like a vacationer on a beach. With wrinkles and scars on his face he reminded me of my father (more so than my offspring.)

"We are so screwed," I muttered with a nervous laugh.

Abby opened his blue eyes for a moment, just enough to glare at me like a child. "Because this is an orphanage in a third world country?"

"Sorry," I said, swallowing a lump in my throat. The last thing I wanted was to come off as a stuck-up, spoiled American girl. "I'm a little out of my element."

With his eyes still closed, he chuckled to himself. "That's not something my mother would ever say."

"I wish I knew her," I said with a shrug. "She was probably amazing. Let me guess, she died doing something heroic, right, like stopping a nuclear weapon by punching it to death."

Abby turned to me, eyes closed, as a single tear dripped down his cheek. "My mother died of cancer. she was a hero, my hero, just not the type that go down in history."

I nodded. I desperately wanted to change the subject. "So, where are we? Whose territory is this?"

Abby sat up, putting weight on his injured hands. "What did you say?"

"Who controls this area? Cleary, by the presence of local soldiers, this is an active warzone. Therefore, someone important to the axis has to be stationed here. We just need to attack them at their home base."

Abby chuckled. "Knock on the door to the hive, to get a meeting with the queen. Not a bad idea."

After a few days of rest and recovery, we learned the country was occupied by Axis forces under the command of General Rin Ito, a small female with the face of a beauty queen. Her publicist made it known she was the descendent of Yakuza leaders. She had posters and advertisements all over the city, proclaiming herself to be the next savior of the land (like the musical Evita or a Disney princess movie.) After talking to various business owners who posted her image, Rin's goal was to drive the city into a state of lock down, to force a 'democratic election' to establish herself as the 'voice of the people.'

This meant she was not shy about public appearances. There had been more than a few assassination attempts, but all failed due to lack of teamwork. It would take more than a single sniper or suicide bomber to get past Rin's security detail.

Under the leadership of Abby (as the experienced American military officer) we established a multilayer plan with the local forces. During the weeks that it took for our plan to come into fruition, I got to know my adult son's tragic past. In this reality I lived long enough to see him graduate from West Point Military Academy at age nineteen (he skipped a few years of school.) He was a tech specialist who later transitioned to special forces, under the guidance of the man who raised him as his father: Julian 'Axel' Diaz. I didn't know what to make of that.

In the days leading up to the attack, a plan was put in to place. Group A would take on the military guards, Group B would attack the crowd causing further disruption and chaos (and ideally, minimal casualties.) Group C would back up Abby, keeping Rin from escaping while he took a shot with his custom sniper rifle. It was the perfect plan; Rin would be eliminated, allowing for the local groups to all take credit for liberating their city. And then Abby got sick.

The injuries to his hands and feet had become infected. He had tried to hide the painful, swollen lesions under layers of dirty bandages. By the night before the mission his hands were noticeably weak.

We had been staying in a small room with a bare mattress and a makeshift hotplate. Our allies supplied us with rice, and dried meat. Abby added some of our filtered water to make a soup, while I warmed my hands against the candle flame. "Did Julian ever cook with you?" I asked. I had never seen Axel cook but I had to assume he possessed survival skills.

"You were the one who taught me how to cook." Abby served the night's meal in our two bowls. His was made from wood while mine was an upcycled metal can.

"I mean, Julian raised you. I just assumed he taught you some of his super soldier skills."

Abby looked at me with a raised eyebrow, as if questioning the legitimacy of my inquiry. "I was raised by you." With trembling hands, he paused to take a sip of the warm liquid. "In this timeline."

"Have you met yourself in other timelines?"

"I haven't really tried, or rather I've never been given the opportunity via any assignments. I have a feeling, the only reason I was able to make contact with you is because you're already dead in this timeline." Abby took one last sip before putting the bowl down and resting on the bed. He motioned for me to sit by his side.

That was the first time I rested my head on his chest. (Prior to that, it felt a little awkward, so we instead slept side by side like siblings.

Abby had lost so much weight I could feel his ribcage; I could hear his breath, and heartbeat. "Did you miss her?"

"When you died, it left a hole in my heart. I filled my days working to be the best soldier I could; someone who'd make you proud." He reached for his soup, attempting to lift his arm, but the pain proved too great for him to take a sip. "I can still remember the day we scattered your ashes on the beach. When the sun hit, I could feel you smiling down on me."

"The beach? In New Jersey?" I couldn't wrap my mind around taking my son to a place where I'd experienced so much pain.

"No, there was a location further south, I think it was somewhere in North Carolina. It was a private beach that we went to every summer, and sometimes over Christmas. We would go camping, hiking."

"Hiking?" I could picture myself going on walks with my baby on my chest. Perhaps, as he grew, we could go on adventures; collecting rocks, climbing trees, like I used to as a kid. Just the idea of having little Abby by my side, as my sidekick and best friend filled me with a sense of joy.

"You introduced me to the beauty of the world." Abby lifted his arm, exposing his badly injured hand. He motioned to a scar on his palm, just below his thumb.

"It kind of looks like a shooting star."

"That's what you told me back then, too," he said with a laugh. "This was from the first time you taught me how to swim. I was five years old, got pulled out by a wave. You always let me play in the water, collecting shells, those creepy little crabs." The exhausted soldier smiled wide as he chuckled at the nostalgia. "I was pretty fearless as a kid; I could walk into water up to my neck. The first time I saw an actual fish, was the first time you realized I didn't actually know how to swim."

I buried my head on his shoulder, as I laughed harder than I ever thought possible. "I'm so sorry."

"That wasn't the worst part. When you pulled me out, I was fighting to keep hold of my little fish friend: a piece of driftwood that was cutting my hand."

"Seriously?" I could visualize the moment; me cradling my sweet little boy as he cried over a fake fish and blood covered hand.

"You bandaged my hand, and gave it a kiss. I took a nap with the wooden fish in my arms, but when I woke up, I just cried and cried, because I thought I'd never get to see a real fish." Abby laughed through a pain-stricken cough. "You went out and found a bunch of empty water bottles and made flotation devices."

"Like a life jacket?" I had seen such a thing on the internet but never had the chance to try it in real life.

"You started with a lifejacket; I remember you wanted to be able to keep my cut out of the bacteria-infested ocean, but then it moved on to making kickboards and other water toys."

I reached out to hold his hand. As my fingers caressed his, I could feel a noticeable, tingly energy. When I closed my eyes, I could see glimpses of the mysterious beach. It was someplace I had never been before. In the distance, I could hear my son's laugh. "Was I a good mom?"

"You were a great mom." Abby paused blinking tears from his eyes. For a moment we just stayed in the position, looking at our united hands. "Promise me something?'

"Of course." I was fighting back tears. He was my son, my child.

"If you have the chance to go back, I want you to take it. I don't even know if it's likely, but if it's possible I want you to have a chance at a life."

"Even if I never see you again?"

Abby turned to me. Looking directly into his eyes, I could see a lifetime of pain. He knew how sick he was. "You'll see me again, I promise."

"Ok." I could only assume he meant in heaven or the afterlife. I held him close, I could feel his body trembling; he was in pain, but at least he was alive. I fell asleep in his arms, but awoke alone. Terrified, I sat up, immediately fearful of having been left behind.

"I'm still here." Abby was already awake, attempting to get dressed in the body armor we had salvaged.

Immediately, my eye was drawn to the massive bruises (and even open wounds on his back.) "Abby?" I couldn't hide the terror in my voice.

He flexed his shoulders, as he put on a shirt and then his bulletproof vest. "I've worked through worse pain."

I knew what that meant; Abby no longer cared if he lived or died. "You can't go on this mission; I won't let you." I knew I was crying but Abby didn't turn around.

"What's the alternative?" he asked as he packed up his weapon kit. "The locals won't follow you into battle."

He was right, I didn't look the part. "Well, I'm not leaving your side. If something goes wrong, I can take the shot."

I expected him to laugh in my face. His sniper rifle was his baby. After getting captured by Faust, his original kit had been all but destroyed. Abby had been able to recover bits and pieces of his beloved weapon and combine them with parts supplied by our new allies.

"I can live with that," he said with some level of confidence.

He would have to.

The mission went ahead with all the teams falling in to position while Abby and I took our place on a nearby rooftop. I watched through binoculars as he lined up the shot, took the shot, and missed. Well, to be fair he didn't miss; he shot her in the shoulder, inadvertently giving away our location.

Abby let out a string of silent curse words as he reloaded. "Prepare for an ambush." He realigned his sights, so I had to assume he had a view of Rin. I readied my knife and rushed at the troops that were already at the door of the office building.

I knew there were people in the office, innocent souls who were about to become collateral damage. Best I could do was try to make sure the bad guys didn't make it to the top floor. I fought a few soldiers, disarming them with well-placed cuts to their hands and arms. Someone reached for a dropped handgun, so I reached for it at the same time. That was how I came face to face with Rin. She was a small woman, no taller than myself. The way our eyes locked, she knew who I was, or at least what I was. She shouted something in her native language before diving for the gun, firing in my direction. Thankfully her arm was too injured to aim. A bullet flew by my head, close enough to singe my hair.

With a hop and a spin, I kicked her in the face. A normal foot would have left a bruise, but my prosthetic left her with a bloody broken nose. Rin charged at me, slamming against a wall. This got the attention of several of her bodyguards. In a few seconds the fight was going to be ten vs one with me most likely getting shot to death or arrested and put in a military prison where I would be begging for death. So, in a moment of panic I grabbed Rin in a bear hug and dive-bombed the nearby window. I didn't feel the breaking glass, the bullets, or even the live powerline.

I felt a calming numbness, followed by a light. Was I dead? Assuming death worked like it did in the movies I attempted to stand up, preparing to walk in the direction of the light. That was when the pain kicked in. I felt like my body was on fire. I coughed once, then couldn't stop despite the fact that my throat was filling with blood.

"Nicki!" shouted a male voice from the light. "Are you down there?"

Down there? "Yes, it's me. Where are you?" The light was taking on a distinct shape: it was a rip in the fabric of time.

A man appeared with blue armor and gold streaks in his otherwise dark hair. It was Baron. "Nicki! Damn girl, I've been looking all over for you!" He held out his hand. "Come on, hurry!"

I grabbed his hand. if nothing else it represented something familiar. For a moment I felt guilty, sick to my stomach. I wanted to take my son with me. Abby didn't deserve to die here. I looked towards the rooftop, just in time to see the building start to collapse. I couldn't see where Abby was. All around me I heard screams, crashes. The layer of smoke, blood and gore framed the clean glowing space where Baron was.

I placed my second hand on Baron's arm, and he (logically) took this as his cue to pull me up. When I was safely in Baron's embrace, I took one last look at the war-torn fiery vision of Hell. Abby was gone (in that one reality, anyway.) I needed to focus on my baby son, who still had a chance.

We flew upward, out of the rift, landing on cold, wet grass. The sensation of the rift closing felt like a gust of wind laced with flickers of electricity.

Baron stood up, stretching his back as he got to his feet. "I guess I can cross that off my bucket list."

I sat up, looking around the park seemed to be normal, modern. "Where are we?"

"Minnesota, I think." He looked down at his wristwatch. "Home base, come in. Axel do you read me?"

"In route," the watch replied.

"How did you find me?" I asked. I was still in too much pain to stand up. "Is Lucy ok?"

"Let's just get you some medical attention first."

That was not the answer I wanted. "What happened to Lucy?"

Baron sighed. "Kitsune has her."

"Oh." I nodded. "So, we failed."

"For now," Baron said, taking a seat beside me. "Much like Feng, Lucy is worth more alive than dead. We just need to head back to Siberia, attack Kitsune at her home base."

"You're right," I said with a sigh. "I'm just ready to go home."

"Home?"

"Are we going straight to Siberia?" I asked, gripping my shoulder in pain. My entire body felt numb. "I don't think I'd be good for much." That, and I wanted to see my baby.

"You've been missing for three weeks," Baron explained. "Searching for you has been my private project, while Axel has been using his TAC network to track Kitsune and her brother."

"Ok," I said with a nod. "I understand." I blinked tears from my eyes. "You need me as backup. I mean, you did save my life, I owe you that much."

In less than a minute the medevac plane arrived. Axel greeted me with a hand shake as he helped Baron put me onto a stretcher. "Get her on an IV," Axel said casually.

"Julian?" I whispered softly, reaching for his hand. "Where's my baby?"

"We need to get going," Axel replied firmly. He would be getting the last word. "We can talk later."

I felt Baron poke my arm to start a saline line, but within seconds I was passed out. I didn't dream; instead, it felt like a blink of an eye, before I awoke in Dr. Toki's lab. My wounds were bandaged; hands, back, shoulders. The skin felt tense, but not unbearable. I took a breath, taking in the cold, sterile air. My heart ached for Abby, I could still feel his warmth, his skin, his breath. Did I really leave my son to die in a warzone? I should have been the one to die, that's what a decent mother would have done. My heart raced as I started to uncontrollably sob. Did he suffer? Was he all alone? I closed my eyes, struggling for air.

That was when I felt a small hand on my chest. "Hi," squeaked a familiar voice. My baby had crawled on to my chest. His bright blue eyes staring into my soul. "Hi, Mama."

"Hello, Abby."

He rested his chubby baby cheek, pressing his soft skin against my bloody bandages. It took me a second to realize what he was doing but once I did, I could not stop laughing. "Are you breastfeeding?" He was. The fit of laughter gave me the energy to sit up (or at least raise the angle of the bed.)

That was when I spotted Baron. My guardian angel was slouched in a metal office chair Asleep wearing his armor. He moved his hands over his arms, freaking out for a moment before fully opening his eyes. "Really?"

Little Abby took a moment to look in his direction, giggling sweetly.

"I swear to God."

"Not in front of my little angel, you don't."

That got a laugh. Baron sighed as he ran his fingers through his hair.

"When I fell asleep holding the baby, he was acting like a normal three-month-old. That thing is like the reincarnation of Agent Deadlock."

"You mean Tony."

"Yeah, Tony." Baron reached for the baby, lifting him from my arms.

Abby scowled. "Ma-ma." He started to fidget and squirm, fighting his way out of Baron's grasp.

I screamed as Abby fell to the ground. I instinctively jerked to the side, to see if he was still alive, causing the wounds on my back to rip open. I bit my lip so hard I drew blood. That was when I saw Abby standing up all on his own.

"Mama!" he slapped his hands joyfully.

I was about to reach for him when he started to climb. "What the?" I knew the grip of a baby was abnormally strong (ask anyone who's ever gotten an earring ripped out by a kid who could barely lift its own head.)

"I'll let Dr. Toki explain," Baron said as he returned to his seat. He knocked on the wall. "Yo, Doc, she's awake!"

Dr. Toki entered the room with the biggest smile on her face. "So, did you tell her?" she asked Baron.

"Tell me what?" I asked apprehensively.

"Abby is coming with you to Siberia."

"Um, no."

"We've learned a lot in the past three weeks," she said patting Abby on the head.

Abby turned and lifted his hand for a high-five. "To-ki!"

Dr. Toki lifted him up, placing my son in my arms. "Your son is the next stage in human evolution."

I had to admit he was abnormally strong. Even when he laid in my arms, his body felt like a doll made of the same material as truck tires. "You mean until he falls into a vat of acid and you strip him for spare parts?"

"That's not going to happen."

"Why? Did you spray him with a bulletproof coating?"

"Even better, he has a robot exoskeleton." Dr. Toki snapped her fingers, causing the door to open again.

I could hear the sound of heavy robotic footsteps. I looked down at Abby who was hopping excitedly. Apparently, he had already met who or whatever was behind the door.

He clapped his little hands, before saying a word that would cut me to my soul. "Nash!"

"Nash?" I cupped my hand over my mouth. There was no way. But there he was, the neon orange robot with the face made of LED lights.

"Hello, Hellion, long time no see." The robot walked over to Baron and gave a high-five. "The band is all here!"

'Except Noah,' thankfully the words never left my lips. The child in my arms was someone special. "Let's go rescue Lucy."

Abby seemed overjoyed at the prospect. Nash picked him up, holding Abby's small body in a sweet, tender embrace. Abby was sucked inside. But since he was still smiling, I knew not to scream. My baby turned around, apparently; he could ride inside Nash's stomach cavity.

"Um, ok." I shuddered. "My mind went straight to 'Teenage Mutant Ninja Turtles.'

Baron laughed out loud. "I know, right! He looks like that one character; the evil alien brain that lived inside a robot body."

"Mama?" Abby looked towards me, his lower lip trembling.

I reached for his soft little face. "You don't look like a scary brain. You look like a hero."

This was what my adult son wanted; for me to have a chance to be a mother, because if I could be brave for him, maybe I could find myself.

CHAPTER

There were so many signs that this was a bad idea, but I ignored them all. (Not that I had much of a choice.) I was still too stupid to understand the science behind Sundra's time travel technology; was she still around, or did she lose her connection to my timeline? I imagined an astronaut tethered to a space ship while going out into the vastness of space. Did I accidentally destroy Sundra's tether? Was she lost in the fabric of space and time, like some kind of trans-dimensional ghost? Or was she about to appear in front of me, to lecture about how insane I am for bringing my baby son to Siberia?

I sat on the cold metal bench-style seating of the small military plane, across from Nash. Abby was already huddled inside the robot's core. I could feel the warmth from five feet away. "Do you have central heating?"

"Affirmative, Ms. Hellion." The robot patted the seat next to him. "There's plenty of room. And I'm sure Abby would enjoy the opportunity to be closer to you."

The whole reason I had chosen the space opposite him was to be able to look at Abby from his little seat. He seemed content, happy, playing with various hanging toys. "Sure, thanks."

I took a seat at Nash's side, temporarily loosing eye contact with Abby. I could hear him start to whimper.

Nash quickly held my hand. "It's ok, Abby. It's ok. Can you feel your mommy's hand?"

"Mama?" Abby squeaked.

As he spoke, Nash's hand gave my fingers a soft, gentle squeeze. "Yes, your Mommy is right here."

Could he feel my touch via Nash's body? The idea seemed crazy, but it also melted my heart. I found myself hugging Nash like a security blanket. "I can't believe there's no heat on this plane," I muttered, in an effort to not look like a weak sentimental female in a plane full of actual soldiers.

Baron laughed at me from the pilot's seat. "If there was no heat, we'd all be dead."

"We're that high up?" I asked. The military aircraft had no windows other than the cockpit, which I could barely see. From where I currently sat, all I knew for sure was that we were flying through a dark purple star-filled sky.

"Yes, little Billy, we're flying in commercial airspace," he replied in his most condescending voice.

"What did you call me?" I didn't know whether to be confused or offended.

"I was thinking of that show, Mr. Wizard, Bill Nye or whatever. There's always a dumb-ass kid asking questions like he needs everything spelled out."

'Oh hell no.' I bit my lip until I tasted blood. "Yes, that is the point of educational television aimed at children."

"Well, Billy," Baron replied in a comically exaggerated voice. "Please, allow me to break it down into terms you can understand. This plane is like a maggot in a bag of breakfast cereal."

"As opposed to dinner cereal?" I snickered.

"A little critter just dipping and diving among the freeze-dried marshmallows, raisins and puffed rice."

"What kind of bizzarro world cereal did you grow up with?"

"Not the point, little Billy."

"Call me that one more time." I stood up, ready to fight (or at least punch him in the back of the head.)

Nash, perhaps sensing my anger, gripped my arm, preventing me from rushing the cockpit. "It would be ill advised to attack our primary pilot, at this time."

"At this time?" I giggled as I sat back down, resuming my warm, comfortable position.

Baron cleared his throat. "Ladies and gentlemen, according to the data of our expected flight path, we will soon be in range of the landing zone."

Since he was speaking normally, I felt safe to ask a question. "How soon is soon?" In hindsight, I could have worded that better.

"Twenty-seven minutes," Baron replied as he glanced upward to check a nearby switch. "Can you count to twenty-seven, little Billy?"

"That won't be a problem." I shot up from my seat, slipping out of Nash's grasp. "1, 2-"

Before I could strangle Baron while ripping out his hair with my teeth, Axel stood up, creating a human wall between me and the cockpit. "Hellion, will you please join me at the equipment closet?"

"Sure, that sounds lovely," I replied through gritted teeth. The weapons stash was at the opposite end of the plane. I watched as Axel selected his pieces, readying his weapon and armor.

"We need to acquire intel on Lucy's location. Baron you take the east, Hellion, you and Nash/Abby take the south, and I'll take the west, doubling back to the north. stay safe and remember; Lucy is the priority, if you have a chance to get her out you take it."

Baron saluted him sarcastically. "Sir, yes sir!"

We landed on a remote airstrip overlooking the all too familiar base. With my robot nanny at my side, we scouted the required area. The layout of the base was the same as I remembered it (in terms of the airfield, landing strip and storage facility.)

The noticeable difference (at least on the side we were patrolling) came in the form of (what appeared to be) a powerplant. "Hey, Nash? What do you think about that thing?"

"Some kind of reactor?" Nash used the camera on his arm to take photos from various angles. "Should we approach or wait for backup?" he asked as he hit send.

I assumed he was sharing the info with Axel. "No, we need a good reason. let me see those pictures."

The building was primarily dark, but there seemed to be a series of windows with distinct red lighting.

The image switched to a text chat; Axel apparently saw something in the corner. He recommended we investigate from a safe distance. I pulled out a pair of binoculars. From what I could make out, there was a figure on the roof; a guard in full armor, walking back and forth. "Nash, are you seeing this?"

"Affirmative, Miss Hellion," he replied, using his own built in enhanced vision system. "What is your plan?"

"We need to get inside, or find a way to the roof without putting a target on our backs."

"We should split up."

The immediacy of his idea came as somewhat of a shock. "Not in your little robot life."

"Listen," Nash said, moving closer. "There's a climbable fire escape on the left side, completely in the dark. One of us can climb, while the other starts inside."

I could see what he meant and it was actually a very time effective plan. "And we can switch every floor, to gain more visual perception."

Now it was just a matter of who would start where. "Do you know how to pick a lock?" I had to admit, my inner child was hoping he had some kind of adorable tech attachment. the robot flexed his hand transforming his fingers to a series of power tools. "Well, that settles that; you start on the interior while I scale the fire escape."

For a moment I forgot about the super powered baby in Nash's core. My son appeared to be asleep, with his head, and arms attached to electronic monitoring nodes. He looked a little too much like an actual, normal baby. What the hell was I doing? "You'll take care of him, right?"

Nash nodded. "Of course, Miss Hellion. I've already lost my dear friend, Noah once. I will not let it happen a second time. You have my word."

His tone filled me with a sense of confidence. "Thank you." I didn't know what he had gone through, but he was as human as anyone on the team. I took one last look at my son before starting the mission. I needed to live for him, I wanted to make him proud.

I headed for the fire escape. With the mechanics of my legs, I was able to make the jump to grab the ladder, pulling it down. I had assumed the fire escape would take me directly to the second floor and I was correct. With my blade I went to work on removing the frame on the window. There was also a nearby door, but I hoped that my decision was less likely to trigger an alarm. After a few moments of prying off screws and metal paneling the entrance opened to an otherwise dark staircase. I flicked on my wrist light giving me just enough power to be able to see my surroundings. I also had a radio and a tracking system to reunite with Nash in the event that we lost each other. Hopefully I wouldn't need it.

The room hummed with the sound of laptop computers, connecting to areas that were not accessible to the public. I just had to assume this place wasn't rigged to blowup. I followed the sound of footsteps, I figured it was either Nash or a armored guard. "Nash," I said with my back to the door. "That you?"

"Affirmative."

We cleared floor after floor, avoiding detection. everything was going great. too great. Why was there no one in the facility? (not even a janitor.)

Finally, we were at the interior door to the roof.

The armored figure stood facing the moon. "Hey, Nicki."

"Anya?" I could feel my heart freeze in my chest.

"How's motherhood treating you?" Still facing away, she removed her helmet revealing her long lavender hair.

She looked as sleek and beautiful as ever, but unlike our past interactions, there was no love in her eyes. "Where's Lucy?"

"Depends who's asking." She had her hand on her weapon but the fact that she didn't pull it right away gave me a small amount of hope.

"I am," I said, with fake confidence. "I've met her family. Her son needs his mother, you know that."

"Actually, I never met her. While Baron and Noah were living it up in Wisconsin, I was being a good girl, donating my body to science."

"Yeah," I said through pursed lips. "I know."

"Where's Axel?"

"We went south, directly opposite of here."

"Call him." Anya stroked her hand just above her weapon, her gloved fingers touching the grip.

"Why? You can just talk to me." I turned to Nash who stood a few feet behind. "and Nash. I know you've met Nash before. He was the reason Baron and Noah even met."

Anya raised her chin, "Hey Nash."

"Hello," Nash replied.

I could hear him take a step backward, into the shadows. I assumed he was trying to hide Abby's presence. "See you can talk to us; we can get you out of here."

"Who says I want out?" With a flick of her wrist, Anya was now pointing her weapon at my head. "I want to talk to him." Her voice was quivering. "Now."

"Ok, sure." I held up my hands. "Nash, put the radio on the floor and kick it over here."

Nash paused, hopefully he understood my cryptic plan. "Certainly, Hellion." He detached his hand and slid it over. The small device landed at Anya's feet.

Anya did not look down, so neither did I. This resulted in ten seconds of silence before static came over the signal. "Hello? Crackle… crackle…Who's on this channel? Identify yourself." The voice was barely audible.

Was that Axel, Baron, or someone else entirely? I knew there was only one way to find out. "This is TAC volunteer unranked Call Sign Hellion. I require assistance against an enemy combatant. Do you copy my location?"

The radio spit out more static before going dead silent. This was followed by (what I assumed was) a smoke bomb.

Knowing my window was fleeting, I quickly executed a leg sweep, knocking Anya to the floor. This was only possible due to my metal legs, since her armor was as steady as a tank.

I knew she would get back up. I needed to get her weapon (preferably without firing it in a random direction.) With all my strength I stepped on her hand. She released the weapon and I kicked it away. That was my first mistake.

Anya sprang back up, punching me in the face. She glanced around, frantically looking for her gun.

I assumed it was an ordinary gun, in a futuristic shell (to match the yellow-orange color of her armor.) I would quickly learn that the weapon was more than just a fashion accessory. She managed to get it back, firing at my knee. The blast sent a white-hot bolt, destroying my prosthetic like a piece of ice being dunked in hot water. "What the hell?" My leg felt uncomfortably warm. Did she just shoot me with corrosive acid?

Hopping on one foot, I scrambled for my own weapon. Slashing at her chest, my blade did little to no damage to her armor. I needed to hit her in the face. I sprang up, with the goal of climbing on her, wrestling her to the ground. Was I really going to stab her? Could I?

Anya laughed. "You were never worthy." She rammed her knee to my stomach, hitting me right in my c-section scar.

I plunged the knife hard, stabbing her in the cheek. The blade got stuck in her jaw. It was, of course, non-fatal but looked painful as all hell. She released her weapon, in an effort to free both hands, to pull out the knife.

I grabbed her gun and fired over and over, until my former friend stopped fighting me. I kicked her in the stomach sending her flying off the building. It was only then, when I allowed myself to take a breath. I looked over the edge to see if she was still alive. (Anya was wearing full armor, anything was possible.) Looking over the lip of the rooftop, I had my answer. Somehow, I had shot her in the abdomen with the acid gun. As a result, she fell off the roof in two pieces, landing in the bright white snow.

I cupped my hand over my mouth. I made sure to sit down on my butt (since I was still missing half a leg,) as I sobbed uncontrollably. I didn't even care if I was alone or not. I pulled my good leg to my chest, trying not to vomit all over myself.

I felt a hand on my shoulder; cold, robotic, likely armored. "I'm sorry, I'm so sorry." I held my breath waiting for the bullet to the head. I didn't deserve to be alive.

There was nothing; no gun pressed to my back, or even a hand on my shoulder. Confused, I turned to see Sundra standing with adult Abaddon. She was in full armor while he wore the clothes, I last saw him in.

"Are you proud of me?" I asked out loud. "Was that the right choice?"

Sundra rolled her eyes, turned and walked in to the fog, leaving Abaddon standing alone.

When his lover was gone, my son sighed, running his fingers through his dirty blond hair. He took a step towards me, walking in slow motion with a glowing blur filter; like a ghost or an angel. "Anya made her choice, you know that."

"No." I shook my head, now sobbing for a variety of reasons. Abaddon was dead, and it was all my fault.

He placed his hand upon my shoulder. "Even with a thousand years and a million tries, you would never have been able to heal her heart."

"I know, but I'm still sorry." I stood up, reaching for his hand. He had been able to touch me but when I tried to touch him, I felt only air. Air laced with electric static. "Are you dead?"

"What?" Abby asked with a smile. "Is that why you're so down on yourself?" His hand caressed my cheek, causing a warm soothing sensation. "In truth, I'm not dead, I'm traveling."

"Prove it.

"Prove it?" he laughed even harder. "Ok, give me your hand."

I lifted my hand, holding it in front of my face. "Ok." I closed my eyes, focusing on my breath. "I'm ready."

I could feel his rough callused hands cupping my fingers. He maneuvered my hand to his face, allowing me to touch his cheek, just below his eyes. I could feel every wrinkle on his sweet smiling face. "Nice crow's feet."

"I prefer the term laugh lines, although some cultures refer to them as character lines."

"I like that."

When he kissed my forehead, I could feel his lips, his skin. even his facial hair.

"I'll see you soon, Mom."

When I opened my eyes, I was standing before my very confused teammates. Baron's head was tilted as if he was looking down a magnifying glass. "Nicki?" he snapped his fingers a few times. "You there?"

"Yeah, I'm fine," I muttered, still noticeably hopping. "Just my busted leg."

Nash took a step forward. "I am so glad." He shook my hand, bowing his head. "I do apologize for my actions. Although it may have appeared that I had abandoned you, I stepped back to a safe location to keep track of Baron and Axel's current whereabouts."

I nodded unable to hold back my grin. My baby son was looking up at me from his space inside Nash. He was happy, proud. For a moment I didn't even notice someone was missing. "Where's Axel?"

"Axel!" my baby squeaked from inside of Nash's core.

Nash waved his hand, opening a window to allow me to see my precious son's face. I would have wanted to touch him but I knew that was an unwise idea in the freezing cold of the artic. Instead, I placed two fingers to the clear window.

Abby lifted his little hand as if saying hello. "Hi, Mama!"

"Did Axel find Lucy?" I asked Nash while looking at my son's big blue eyes. Abby's joy was palpable and contagious.

Abby nodded, looking up at Nash to supply the details. "Axel! Lucy!"

"Yes," Nash explained, "Axel located Lucy within Kitsune's personal living quarters."

Baron sighed, taking a seat on the edge of the roof. "That sounds about right." He hung his legs (clad in his usual anti-gravity boots) over the side. "Now we know where all the security forces disappeared to."

I knew he was looking at Anya's corpse. The kind thing would be to take a seat by his side but I wasn't sure I could manage that without puking. Instead, I opted for a comforting hand placed upon his shoulder. "Will you be alright?"

"It's not about me, Nicki." His voice was serious yet calm.

"I know." Now I had to sit by his side, if only to not appear frightened of the bisected corpse of our former friend.

Baron placed his hand in mine. "Poor Anya, she was a good kid. Hopefully in death she can finally find the peace she was looking for." He sounded as numb as I felt.

"I guess we'd better go find Axel, before that dumbass gets himself captured," I muttered. My voice added an involuntary giggle.

"What's so funny?" Baron asked, still looking down

"Nothing." I bit my lower lip out of both frustration and shame.

"You were never going to side with her. Axel, or Julian, or whatever, you see him like the father you always wanted." Baron stood up and proceeded to attempt to repair my leg while I was still standing.

"Noah knew him," I said quietly. "They were friends."

"I'm not saying your loyalty is a bad thing. I'm just saying that given the choice; and you had a choice, Anya would never have won over your loyalty to TAC." He used a pocket knife to assemble a temporary solution; a piece of scrap metal attached to my broken stump. I would be balanced but unable to walk without a limp.

"Says the person who left Noah to die!" I didn't mean to raise my voice. And I certainly didn't want to cry.

Thankfully, Nash made a comically adorable robot throat clearing noise. "If you two are finished arguing, I have intel to share."

"Sure," I said taking a comforting, deep breath. "My apologies."

Nash, having retrieved his hand, was typing something into a small screen. "Well, team, according to the ping of his last communication, Axel appears to be holding still at his last known coordinates."

"What do you mean by 'holding still'?" I looked over his shoulder to get a better look. The tracking ping showed Axel's coordinates as paused for well over twenty minutes. "That's weird. Do you think he's talking to someone?" (Or dead.)

Baron stood up, putting away his tools. He shook his head with a look of indifference. "He's frozen in place? Yeah, that doesn't sound like a trap at all."

"Only one way to find out," I said in my best superhero impression.

"Um, what was that, little Billy?" Baron looked at me like I was a mentally challenged reality star running for president.

"Well, you're free to stay at the plane. In fact, you can fly back to Dr. Toki and get a head start on corpse retrieval, because you always like to be on the winning team."

Baron laughed, "What's that supposed to mean?"

"You hop the fence like," I pursed my lips struggling for a word that would make sense. "A volleyball!" That was not the right word.

"Because volleyball is played over a fence?"

"You know what I fucking mean!" The anger was boiling over.

"I recall betraying some very powerful people, to pull your immature ass out of the fire."

I was taken aback by his choice of words. I had been expecting him to play the race card or even make fun of me being the weaker gender. But then I realized, no; Noah was white and Anya was a girl. He had no problem with teammates who could pull their own weight. I was just a little bitch.

Our argument was interrupted by the sound of crying. I turned to see Nash, swaying side to side, like a baby swing. "There, there, little one." Nash looked up at Baron and I with his digital eyes. "If you two are done bickering, we have some ground to cover."

"Fine, let's go." Baron took a running start before taking to the sky.

"I guess he'll meet us there." I walked to Nash's side. "Do you want to take the stairs or the fire escape? Fire escape seems faster, but I'm not sure how well I can climb with one functioning knee.""

Nash gently gripped my arm. "Will you be ok?"

I nodded. "Yeah, of course. It doesn't even hurt, it's just a pain in the ass to balance on."

"I'm serious, Ms. Hellion. I need you to be ok." He placed a single finger under my chin. "I'm not going to say if you are skilled or if you are simply lucky. Luck and skill contain many overlaps. However, what I know for a fact is that in this life we take what wins we can get, regardless of the aftermath."

I understood. That was the kindest way to call me an immature newbie for getting so emotional at the sight of a corpse. "Can I ask you something?"

"Certainly, Ms. Hellion, we are friends."

"How much of you is being controlled by Abby?"

Nash nodded and paused for a moment, as if truly thinking about the philosophical nature of the question. "From what I understand of my programming, Abby offers me suggestions in regards to direction, combat and other ideas, but my body has the final say."

"That was why you made the choice to throw the hand. You took a step back instead of engaging with Anya." He had been protecting Abby, just as he said he would. I smiled; a light breaking through a wall of tears as I reached for his hand. "Let's go be heroes."

CHAPTER 18

"Come on, Nicki, just stop thinking about the pain," I groaned out loud with every step. Walking with only one functional knee was difficult in itself, but to do so in thick snow was quickly becoming annoying. I was beaten and bloody, with a sharp pain in my side (what I assume was broken ribs, as opposed to a punctured lung.)

"Ms. Hellion," Nash said, slowing down to walk by my side. "If you don't allow me to assist you, we risk freezing to death before locating the apartment complex."

"Are you being serious?"

"I may be a robot but even my electrical components risk damage at critical temperatures."

"Fine, you may carry me, but only if we can stick to the shadows.

"That had always been my intention," my robot partner said with a regal bow. I could hear my son giggling from inside Nash's heated core. "See, even Abby likes the idea."

"Mama!" Abby squeaked gleefully. There were no speakers or even airholes, but somehow, I could hear his tiny voice over the roar of the wind.

Nash took a knee allowing me to climb on his back. With my arms around his shoulders and my legs on his hips, I felt like a sidekick character out of a late 90's anime. Nash broke into a run, and within moments, the crystal blue building came into sight. Framed in the glow of the pure white snow, the building looked like the world's most silent nightclub. I was mesmerized by its beauty when suddenly, a hit to the face sent me flying.

I landed in a soft snowbank which immediately collapsed on top of me. Resisting the urge to scream in agony, I dug myself out. Freezing cold, I blew on my hands, if only to keep my mind focused. All I had to do was find the building and I could easily catch up to Nash. Unfortunately, the man that stood before me had other ideas. "Hey, Faust. It's been a while."

He stood over me wearing dark sunglasses paired with a tactical designer suit. "You were never the worthy one."

"What's that supposed to mean?"

"Lucy is the chosen one, and I need to collect her for my team. Ideally, I would have liked to prevent Sundra's creation but unfortunately, that plan faced an insurmountable paradox. Noah inspired Lucy to pursue coding, but he also inspired her to get pregnant with the son of a high-ranking official."

"Why not go after Denny's father?"

"The father is unknown to history. And not just because Lucy was a slut," he said with a sexist laugh.

Since the time-traveling wizard clearly was not going to attack, I felt a little more comfortable. "What are you talking about?"

"She purposely led on multiple high-ranking men; both police, and gang members. She used this to rise to a position of power but also to protect her son's future."

"Why do you look so much like my son?"

"Why does it matter?"

"I'm not feeling very good about myself, at the moment." I knew my choice of words made no sense. I looked up at Faust with sad, innocent doll eyes. My goal was to appear emotionally defeated.

It appeared to be working. Faust crossed his arms, taking a seat beside me in the snow. He was smiling less like a comic book villain and more like a disappointed father figure. "You've come a long way from when we first met."

"So, have you. You're certainly more than a Russian pimp with a fetish for little girls." I didn't know if I wanted to laugh or cry, so I did a bit of both. "Now, will you answer my question? Why do you look like Abby? Is this just one of your costumes? Or-"

"You want to know if we're related."

"Well?"

"Have you ever heard the saying, 'you're one in a million?'"

"I guess."

"With nine billion people in this world that makes us all doppelgangers to someone."

"You're saying it's a coincidence?"

"Never said that."

"Are we going to fight or can I go now?" I stood up with a sickening realization; he was stalling me, that had to be his endgame. I sprang into a run. For the briefest moment I forgot about my damaged leg, managing a good hundred feet before falling on my face.

Faust easily caught up using his teleportation. He stood over me, looking down like a horror movie villain staring down its prey. He didn't want to kill me or even fight me, he just wanted to watch me struggle. "I figure Lucy and I; we could have a 'Beauty and the Beast' type of relationship," he said casually. "Some people call it Stockholm syndrome but those people just don't believe in true love."

"You love her?"

"Given enough time you can't help but fall in love with someone."

"You can't be serious." He was, he wanted me to suffer. "Lucy would gouge her eyes out before she ever loved you."

"That's where you're wrong." Faust ran his fingers through his hair, causing it to grow to shoulder length. He lowered his sunglasses, looking at me with familiar eyes; Noah's eyes. "I can choose to look like him, as little or as much as I like. I can pull traits from any timeline, to give her the vision of Noah she always dreamt of." He patted my head like a puppy. "Now, be a dear and play your part." With that, he snapped his fingers and teleported away.

"Well, crap." I looked ahead towards my target. Faust was likely already at the apartment, just waiting to pick through the remains like a vulture.

I knew what I had to do, but I sure as hell was not fighting for Faust. When I made it to the fire exit of the building, I could hear the sounds of gunfire. Since I had never actually set foot in Kitsune's home I had no idea how many floors there were. I guess I would just have to follow the sound of combat and attempt to not get myself killed.

I was about to attempt to jump for the ladder but that proved difficult. Out of frustration, I stabbed the wall with my knife. The wall was climbable. I only had to make it about thirty feet, and with all of the commotion inside (and the roar of the artic wind), I had more than enough cover. The idea of death, loss, and sadness: it all got pushed to the back of my mind. And with it went the fear. Once I achieved a handhold, I swung up to the ladder. It was actually pretty fun.

My mind started to wander; was there life after death, or were we all just plastic pieces on someone else's gameboard? Most importantly: what did Faust mean by playing my part? Using the back of my knife, I easily shattered the window. Apparently, it was made of the same material as a typical car windshield. There was an inner layer that appeared to contain a heating element. This left behind sharp shards, but I had nothing but time to chip away at the odd metallic fibers. I could hear voices in the distance; screaming and cursing in Japanese, interlaced with English and some Spanish (hopefully that was Axel.)

Upon entering the space, I was faced with a path that split into three hallways. The first one had lights; flickering red, yellow and orange, possibly a fire. The second had sound; gunshots, voices, this path seemed to lead to the main battle. Then there was the third; a pitch-black path with no discernable end. With one hand on the wall, I blindly followed the third path.

The hallway was straight, with a single sharp turn, leading to a mysterious sliding door. "A cleaning closet?" Using my wrist com as a light, I could see there was a hotel cart and an array of supplies, but something seemed off. The walls were covered in cabinets and drawers. This was for something other than storage; one of these was a hidden door. And if I was wrong, I could still use the cleaning chemicals to make a weapon of some kind. I started to open every latch; some were locked, some had hand tools (hammer, screwdriver, wrench.) Upon collecting a variety of tools and spray bottles, a previously locked door opened all on its own. It was a staircase.

The upward journey was long and winding, like something out of a fairytale (or a horror movie.) Without any lighting, the climb seemed to go on forever. After what felt like hours in the silent darkness, I saw a soothing blue light. Was this a server room, maybe a theatre? No, when I passed through the threshold, I could see it was a studio; the digital studio of a mad scientist.

"Lucy?' This had to be where Kitsune was storing her secret weapon. Walking around the black-painted space I could see the home was the size of a typical hotel room. There was even a miniature kitchen and a bathroom:

Everything was lit up with digital neon lights; no windows, or even normal lightbulbs, just wave after wave of calming blue light. "This must be what those flying turtles see before they meet Super Mario." The main source of the light appeared to be a floating wall of text.

"You are such a fake gamer-girl." Lucy was giggling from behind a virtual keyboard. Her long manicured fingernails tapping on the glowing plastic.

Her magic was on display for all to see; line after line of coding that seemed to be crafting the world around her, from the art on the walls to her very appearance.

"Hey, Lucy," I said, more nervous than I intended.

She stood up, wearing a black shimmery gown, like something out of a beauty pageant. "Hey," she replied in a sultry Spanish accent. The light caught her long, shiny black curls, then with a stroke of the keyboard her makeup changed from dark and smoky to metallic (like some kind of robotic cyborg angel.) She walked towards me, the holographic color of her clothing shifting with every step.

"Are you wearing digitally generated clothing?"

"Don't you just love it?" her accent changed to British. "This is my world. I can be the princess, the queen, I can have everything I ever wanted."

I had a feeling I knew what she meant by that. "Show me."

She stroked her hands through the screen projection, drawing the outline of a male figure. A man materialized by her side; a younger, healthier, clean-cut version of Noah. His long hair was pulled back in a braid, highlighting his sparkling eyes, and sexy groomed facial hair. It took a second before I even realized he was in a dark blue suit, complete with a cape.

I wanted to laugh, but in my heart, I knew that would be more hurtful than anything. "You know this isn't real, right?"

"Do you think I care?" Lucy's voice was filled with happiness, innocence, and pure joy.

"You can't stay here." That wasn't what I had meant to say. If I had the technical ability to mold my own world, with the man of my dreams, I would do it in a heartbeat. "I mean, what about Wisconsin?" All I could picture was the sight of her precious son in the arms of her heartbroken father. She had people who loved her, people who wanted her home.

"What about it?" Lucy took a step towards the male figure, allowing him to hold her hand. "There's nothing for me in that truck stop town."

"Your family; your son, all the people waiting for you?"

Lucy's reaction was a little too real. "My father only wants to keep face; it would look bad if he admitted just how little he cared about my disappearance." She blinked her eyes, causing a single tear to roll down her cheek, over the digital makeup. The actual, physical droplet cut through the light causing a line of darkness.

The male figure smiled as he caressed his hand to her cheek. "This is what she wants." His voice was clearly Faust pretending to be Noah. There was no way she didn't notice that.

Lucy leaned back allowing him to put his arms around her. "Sometimes family isn't enough. I want what I want, what I deserve."

I could feel my hands shaking. This was not happening. "There is no way you're this stupid." I refuse to believe Faust was completely correct about the human psyche.

Lucy cupped her mouth in anger and offense. "At least you got the chance to make love to him. He was my teacher, my mentor. He believed in me more than my father ever did. I guess I just wasn't worthy of his love."

"You were a kid." Again, that was the wrong thing to say.

She swept her hand in front of her face, conjuring up a keyboard. I suddenly felt fishing wire grip my arms, pulling me into what could only be described as a crucifixion. The wires lifted me off the floor. Holding me just high enough to keep me trapped.

The male figure pulled Lucy close in a loving embrace. He looked up at me, locking eyes. With a sickening smile, followed by a flirty wink.

This pissed me off worse than anything. "You," I coughed in pain the string of curse words choking in my throat. "Tell her who you really are!"

Lucy giggled. "I know who he is. Faust; the big bad wolf who wants to devour my brain. That's what you were going to say, right?"

Something broke deep inside me. "Do you really love the idea of playing house more than your son?" I needed to get back to my team, my own baby son, but above all, I needed to return to Wisconsin. I wanted to scoop Denny up in my arms while he called me Ms. Iron man; I would be the hero he deserved, I just needed to find a way out of this virtual spider web. "You're such a freak!" My mind had gone straight for schoolyard bullying, hoping I could provoke her into a fair fight.

"Excuse me?" Lucy placed her hands at her sides as if trying to show off the fact that she was in control, and had no intention of letting me out.

"What are you going to do kill me?"

She pursed her lips, turning briefly to Faust. "I don't know. I actually hadn't thought that far ahead. Maybe I'll keep you around like a trophy; cut off your arms and legs, just keep you alive enough to revel in my glory."

'Ok, you're completely insane.' I had one trick up my sleeve; my wrist radio. If I could knock it to the ground there was a slim possibility it would send out a signal to reveal my location. The way my arm was bound, I would need to attempt to dislocate my shoulder. I was so focused on knocking it off my arm, I barely noticed a new figure wearing familiar purple armor.

Sundra appeared, firing a single round. The sound of the bullet hitting its target caused me to pause my actions. Within seconds I was falling, landing hard on my shoulder. This caused me to crush my transmitter under my ribcage. 'And holy crap did that hurt.' I flinched in pain, closing my eyes for what felt like only a few seconds. But the next thing I saw was a plain, white room. The plaster was cracking exposing a colorful array of wires.

Lucy collapsed, falling into Faust's arms. It was clear what I was looking at; she was frail, haggard, possibly starved. Lucy had been living in the virtual world, ignoring the state of her physical body. Even without the bullet, she would have been dead in a few weeks.

Sundra patted my shoulder as she turned to leave.

"Why?" I shrieked.

With a wave of her hand, Sundra opened a portal; a dark black void, leading to nowhere. "Blood is all we have."

With Sundra gone I turned to Faust who was now carrying Lucy's body like a lover. Was he taking her? The sickening idea (that was now stuck in my head) gave me a burst of strength. I charged at

Faust, punching him as hard as I could. My wrist radio (which had been sending out a distress signal ever since getting crush by my ribs) collided with his sunglasses.

I'd like to think this act was what triggered the teleport. Either way, I was stopping Faust from harvesting Lucy's brain (and whatever else he had in store for her body.

What I didn't count on was where we landed. Looking around we appeared to be in a large ballroom covered in blood, broken glass, mirrors, and sculptures. It took a few seconds for me to realize this was Kitsune's living room.

Kitsune and Axel stood frozen, at the sight of Lucy's dead body. With Sundra long gone it was now a question of 'How the hell did this happen?' Thankfully they both seemed to assume Faust was at fault. The moment seemed almost unfair. I rolled to the side as both leaders opened fire at Faust.

When the world went silent again, Kitsune doubled over with laughter. "Wow, just wow." She threw down her weapon, sliding it to the corner of the room. The heavy butt of the weapon thumped against one of many dead bodies, firing a single shot into a random wall. This was enough to bring out all remaining survivors.

First came Baron, dropping a body into the pile of dead guards. This was followed by Nash who was carrying a dozen or so swords that (I assumed) he took off his opponents. Nash's core section was completely opaque, hiding Abby's presence. (I just had to accept my son was still alive, until we were someplace safer, where I could physically check.) One thing was clear; Kitsune was outnumbered.

Faust started to stand up, gripping at his chest. The once-powerful sunglasses fell from his face, revealing blue eyes, cracked with sadness. He was injured, close to death. Was he going to apologize, beg for mercy?

Baron didn't give him the chance. He flew at Faust, pummeling him with armored fists. I assumed this raw reaction was an emotional mixture of grief combined with the desire to make sure Faust didn't have the chance to teleport.

Unfortunately, Kitsune took this opportunity to flee the room. Axel went after her, while Nash stayed behind. I could hear the sound of a motorcycle leaving in one direction while Baron and Faust continued their hand-to-hand combat down the hallway. Nash gripped my shoulder, helping me to my feet. "Are you alright, Ms. Hellion?"

I wanted to ask to see Abby. Nash was covered in blood, any part of which could have come from my son. Would he have told me if Abby was dead? Or would he want to wait until we were at a place where we could be alone? (That seemed like the human thing to do.)

My thoughts were interrupted by the sound of a body being dumped at my side. I flinched as a splatter of fresh blood hit me in the face. "Ew!"

Baron had tossed the limp body of Faust before me. "What's the matter, Nicki? You look surprised? Was it the blood?" He kicked Faust in the gut, causing the body to groan. "He's not a God, just a man." Baron chuckled, stretching his back. My teammate appeared relaxed as he started to remove his armor.

To me, this seemed more than a little strange. "Why are you getting naked?"

Baron laughed. Clearly, he was not getting naked, just sheading TAC property; weapons, armor, etc. "Because the last move is up to you. I'm out of here."

"You're out of here?" I asked with a forced giggle. This could not be happening. "What about the plane?"

"Nash can fly." Baron took a look at Lucy's body, paying close attention to her hands.

"Are you trying to decide what to bring to her father?" I could hear my voice breaking with emotion. My impending tears seemed to inspire him to find a way to take the entire body.

"I guess so," Baron said calmly as he wrapped the body in a nearby rug. Lucy was small enough for him to carry like a bride, so there was the real possibility he was going to fly her back to Wisconsin.

"Where are you going to go?"

"That's none of your concern." Baron fired his weapon, opening a hole in the wall. His boots were active; he was going to fly off into the snow.

"Are you coming back?"

"To Siberia?" He asked with a chuckle.

This was all a big joke to him. "Never mind."

Baron turned back one last time. A soft gust of wind blew his hair over his face, giving him a raw ethereal appearance. "If you're ever in the neighborhood, be sure to ask for Leo."

He took off towards the airfield, likely to steal a plane. I forced myself to my feet, but I couldn't make myself go after him. Leo could tell Lucy's family that we failed; they were his friends, his priority.

Nash put his arms around me, holding me close like a true human friend. "You have to let them go." His voice was calm and serene. "We need to get back."

"Back to what?" I asked, my mind, body, and soul were all too tired to move. "TAC, Dr. Toki? And to where? Vancouver, Washington?"

"Yes." Nash's answer was quick, direct, and precise.

With no sensation in my legs, I was unable to verify the location of Faust's body. Was he still alive? Did I want to know? "It's too quiet." The moonlight sparkled off the fresh snow. 'Why were there no alarms? Where were the rest of the base's employees and staff?'

"Ms. Hellion?" Nash tilted his head, looking in the same direction. "What do you see?"

"We need to run." I put my arms around Nash, gripping his back. "Now!"

At the moment, Faust was an afterthought. I wanted to be as far away as possible before this base started its self-destruct sequence. "Affirmative," Nash replied, breaking into a run.

In the distance, I could hear the sounds of multiple aircraft taking to the sky. We needed to get to the plane and get airborne. The thought, of course, crossed my mind: what if Axel wasn't there?

Could I really leave him behind? He was older, stronger, Axel could take care of himself. I needed to believe that.

With Nash's speed, we made it back to the plane in record time, but my worst fears were realized: Nash and I were alone. 'What do we do?' I wanted to ask, but the words that came out were, "So, can you get this bird in the air or not?"

Nash paused for a moment, "Should we attempt contact with our commander?

"I'm your commander now and I want to go home."

"Setting a path to, 'home,' Commander." Even with his robotic voice, I could hear his sarcasm. "And by that, I mean Abby."

"I'm sure you do," I replied with a smirk. I took a seat beside Nash. I put on my seatbelt in preparation for takeoff. I could hear groaning, but within seconds we were in the air. Judging by the radar map I could see we were heading back in the direction of Vancouver. "Do you think Faust is human?"

"Dr. Toki will let us know for sure."

"What?"

"Dr. Toki will be able to dissect Faust; relieve him of his blood, flesh, and tissue.

"How?"

Again, he spoke calmly as if his actions were an afterthought. "I attached a teleporter ping, sending his remains straight to our cargo hold."

"Oh, ok." I closed my eyes, reaching my hand to the opaque window. Was Abby controlling Nash? Was he flying the plane? I wasn't about to ask to see him, especially if Faust was still alive somewhere on the plane.

<h1 style="text-align:center">CHAPTER 19</h1>

When we landed back at the Vancouver base the first thing I did was reach for Abby. I pinned my arm over my robot companion's chest preventing him from leaving his seat. "Nash! Give me the baby, please."

"Sure, why wouldn't I?" Nash rolled his shoulders, popping his neck, prompting his chest cavity to open.

My little son had been asleep for the majority of the flight. He looked so comfortable I almost felt guilty about picking him up.

My baby blinked his big blue eyes. "Ma-ma?" With a sleepy yawn, he looked up at me with the sweetest smile.

"Hi, Abby."

"Ma-ma!" Abby sat up, flailing his arms, just begging to be held.

At that moment I knew what people meant by, 'my heart literally melted.' I truly felt like I was going to die from love. "I missed you too."

With my son in my arms I skipped, twirled and danced in the direction of Dr. Toki's lab. My soul was filled with joy, love, until the physical pain (and my damaged leg) took hold and I nearly dropped my baby. 'Shit!' I leaned against the wall, steadying myself before knocking on the door. No answer. This seemed oddly familiar; just like when Tony died.

Where was Axel? I pounded harder on the door. "Dr. Toki!" I felt a sharp pain in my chest. Leaning my ear to the door, I could hear soldiers, shouting orders as they ushered in heavy machinery. 'Where was Faust?'

After a while the door opened and Dr. Toki greeted me with open arms. "Nicki, Abby!" there were tears of joy in her eyes; she was truly astonished that we made it back alive. "I'm so proud of both of you!" she quickly shut the door behind her, keeping us in the hallway. "Excuse the interruption, we're in the process of moving Faust to a secure holding cell."

"More secure than the last time?" I asked with a forced smile. I didn't want to accuse her of incompetence but my prosthetic legs were a constant reminder of what happened last time Faust was in custody.

"I am well aware, there have been several instances where Faust has escaped TAC custody, but rest assured we've learned and evolved." The way she smiled sent shivers down my spine. What did she have planned?

"Can I speak to him?" I asked as innocently as possible.

"Only after all precautions have been taken."

"That's fair." I wanted to ask more; what was Faust, why did he look like the adult version of my son? Was Dr. Toki going to kill and dissect him? I couldn't think about that. "So, where's Axel?"

"There was an explosion at the base." Dr. Toki's voice began to trail off. "Axel had gone into shock; his heart was weak. And there was so much blood. We brought back what we could." She led the way to a ward of patient rooms (the base's personal ICU.) While I mentally prepared for the worst.

Axel had a brace on one leg and the other was simply gone. "Hi, Nicki, I guess we match now." My older mentor smiled big and bright despite the fact his face was badly bruised with several notable lacerations.

"Hi." My heart was in my throat. Julian seemed alive, happy even, but I felt so guilty for leaving him behind. "What happened?"

"Kitsune is dead," he said with a confident shrug. "that's all that matters."

I made my way closer, walking my fingers along his chest. His body was held together with bandages caked with blood, under which I could see staples, stitches. He had to be in an unbelievable amount of pain. "So, um, you blew up the base?"

He nodded proudly. "There will always be others, but that's a task for another day."

All thoughts of meeting with Faust were pushed aside. I'd been so close to losing Julian. All I wanted to do was hold him like an emotional support animal.

Julian placed his hand on my shoulder. "Dr. Toki, please Close the door on your way out. I don't want us to be disturbed."

Once I heard the door shut, I started to sob uncontrollably. "I'm so sorry!"

I could feel Julian's hand on my back, patting my shoulder. Abby leaned against my chest, attempting to nurse through my sweaty clothing. "Ma?"

Since I was still hysterical, I shifted my weight placing Abby in bed between Julian and myself. This gave me just enough time to get up and walk around. "I need to splash some water on my face." I rushed to the in-room sink, soaking a piece of paper towel in cold water. I paused, taking deep calming breaths.

"Will you stay with me?" Julian asked. His voice was weak, timid, even a little scared. "If you need to leave, I understand."

"No, I'm fine right here." I started to remove my sweaty clothing to reveal my nipple (and the fact that I was overdue for a shower.) I dragged over a plastic visitor chair, close enough to hold Julian's hand while breastfeeding. "Hand me my little gremlin, if you please."

Julian placed Abby in my arms and I proceeded to feed my superbaby, like a normal human mother. "Your little boy is truly something special."

"And he knows it." I looked down at my son's face. He didn't need me; he was a truly unique soul destined for greatness. It was actually kind of scary. Would I be able to teach him anything? Would he eventually grow to resent me?

Abby released my nipple, giggled and squirmed. At first, I thought he was being playful, then I realized Abby was a normal human baby who'd just soiled his diaper.

Julian laughed at my noticeable discomfort. "Let me guess, you've never changed a diaper before?"

"Well, he's been with Dr. Toki for the majority of his cute little super powered life," I pointed out. "And I never had the chance to earn money as a babysitter."

"Give him here." Julian held out his hands. With one arm he took hold of Abby while the other moved a rolling medical trolly closer to the bed.

"Don't tell me you're making a diaper." I had to admit I was impressed.

"Yup," he replied with a genuine smile.

"And how do you know how to make a diaper?"

Julian laughed. "You know, I'd like to tell you I did it for the first-time while doing volunteer work in Rwanda."

"You didn't?"

"Growing up the oldest of six kids, plus all my distant cousins, I learned a lot. And by that, I mean, I had to help out or else my mamma would beat my ass. Bless her soul."

"Lucky you." I laughed out loud. Feeling happier than I had in a while.

"Before I begin will you grab that tub of wipes over there, near the sink?"

"Sure." I brought over a package of hand wipes, first testing them on my hands to make sure they weren't bleach.

"Did you just check to make sure they weren't bleach?"

"And to make sure it's not alcohol or anything that would hurt my little cutie pie's skin."

"How very maternal of you." Julian proceeded to clean Abby in a sweet, gentle way. I watched in awe as the wounded soldier laid out a clean towel to use as a changing mat.

"Da!" Abby calmly allowed Julian to clean him off and create a make-shift diaper out of a second towel.

"Be careful when you hold him," Julian said as he cuddled the overjoyed little boy in his arms. "I don't have actual pins or tape." He shifted Abby's body, holding him close in a way that allowed my baby to comfortably stay in the diaper.

I couldn't help but smile. He looked like a father. "That comes so natural for you."

Julian froze, his voice went silent as his eyes drifted off in deep thought. "I've lost a lot of good people in my life."

I didn't know what to say to that. There were several possible answers; 'yeah me too,' or 'life is unfair,' but they all seemed to come off as condescending. "You have me." I reached for his hand, blinking back tears. "You have us."

Julian leaned back, looking up at the ceiling. There was a long silence, as if he was trying to decide if he believed my words. "Is it true you would have married Tony?"

"Are you asking me to marry you?" I said with a smirk, walking my finger along his sexy jawline. His face was rough; coarse, a map of a life well lived.

"If that's what it takes for you to stay."

"I have a feeling Dr. Toki wouldn't let me leave with Abby. I mean at least if I stay, I get to be with Abby, Nash and you; my family." My words were the truth, I literally had nowhere else to be. 'I mean, I guess I could walk away if I had to.' Looking at my sweet little boy and my beautiful Latino soldier, I knew that would never be an option; I would die before leaving them.

Julian looked at me with his deeply emotional eyes. "Would you marry me out of pity?"

"Marry you out of pity?" I had to assume he was joking. Or was he truly that lonely.

"I've lost so much." Julian clenched, gripping at his thigh. I watched as he swallowed hard, choking back emotional discomfort. "I might need something for the pain."

Even I knew his tears were for more than just his leg. "Can I see?"

"Sure," Julian said with a sigh. He probably knew the only alternative would be to call back Dr. Toki for advice.

As he held Abby, I lowered the hospital issue blanket to examine the full extent of his disfigured legs. "Wow."

"For the first few moments I couldn't even feel the pain," Julian said with a forced laugh. "I wanted so badly to die." He blinked once then allowed his eyes to close. "Maverick, bless her heart she was one cold bitch but she was still the love of my life. And Tony," a soft chuckle slipped from his chapped lips. "To me he was just a little boy playing superhero. He was so strong, with such an admirable spirit and a level of courage I'd never seen in anyone."

I could feel his damaged leg muscle throbbing, as if calling out to the missing portion of Julian. Ironically that was what Julian himself was doing; calling out to the lost. "Tony was the way he was, because of you. You taught him to be a soldier, a hero. Hopefully you can do the same for Abby; train him, teach him, love him." I placed my hand upon Julian's bandaged limb. his leg was packed with gauze, but I could feel where the bone was amputated. "You can be the father he deserves."

"He deserves more than a washed-up cripple."

"Ok," I said with my hands on my hips. "You just said we were twins; are you calling me a cripple?"

Julian laughed so hard he gripped his side in pain. He flinched, briefly shifting his weight, and then he laughed some more.

I tickled Abby's cheek. "Is our papa down in the dumps?"

Abby giggled.

"That settles it, we'll heal together, as a family."

I stayed with Julian for the rest of the night, awaking to coffee, oatmeal, and a package of store-bought diapers. I had to admit, it felt nice.

It was nearly a month before I visited Faust and when I finally did, it was only because Julian was in physical therapy for the day. I left him with Abby (who still had access to the Nash suit, making for an ideal training partner.)

Faust was strapped to a table. There were IV lines in his arms and chest, but my attention was drawn to his freshly shaved head, where a blue liquid was being pumped into his brain. I also noticed fresh surgical stitches on his forehead; he had a brain injury, or perhaps he had been lobotomized prior to my visit. I was about to touch his skin when his lips opened.

"It's a chemical lobotomy." His voice was weak, scratchy. "What do you want? Why do you care." His fists clenched as I watched him suffer a grand-mal seizure. The pain was evident.

I simply took a seat watching his body writhe in agony. Looking around I could see a wall of screens observing his vitals. "You done?"

It took him a few moments to be able to speak, but it was clear he had heard me. "What do you actually want?"

"I want to be happy."

Faust chuckled. "Good luck with that." He turned his head to face me. "So, pray tell, where is your little genetic miracle?"

"With his father."

"With, Noah?" he asked with a smirk. "So, you killed him as a way to free yourself from these people?"

"Very funny," I stood up, walking around the room, marveling at the array of data being processed. "I meant Julian."

"Axel? You're in love with a man old enough to be your father?" Faust laughed until his chest started to spasm. "And you see that as wise?" He added between coughs.

"Julian is nothing like my father." The very comparison made me sick.

"That may be true, but are you like your mother?" Faust asked with a confident grin.

Would I choose my partner over my child? Absolutely not. "If Julian or anyone in TAC ever hurt my child, I would not hesitate to destroy them."

"You say that now, as you are still only a child yourself."

Now he was getting annoying. I was tempted to leave when something caught my eye. This equipment seemed oddly familiar. Was this the same set up used to dissect Tony's body? Was TAC going to harvest Faust; his powers, his mind, his intellect? Were they trying to port his consciousness? I placed my hand upon one of the screens, just close enough to feel its warmth. This was not a touch screen, but for whatever reason it started to shimmer. The movement, an animation of sorts seemed to spread to the other screens.

At first it seemed like just random motion; flowing water or bending light, then it started to form a human hand. Faust continued to speak, possibly asking what the hell I was looking at. But I didn't care. I knew who this was. The hand guided me to a locked drawer. (Or rather a drawer with a six-character scrolling lock.) I didn't know the code, and the hand seemed to already know that.

Five lights, in the position of fingertips appeared. The now human-sized hand traveled from my eye line, down to where my fingers were. It drew a heart and then a star. This glowing digital finger painting was followed by a diamond, a moon and a clover. I started to hum the Lucky charms commercial, "Frosted lucky charms, they're magically delicious." Wait a second. 'Lucky charms? That had to be it.'

I scrolled through the wheel of letters on the lock. L, U, C, K, and Y all resulted in clicks. But the last character had me at a loss. Was it a letter? I stroked my finger to the screen over and over until the letters turned to numbers. I looked back at the computer screen, hoping for some more help from the mystery hand. Looking up I was face to face with a glowing silhouette. The figure held up five fingers.

"Lucky five?"

He twisted his hand, folding his fist before briefly flashing four fingers. The figure then moved one hand above his head, creating a pose reminiscent of a very specific videogame character. The code was 'Lucky9.'

I silently fixed the final character of the code, causing the drawer to slide open half an inch. Inside was a cobalt blue pistol-sized weapon. I picked it up, wrapping my fingers around the hilt. Without a second thought, I turned to Faust and fired a single bright red blast. The projectile destroyed his head, leaving behind a smoking stump.

I gasped for air, laughing, crying. "Tony, are you here?"

The room lights flickered. "I'll always be here," the voice sounded like static mixed with the auto voice from a word processing program.

An energy rippled through my hands, up my arms, holding me in a loving embrace. It was Tony; he was here, he was everywhere. "Thank you," I said in a whisper, "but am I going to be in trouble for well, you know..."

"Nah," Tony's voice echoed, as if spoken through a seashell. "If the good doctor has anything to say she can talk to me directly."

"Ok, sure." Was this really happening?

"Because there was no way in Hell, I was going to share my digital eternity with Faust." Tony's voice started to sound more and more human. He was frozen in time as his teen gamer persona.

"Understandable," I said, blinking back tears. "I miss you so much."

Tony's energy tickled my arm. "I miss you too, kiddo."

His touch felt like when we used to share a bed. At that moment, I wanted so badly to live forever in his arms. "Will I see you again?"

"I've been watching over you this entire time," he said in a soothing whisper, sending shivers down my spine. "You, Abby, and Nash."

"And Julian?"

Tony went quiet. "Um, yeah… about that."

"About what?"

Tony chuckled nervously. "I might have been the one who sent the command to set that particular protocol into motion."

"What do you mean?" Part of me knew fully well what he meant.

"Once you and Abby-Nash were airborne, I may have authorized a drone attack resulting in a scorched earth protocol command."

I laughed, assuming he was adding extra words to sound important. "You can do that?"

"I'm a human soul living on a massive server connected to the internet; I can do whatever, wherever."

"Like what, babe?"

Tony's voice swirled around the room like a stereo system. "Hack the stock market in Hong Kong, rigg an Ebay auction in Ohio, maybe even rob a few hundred bitcoins from the dark web, all while I'm talking to you."

Wow, just wow. "But you didn't mean to hurt Julian, right?" I needed the clarification, otherwise, this moment was a little too 'horror movie' for my liking.

"No, of course not. He's my mentor, my partner." Tony's sadness and remorse was noticeable even in his digital form. "Julian has been nothing but good to me; kind of why I feel extra shitty about the loss of his legs."

"Legs, as in plural?" My stomach sank. His one leg was gone but, Julian had been doing well, regaining balance and strength with the use of prosthetics.

"That will all depend on what Dr. Toki can do for him; cybernetics and all that shit."

I wanted to ask why he assumed Julian would be losing his other leg. "Have you spoken to him at all?"

"I tried," Tony replied with a sigh. "A few times, in his dreams, because he sleeps with headphones on."

I nodded, knowing what he was referring to. In an effort to combat anxiety and panic attacks, Julian slept wearing wireless headphones connected to a playlist on his laptop. "What has he said to you?"

"I know he still blames himself for my death. I tried to talk to him, to tell him where I was, how I was ok, but he just starts to cry or even pray. I don't think he believes I'm really here. And I figure, if I push too much, he'll think he's losing his mind."

"I can see that."

"Anyway, I should probably let you go; run outside, get a head start, before I allow this bastard's lack of vitals to be visible on the network. With any luck I can convince Dr. Toki that I did it all on my own."

"That your spirit possessed the gun via some kind of Bluetooth signal?" I guess that wasn't the craziest thing I'd seen. "Will I see you again?"

"Of course," Tony said happily. "All you need to do is click your heels together and declare your belief in Tinkerbelle."

"For real?" I asked. I knew he was kidding but I genuinely wanted the truth; if he could travel anywhere on the internet how was I supposed to find him?

"I'm kidding. Just log on to any device with wi-fi and look for my name listed as a possible connection. I'll fine you; I promise."

I felt a tingle going across my neck, to my lips. "Thanks, Tony." I did as he requested, running for the door, leaving my digital guardian angel to handle the mess.

I knew where my family would be. I headed straight for the outside track. The circular running track was surrounded by bleachers and in the center was a small playground area. Julian was jogging, practicing with his new prosthetics. His missing leg had been replaced with a high-tech model with fully functional joints connected to his remaining muscle and nerve tissue.

I began to job by his side, our mechanical legs matching stride for stride.

"You ever heard of Neerja Bhanot?" he asked as he maintained a stable pace.

"No, I don't think so." The name seemed familiar.

"She was a famous Indian model who saved a plane full of people."

"In the eighties, right!" I could picture the internet famous image; a model turned flight attendant with feathery pageant queen hair.

"I fell asleep watching her bio pic. She reminds me a lot of you."

"Bullshit," I chuckled, as we stopped for water.

"Do you know why she was honored by three different governments?"

"Something about tossing out American passports, and dying while saving a bunch of kids." Those were the stories I'd heard on true crime YouTube channels. "Although, later on, the four men who got arrested escaped prison and disappeared."

"As far as the United Nations are concerned," Julian muttered.

"What?" I asked sarcastically, already knowing the answer was out of my paygrade.

"Anyway, over the course of a nearly twenty-four-hour ordeal Neerja Bhanot did three things that reminded me of you."

"Just three?"

"To start, she warned the pilots, allowing them time to escape."

"And how did she do that?"

"There were only four bad guys compared to her entire cabin crew. She took the opportunity to pick up the phone and radio the cockpit." Julian took a seat, looking out at the playground. "Nothing too heroic, but she kept a level head."

"Fair enough."

"The second thing she did was what made her a hero to all America. The terrorists asked the cabin crew to collect passports from the hundreds of passengers. Neerja Bhanot made it a point to not hand over American passports and she convinced her entire crew to do the same. I mean, can you imagine?"

"How does that remind you of me?"

"I think you would have done the heroic thing, and convinced the rest of your team to be brave." Julian patted the seat next to him.

"Are you sure you're not thinking of your wife?" Being a bad-ass hero seemed to be more of Maverick's thing.

He reached for my hand. "I guess I am."

It took me a second to realize what he had done. There was a weight on my hand; a gold band with the word, 'my hero,' engraved on the top (where a diamond would typically be.) "Wow."

"As the lead flight attendant Neerja Bhanot was the one who opened the first escape door. She could have been the first person off the plane; it would have been that easy. Instead, she chose to make sure everyone who could still walk got off the plane. And as you know, she went down in history for taking a bullet to save a group of terrified unaccompanied minors."

I looked out at the playground. Nash and Abby were playing in the sand, appearing like a happy normal baby with his robot nanny. I knew in my heart I would give my life for the ones I loved. "It was her job as a flight attendant to watch over the passengers." Just like it was my job to be a mom, a teammate and a friend.

"We make choices in our lives," Julian said as he held my hand, lacing his fingers through mine. "And despite how badly we might want it; we can't go back, only forward to a new day."

Nash turned to me. "Nicki!" He stood up happily, scooping up Abby in is arms. "Come see our sandcastle."

There were a few other children playing in the area, mothers, fathers, nannies and other caretakers.

Fuck you, Faust and all the other assholes who've tried to keep me down:

I'd found my happiness.

The end

9 781956 010527